A SOLDIER REBORN

DAN McCARTY

BEAVER'S POND PRESS

ISBN 10: 1-59298-443-6
ISBN 13: 978-1-59298-443-5

Library of Congress Catalog Number: 2011941125

Printed in the United States of America

First Printing: 2012

16 15 14 13 12   5 4 3 2 1

Cover and interior design by James Monroe Design, LLC.

BEAVER'S POND PRESS

Beaver's Pond Press
7104 Ohms Lane, Suite 101
Edina, MN 55439–2129
952-829-8818
www.BeaversPondPress.com

To order, visit www.BeaversPondBooks.com
or call 1-800-901-3480. Reseller discounts available.

Dane Joseph Ableidinger

He came to this earth as a baby boy
and left three months later as an angel.

His loving smile and beautiful blue eyes
will be missed forever.

PROLOGUE

30 September 2005
Project Black Thorn

The sound of the rotor blades from the UH-60 Blackhawk helicopter formed a metronome in Master Sergeant William Connelly's heart. Sitting bleeding against a mud wall, he hung onto life. Every breath he took was more labored than the one before, filling his lungs with the acrid dust and dirt of the godforsaken country where he was going to die.

Their target had been Abdul Aligazhar, leader of the Jihad Brotherhood, a group of terrorists claiming responsibility for more than a dozen recent car bombings in the United States and countless other terrorist attacks worldwide. The U.S. military's attempts to track him throughout the Middle East had resulted in a half dozen raids, all coming up empty.

The Alligator, as he had been codenamed, was more like a ghost. Latest word to come down from higher up was that an eyewitness had seen the Gator in a building on the outskirts of a village.

The village was nothing more than eight clusters

of mud huts that sat unevenly along both sides of a potholed excuse for a desert road. Six-foot mud walls around each of the compounds prevented access to the buildings via anything other than the small wooden or metal gates set into the barriers.

Spy satellites zeroed in on Aligazhar's supposed compound; intelligence indicated no enemy movement away from the building. Connelly's team activated, and fifteen minutes later they were ready to go. The plan had been to go in hot and secure Aligazhar for transport and interrogation.

The Alligator never traveled without a personal army of a dozen or so of the most deadly men in the Middle East. These combat-hardened soldiers had been guerilla fighters against the Russians during the 1980s. Connelly knew this mission would be far from a walk in the park, but it had to be accomplished at all costs.

The A/MH-6 Little Bird helicopters took off at 1300 sharp, the proverbial thirteenth hour, an omen Connelly did not want to think about. His men were ready, and this was a chance for some of the new guys to see combat. Most of his friends from his earlier years had left the military, opting for high-paying civilian jobs as advisors and security experts.

As stubborn about leaving the military as Connelly, Sergeant First Class Timothy Maddox, seated next to Connelly, bobbed his head to internal music. The former college linebacker's large frame had earned him the nickname Ox.

"How long have we been doing this?" Connelly shouted above the sound of the helicopter's engines and rotating blades.

"Too long," Ox answered. "You get a chance to talk to Abby before we left?"

"Briefly. Her mom is back in the hospital. It doesn't look good."

"Sorry to hear that. Maybe after we take down the Gator you can use up some of that leave. Get the hell out of here and head home."

"That's not a bad idea. You know how she was when she lost her dad a few years back."

"Those were some rough times."

"I know, I never got over my father's death."

"Your old man would have been proud of you. From what you told me, he was one hell of a cop."

"Yeah, he died doing what he loved. My mom wasn't the same after. The depression fueled her drinking and it was only a matter of time before I buried her right next to him. I joined the Army to get away from what little family I had left."

"You found yourself one hell of a family here in Delta. Hell, our wives are practically attached at the hip."

"No kidding. I think it would have been easier on my credit cards if we had never met."

"True. But then I wouldn't have had to put up with your sorry ass through basic, Airborne, RIP, Ranger Batt, Ranger School, and Delta."

"You would be lost without me. Hell, I saved your life in Mogadishu. Remember when they decided to send us into a lawless city in the middle of the day with a half-baked extraction plan?"

"And you claim there was a sniper on a rooftop that was about to shoot me before you put three in his chest? We've discussed this. No one else saw it."

"My word is golden."

"So is the bullshit you've been trying to pass off as fact for the last fifteen years."

"Whatever you want to believe. You have to admit, those were the good old days."

"You mean spending the night in an enemy-infested city?"

"I mean the days when we dreamed about becoming Delta. We watched those guys lay down their lives to protect their own. Our Ranger buddies put up one hell of a fight, but those Delta guys kicked some serious ass."

"Speaking of kicking ass. Touch-down in sixty seconds," Connelly advised.

The men on his team checked their weapons one more time. The majority of them carried either a M4 or AKS-74 assault rifle. At just under thirty inches, the M4 is a shorter, more maneuverable version of the M16 or AR15. Introduced in 1963, the M16 lineage has been the primary service rifle of the U.S. Army.

At twenty eight inches, the AKS-74 is a compact and updated version of the widely popular AK47 assault rifle. Named for the year it was developed, the AK-74 was used by the Soviets in Afghanistan and became a staple throughout the Middle East.

Both weapons are deadly accurate in the right hands. Connelly's men outfitted each of their guns with a variety of accessories. The combination of electronic sights, flashlights, night vision lasers, grenade launchers, and custom paint jobs made each soldier's rifle look like something out of a futuristic science fiction movie. The soldiers inspected their well-oiled machines of war and looked over the rest of their equipment.

Confident they were ready, each man performed his pre-combat ritual. Prayers were said, dog tags were rubbed for luck, and pictures of loved ones were kissed as the chopper flew low to the ground to avoid being seen from the distance.

Connelly shared his bird with Ox and two other operators. A second helicopter with four more operators flew at his five o'clock. With a feather touch, his chopper touched down on the roof of the target building. Connelly's team jumped out, fighting through the dust storm created by the rotor wash.

They would clear the building from the top down, followed by Bravo Team, with the Little Birds providing air cover and preventing anyone from running too far out of the complex or entering it from the ground level. The reserve element was already in the air, having lifted off from the strike base a mere ten minutes after Connelly's raiding squad. The reserve's mission was to assist with detention of any prisoners and provide medical aid as needed for either side of the small conflict.

Staff Sergeant Michael Thomas, a young operator nicknamed Tex for his love of cowboy boots and big belt buckles, aimed his M4 at the small wooden door that led from the roof to the second floor of the building. Behind him Ox pulled out a flash-bang grenade. Staff Sergeant Patrick McKenzie, nicknamed Mack, was the last member of the team. He opened the door just wide enough for Ox to toss in the flash-bang. The stunningly loud bang from beneath was the cue for the team to enter. As Mack threw open the door the second bird touched down, dropping off Bravo Team. They had done this hundreds of times. Their movements were synchronized, fluid actions composed by the likes of Mozart or Beethoven. Each man knew every other's movements, timing, weapon capabilities, and equipment load. They thought they were ready for anything, but what awaited the team at the bottom of the stairs was nothing short of hell on earth.

The terrorists lay in wait, knowing the exact response the military would make to Aligazhar's presence. The leaders in Washington could not have known that the Alligator and his men had decided to make themselves martyrs in the eyes of the Middle East. Their deaths would bring an end to their running and inspire renewed passion in others fighting against the West. After years of ducking and hiding, they would make their stand. Aligazhar planned on killing some of America's best before Allah accepted him and his men with open arms.

Tex was the first one down the stairs; his job was to clear a path through the room, taking out any enemy combatants in his sight. Mack was next, tasked with clearing the other portion of the room. Connelly and Ox would join them and establish a foothold in the building for Bravo Team to sweep the remaining rooms before heading to the ground floor.

The team reached the bottom of the stairs without incident. The stairs were nothing more than dried mud over a rough wood frame. There was no handrail, and the dimly lit room was open to Connelly's right side. A few small pieces of wooden furniture and a makeshift bed occupied the room. The only exit from the room was a rusty metal door, just past the base of the stairs. Reaching the bottom step he saw the door open slightly. A small dark object landed with a thud as it hit the wooden floor.

In a fraction of second, Connelly watched the grenade roll to the right side of the room before he was thrown against the wall by the explosion. He struggled to breathe against a crushing sensation throughout his chest, but he was still alive and trained to respond.

Connelly had uncontrollably rolled down the last few stairs, ending up on his stomach next to one of his teammates. Still woozy from the attack, he located his weapon, pushed himself off the dirty floor, and dove behind a nearby wooden desk.

Bringing the barrel of his AKS-74 over the desk, he watched the door open and two enemy soldiers rushed into the room. Instinctively his finger moved into the trigger well and squeezed. The first target looked like he was being punched by a phantom boxer as Connelly's rounds found their marks in his chest. Crimson splattered the dusty yellow wall behind the adversary, who fell backwards and collapsed in a heap on the floor.

The other soldier turned toward the desk. Connelly didn't hesitate as he inflicted multiple head shots on the enemy and then focused his weapon on the doorway.

The firefight had lasted a matter of seconds. As he regained some of his hearing, Connelly picked up the faint groans of Ox, who lay at the bottom of the stairs. Quickly scanning the room he saw Tex and Mack lying on the floor in the middle of the room. It did not take more than a quick glance for Connelly to know there was no life left in the mangled piles of flesh and bone that had once belonged to his teammates. Their bodies most likely took the brunt of the shrapnel, allowing Connelly to escape the grenade attack with minor injuries.

"Bravo!" Connelly yelled, keeping his rifle trained on the doorway. A bearded, middle-aged man appeared, taking two shots in the direction of Connelly's voice. They were near misses, and Connelly was able to eliminate the latest threat with another short burst from his weapon.

"Bravo!" Connelly shouted again. He desperately needed Bravo Team to assist with security and get Ox some medical attention. Boots thudded on the steps above.

Just as Bravo Team reached the bottom of the stairs, the now repetitive sound of heavy metal on wood reached everyone's ears. "Frag!" everyone yelled as they dove for cover. Another well-timed grenade exploded before Bravo Team could hit the floor.

Connelly felt the searing hot metal enter his flesh, his whole body erupting in pain. The desk had splintered under the force of the explosion. Filled with rage, he managed to stand up and run to the wall just right of the open door. His whole squad was down, and those who weren't dead were minutes from it. He could do nothing more for them than exact some revenge.

He grabbed a fragmentation grenade from his tactical vest, pulled the pin, flipped the spoon, and cooked it off for three full seconds. That gave him just enough time to lob the grenade into the unknown beyond the door. Screams of pain told Connelly there were still enemies alive. Removing a second grenade off his vest, he cooked it and lobbed it through the door.

As the second grenade exploded Connelly loaded a fresh magazine into the assault rifle. Using his thumb, he flipped the thin selector lever on his weapon to fully automatic fire. Reaching around the open doorway, he sprayed the freshly wounded combatants with thirty rounds of 5.45mm ammunition.

Receiving no return fire, he dropped his magazine and inserted a fresh one. Stumbling through the door,

Connelly stepped over the unmoving bodies of four terrorists. The narrow hallway had two empty rooms on each side before ending at a stairwell that led to the ground floor. He threw his two remaining grenades into the room beneath. Each grenade sent deadly shards into the terrorists lying in wait at the base of the stairs.

Connelly willed his injured body forward and half fell down the stairs and into the gator pit on the heels of the explosion. The large open room was filled with smoke and dust. The grenades had done some damage, but there were still a few enemy soldiers fit for combat. He took two of them out as he entered, placing two chest shots in each with a fatal sweep of his rifle.

Now there were only two men left standing, one of them Aligazhar. Before Connelly could set his sights on the target, the last of the Alligator's men opened fire. His injured leg gave way beneath him and he fell to one knee as the slugs sliced through his flesh. Reaching into his leg holster as he dropped, he produced a USP .45 handgun. He squeezed off a couple rounds and took down Aligazhar's last bodyguard.

It was now down to Connelly and the man responsible for ending hundreds of innocent lives all over the world. In slow motion Connelly saw Aligazhar lift his rifle. They were no more than ten feet apart, and Connelly knew his life was about to end. Disregarding his certain death, Connelly watched the Alligator pull the trigger.

Connelly used the last of his strength, driven by pure adrenaline, to swing his handgun in Aligazhar's direction. As the rounds from his enemy's gun entered his body, he fired three rounds. The first two missed their mark, and he slipped into unconsciousness before seeing the results of the third.

A white light appeared and he moved toward it. He felt a peace fall over his body, like a hot shower on a cold morning. As the beads of warmth struck his skin he began to think that death wasn't that bad after all.

"Oh, fuck! It's Connelly. Get down here guys. It's clear, help me out!" a voice yelled in the distance. Connelly opened his eyes and saw Rodgers, the medic from the reserve element. "Stay with me, Connelly, don't you fucking die on me!"

The searing pain came back, and Connelly felt himself being loaded onto a stretcher. Within seconds the dirty green canvas was stained black with his blood. Suddenly he was floating. Lifting up his head, he realized they were carrying him out of the room. His head fell against the blood-stained stretcher and rolled to the right. He was losing focus, but in just that brief second he had seen what he needed to see. Aligazhar was dead. Connelly's final round hit him right between the eyes. Satisfied that his mission was complete, Connelly closed his eyes and made the journey into the white light.

★ ★ ★ ★

Abigail Connelly opened the door, and the blood drained from her face. A four-star general at her door meant only one thing. William was dead. She had been preparing herself for this moment for over a decade. She had told herself she would stand strong and remember what a great man he was. Today she couldn't do that. Today she cried, fell to her knees and rocked back and forth. They tried to comfort her, but in the end she sent them all away.

PROLOGUE

They had given her two letters. After she had cried what she thought was every tear in her body, she opened the first.

To the love of my life,

If you are reading this letter, then I didn't make it home from this mission. I never wanted to write this letter and never intended on you reading it. I hope that my words can bring you comfort. I died doing what I needed to do. We live in a great country, one where opportunities abound and hard work is rewarded with the chance to own a house, raise a family, and love life. I leave this world knowing that my life was well spent. I accomplished a lot of things, and best of all I was able to fall in love. I want you to remember that everything happens for a reason. We met in Atlanta for a reason, and I died on this foreign soil for a reason. We will be together again someday in Heaven. I firmly believe that. I want you to do the best you can to live the rest of your life. If you meet someone and fall in love again and it makes you happy, then I promise I will be happy for you. I am in a good place, probably causing trouble with some of my Ranger and Delta buddies who got here before me. Just know that you were the best thing to ever happen to me. Don't short the world by letting this ruin your life. I am sorry for leaving you, but I will always be in your heart and I will always love you.

Always,
William

The second piece of paper almost crackled with military formality. It was the official record of his death.

> Dear Mrs. Connelly,
>
> It is with great pain that I bear to you the news of the death of Master Sergeant William E. Connelly. William was killed in action while performing an essential security mission in a foreign country. Due to the sensitive nature of the mission I cannot provide you with many specifics. However, I will do my best to accurately report his last minutes of life. Before I begin, I want to tell you that William died a hero. His squad was assigned to capture a known criminal in enemy territory. His entire squad fought valiantly, with William leading the charge the entire way. His actions ensured the mission's success.
>
> It is also with great pain that I must inform you that after the mission was complete and before reserve elements could arrive on scene, a fire broke out. The entire squad was lost to the fire. Based on lack of radio contact and the inability of William and his squad to extract from the fire, it is believed that they were killed during the initial engagement. The reserve element was forced to wait for the fire to burn out and then retrieve what remains could be found. William's ashes are being flown to America to be turned over to you for burial.
>
> On behalf of the United States Military and the President of the United States, I offer my

condolences for your loss and advise you that we are forever in debt for William's sacrifice. Please do not hesitate to call or write me if you have any concerns or questions.

Sincerely,
Henry Miller
Secretary of Defense

Abigail folded both letters, lay down on the sofa, and cried a million more tears.

From that day on she prayed for just one more chance to see his face and feel him touch her skin. Leaving her military family behind, she moved halfway across the country and started a new life in the mountains of Colorado. William had always loved the mountains, and after moving to the small town of Frontier she felt him beside her once again.

Every Sunday she drove deep into the mountains and shed a few tears for William. Among the pine trees and rocky outcrops she found her solace. She often stared at a prominent mountain peak, feeling a connection to her lost love. The letters became worn and tattered, so she re-wrote them and carried the copies with her.

While William's good-bye letter always left her with some warmth in her heart, there was a cold feeling associated with the secretary of defense's letter that sent her mind in darker directions.

"Why couldn't I just have seen his body one last time?" she often asked herself. *What if he is out there somewhere?* she often thought. She had seen his ashes but the charred remains did little to suppress her delusions.

An uncontrollable emotional current propelled her heart through both serene waters and painful rapids. Dreams and nightmares clashed during her nights, and on the best of mornings she awoke and swore she could feel William's body next to hers. It was on those dawns she could almost convince herself that her lover was still alive.

Everyone she told about her hopes quickly dismissed them as denial. They told her she needed to accept the fact that William was dead. Ox's wife had told her to accept reality and understand that she would never see William again.

Abby tried to believe her husband was dead. Weeks turned into months but the feelings never faded, and she often wondered if everyone else was right and she was wrong.

In reality, they were all wrong.

1

Frontier, Colorado
0215

Colt Sullivan stirred in bed, his body awash in a cold sweat. His stomach struggled to contain its contents as the room spiraled in and out of focus. He clasped his hands over his temples in a futile attempt to steady his head. Slowly the spinning stopped, but his nausea remained. He swung his legs out over the side of the bed and sat up, drawing in long, deep breaths of the cold mountain air. The nearly full moon bathed the room in a silvery glow, and gradually he made out his own ethereal reflection in the dresser mirror.

He found himself squinting, studying the image. There was something alien about the handsome man peering back at him. Lost in confused thought, he rose and moved toward the mirror. Suddenly nausea overwhelmed him, and he barely made the short sprint into the bathroom in time. Hugging the rim of the porcelain toilet, he expelled what remained of his dinner.

Exhausted, he fell to his side, wedging himself between the toilet and the shower stall. His body folded tightly into the space like a marionette tossed aside by a forgetful master. Walls that had once seemed distant and full of color began to spin. A gyroscope of gray slowly closed in around him as he struggled to maintain consciousness. It was a battle he was going to lose. As suddenly as the nausea had overtaken him, the world went dark.

The brick house sat in a small, quiet neighborhood. The deep red hue of the masonry contrasted sharply with the bright white of the shutters and trim. More than likely, the neighbors here all knew each other and he would stick out like a sore thumb. That did not bother him. He was not planning on being seen. He stuck to the nighttime shadows, his dark clothing blending into the night. Stealth would be his focus for the mission. A suppressor-equipped Glock .45 strapped to the side of his leg would be his tool. As his administrator of justice he would trust nothing else.

Before making a move toward the house, the killer scanned the surrounding houses. Prior trips to the house had given him intimate knowledge of the entire block. Most of the residents were elderly; the chances that any of them would be up and moving around at 3 a.m. were not very good.

His extra caution tonight was the result of his carelessness during the last recon mission. Operating under the assumption that no one would be awake, he had recklessly moved around the target house and stepped into an area of light. For a brief moment he had been visible to an old man next door—a critical instant of failure before he could retreat to the shadows and out of the neighborhood.

Tonight he could not afford another screw-up. Tonight had to be perfect. He looked for movement in the houses, for vehicles coming down the road or pedestrians walking along the sidewalks. The neighborhood was quiet as he made his move. He could hardly contain the excitement growing inside him. Tonight was the night he had been waiting for, a night of absolute justice.

The blackness left Colt as quickly as it had come. Like a college student recovering from a night of binge drinking, he eased himself up from next to the toilet. He fumbled through a bathroom drawer for a bottle of aspirin and poured a couple tablets into his hand. The nausea and dizziness had now been replaced by a mild headache.

"What the hell is going on?" Colt asked himself. "Goddamn dizziness, nausea, and now this headache?"

It was unlike any headache Colt could remember having in his life. Not a stabbing headache, like the kind that felt as if someone was sticking a knife through his eye socket. Nor was it tension that felt like his brain was going to burst out of his forehead. It was a dull burn, like the muscle buzz weightlifters feel the morning after an intense session with heavy weights.

From next to the sink, Colt grabbed a cup, filled it with water, and gulped down the pills. Sucking down a breath, he looked into the mirror and jumped back. He swore something was not right. The man in the mirror was undeniably himself, and yet gut instinct told him he had overlooked some difference.

Rubbing his eyes, he caught his breath and took a step forward. When he looked into the mirror again, Colt saw a reflection he recognized as his own. "Man, am I messed up," he said to himself as he started the cold water running. He splashed some onto his face and let it run off.

The smell of the vomit in the bathroom lingered in his nostrils. Remembering his quick dash to the bathroom, he found that the timing in his head had gone fuzzy. He wondered how long he had been jammed in between the toilet and shower. Feeling no bruises or pain, he believed it had been a short amount of time. It had felt like mere seconds in his mind, just darkness and then the present.

He assumed he had fallen asleep and tried in vain to remember any dreams he may have had. The problem was, he never could remember his dreams. His mind was always a blank slate, and as usual it failed to provide him the smallest clue to his previous night's mental adventures.

Grabbing a towel, he dried his face and then flushed the toilet. The fatigue set in, landing deep in his body, sapping even his bones of energy. He hadn't had a good night's sleep in many years, always getting just enough to keep him going. Fighting the exhaustion, he willed his body back to the bed and collapsed into the sea of blankets. "It's going to be a long day," he mumbled as sleep overtook his weary mind.

2

The Vault
0700

The fluoride-bright walls of the lab closed in upon Samuel's soul once again. "Just one more day," he whispered to himself. The constant hum of electrical equipment and the faint sound of voices from outside the room were his only company. In Lab 232 he was alone, but they were always watching him, listening to him, and they knew his every move. At least they thought they did.

Doctor Samuel Mitchell had been planning his escape for quite some time. Here he was, one of the most brilliant people on the planet. Yet he was caged up, imprisoned by his own intelligence.

When he was born, his life expectancy was twenty years. The healthy child of a prostitute who called the projects of Washington, D.C., her home, his odds were not good. A miracle came in the guise of his mother's fatal overdose three months after his birth. His father was nowhere to be found, so he was put up for adoption. Fate delivered him into the arms of a very wealthy and well-known family with many political connections. His adoptive mother had been infertile, and the couple used the adoption as a chance to draw the limelight. They decided early on that Samuel was destined to enter politics and they would do whatever it took to get him elected to office.

He was put through the best schools, had the best teachers, and absorbed it all. After graduation from high school he was pre-accepted into the college of his choice, a byproduct of his family's wealth and political stature.

Before he made his choice of college, his mother took him to New York to catch a show on Broadway. She fell ill that night, and they headed home early. They walked in on his father having sex with his secretary in front of the living-room fireplace.

His family life, what little there was of it, fell completely apart. The affair leaked to the public, and the media set up camp outside their house. With the family name splashed across the tabloids, any political dreams he might have treasured were soon forgotten.

His mother pushed for him to enroll at a different college, a small, private school far from the influence of the Beltway. Focusing on his studies, Sam kept his nose to the books to avoid focusing on his father's rapid fall from grace. After college, the MCAT, and medical school, his hard work paid off as he entered into the world of medicine.

Having found a fascination with the human brain, Sam geared his career toward neurology. It was risky, and he knew that even the smallest mistake could open the door to a malpractice suit that would target both the hospital and Sam's family fortune.

By age thirty he was working in smaller hospitals and soon performed his first brain surgery. He was happy with where his hard work had landed him, but over time he found himself craving more challenges. There were limitations on what surgeons could do with the human brain.

One day, a mysterious man showed up at his door and offered a cryptic but exciting opportunity to work for the government. The stranger in the all-black suit offered him a career filled with medical breakthroughs. Sam accepted the job and was flown to Colorado the following day.

The next twenty years in the military provided him with plenty of change and many challenges. He could never deny that his decision to work for the government had brought an abrupt halt to his string of mundane surgeries. Door after door opened for him in the military field as he was shuffled from military hospitals to government research bases. Eventually he landed here at the Vault. At fifty-six years of age, he was now the most valuable doctor in the facility. His expertise in the area of memory loss and manipulation had grown exponentially over the two decades.

The only issue was that the base commander, General Frank Harrison, ran the Vault as a top-secret maximum-security prison. His military history included leading infantry troops in Vietnam, Panama, Granada, the Persian Gulf, Somalia, Kosovo, and a dozen top-secret operations. At the turn of the millennium he had been given the opportunity to head a new project and build it from scratch. The only people he reported to were the secretary of defense and a committee of specially selected leaders from the fields of science, business, and the military.

"Good morning, Doctor," came the growl of a voice from Sam's left. "How are you doing today?"

"Can't complain, General, and yourself?" The repercussions of any complaint were terrifying.

"I'm fine," barked the general, his tone making no effort to hide the fact that this was not going to be a pleasant conversation. "I want the latest reports, compiled and analyzed. And I want them on my desk by noon."

Straight to the point, that's the general, Sam thought. Out loud he said only, "I won't let you down, sir. I'll have a copy on your desk by noon." Sam looked away from his work just long enough to catch a glance of Harrison. Just looking at the man was unsettling. The general stood just over six feet tall, with salt-and-pepper hair and a solid build. His face was a spiderweb of scars, evidence of a grenade attack that had claimed the lives of two of his best noncommissioned officers in Vietnam.

"Good, I have to report to Washington this afternoon, and they expect results," the general stated. "If they don't like what they hear it's my ass, and if that happens I'll make sure I don't go down alone."

"I won't disappoint you, sir. They will like what they hear."

"You had better be right, because if you're wrong they'll be sending everyone they have down here to shut us down and fuck up five years of work. Get me my results, Doctor."

"I'll do my . . ." Sam said to the slamming door.

Another cheerful encounter with the local warden, he said to himself. The project was failing, and there was very little he could do to fix it. However, that did not mean he was throwing in the towel. His options were bleak: give up and face the wrath of Harrison, or find a way to save himself and many others from what was a life sentence in prison or worse.

The knock on the door almost gave him a heart attack. "Come in."

"Hey, Sam," Denise said gently. "You doing okay?" Fearing that someone was listening in via the microphones hidden throughout the room, neither of them mentioned Harrison's visit.

"Yeah, just another day in the office," he joked, but he was unable to quell the fear in his voice. "How are you doing?"

"I'm doing okay." Denise was the sweet ray of light in Sam's day and life. He was twenty-five years her elder and simply enjoyed her company. She was smart, funny, and compassionate, and although most guys wouldn't take a second look at her, Sam thought she was beautiful. It often made him wonder why he had not focused more on women and less on his studies. He could have had a family, children, and almost grandchildren by now . . . but it was too late for that.

Sam had no romantic interest in Denise, and he reckoned she had initially befriended him to expand her knowledge of the human brain. However, over time their friendship had developed a high level of trust in this most untrusting place.

The temperature in the room was fine, but Sam wiped his brow, loosened his top button, and then turned on a fan. He waved Denise over to his desk, leaning over to point out some data on one of the papers strewn about his desk. As she leaned over the tiny type, he whispered in a voice barely audible above the fan, "Honestly, the project is failing; Connelly is reverting. I told the general I'd have the results to him by noon, but there is no way I can accomplish that."

"Why tell him that, then?" Denise's face showed fear and a hint of anger. Her voice was well above the level of the fan, and Sam gulped as he muttered, "Relax, Denise, and keep your voice down, please! You know they have this place bugged."

"Sorry," she said, her voice now barely a whisper. "When he finds out the truth, do you realize what they will do to you? You could end up measuring the temperature of ice in Antarctica or worse . . ."

"I told him I would have positive results so he would get off my back for the rest of the morning. I need some time without him looking over my shoulder. I am going to falsify the results until I can figure out what to do."

"Sam!" she exclaimed, then quickly lowered her voice again. "Are you crazy? You can't just—"

"Denise, listen to me," Sam interrupted. "I trust you, but what I tell you can't go beyond this room. I need to get us off this base."

"You really are crazy, Sam. They will never let you leave. You are a walking top-secret hard drive. You know more about confidential projects in the military than the president of the United States."

"I know, but this is something I have to do. Don't you ever feel that your life is already over here? That you are going nowhere, that your life is a waste?"

"Well, we all do at times, Sam. But what you are talking about doing is crazy. If they catch you, you will be thrown in prison. Have you thought of that?"

"Yes, I have. And I think I would prefer prison to this place. I can't take it anymore. I wish you could come with me, Denise, I really do."

"I can't, Sam. I can't spend my whole life running. I wouldn't survive."

"I understand, but running is the only chance I have. I won't survive here, not once my project fails. You know I don't exist anymore. And when Harrison finds out that the premier project in this facility is not a success, I'm through."

"What are you going to do?" Denise asked. Sam could see the worry in her deep brown eyes.

"I am going to see that my project only partially fails, and then I am going to expose it to the world. It's the only chance I've got."

"You mean bring down the whole program? You can't do that; it'll be the end of all of us."

"No, Denise, it will be the end of the general and his goons. It will give the rest of us a new beginning. It's the only hope we have, you have to see that!"

"I will keep my mouth shut, but I can't do anything else for you, Sam. Good luck. If this all works out, find me on the outside."

"Of course," Sam said, his voice barely audible. With that Denise turned and left the room. He shouldn't have told her, he should have kept his mouth shut. Now she was in on this, and Sam had not even given her the choice.

Sam spent the next few minutes filling out a bogus daily agenda. The general was a control freak, and everyone was under orders to provide daily agendas so he would know what every person on the base was doing at any given time. Sam printed off the completed schedule so he could hand-deliver it to the general's secretary. Normally he would have just e-mailed it to her, but he needed to be mobile today and it gave him an excuse to be out of the lab. The agenda, together with his promise to have a report ready by noon, would keep Harrison off his back for most of the morning.

The walls inside the base were half stainless steel and half flat white paint. The general tolerated nothing other than sterility and order, the two things repeated horrifically throughout the building. The tile floor was black and maintained at a spotless shine thanks to Walter Brown, the janitor.

Walter's chores were limited to cleaning and taking out the garbage, and since all documents that needed to be removed were shredded and burned, there was no threat that he could remove any paperwork, on purpose or by accident. As long as the garbage was emptied and the building looked cleaner than a hospital on opening day, Walter kept his job and no one bothered him. Sam walked past Walter and gave him a nod and a smile. The old man smiled back and went back to buffing the floor.

Sam continued his walk to the general's office, passing the string of multipurpose utility rooms. Years ago he had worked there, before he was given his own lab. They were designed to function as workshops, extra laboratories, or medical rooms for testing and experimentation. Silver and white, sterile and spotless, like everything else here.

"Hello, Doctor. Do you have your agenda?" Anna

Bigsby, the general's secretary, greeted him as he walked into the officer area. She was a true southern belle with an elegant air that enhanced her beauty. Her long, glimmering blonde hair had been pulled into bun behind her head; Sam preferred when she wore it down, but the general hardly let that happen.

"Here it is. If the general needs me, I will be in my lab," Sam replied as he handed her the paper. "Have a good day."

"You too, Doctor." Shc smiled and her cheeks fell into two dimples right beneath her enthralling blue eyes. Sam smiled back and retreated from the room. He had a lot of work to do and not a lot of time to do it in.

His first task was to get the sensitive information off the base. He hoped to have this done at the same time the general was receiving the report. The second part of the plan was the all-or-nothing gamble. He had not told Denise the specifics of the plan because there were only two people who could know, and she was not one of them. Everyone knew Sam and Denise worked together, and as soon as he went missing they would talk to her. The less she knew the better.

If he managed to get off the base at all, a team of special agents would be on his tail. These were no normal FBI agents or even CIA agents, they were ghosts. They did not exist in the real world, and they were held to no rules of engagement.

Once away from the base he would set in motion the final part of his plan. But he needed help on the outside, and for that Sam knew exactly where to turn. Only one person had survived an escape from the Vault, and only Sam knew where he was.

3

Frontier, Colorado
0722

Colt's dreamless sleep was interrupted by the ringing of the phone. At first all Colt could focus on was the blurred luminance of the blue digits on the alarm clock. "Jesus Christ. Who's calling this early on a Saturday?" he muttered aloud. Before he could think of any potential callers, his mild headache exploded into a migraine. It felt like some internal force was knocking against his cranium, yearning to escape to the outside world.

Grabbing at the nightstand, still half asleep, Colt reached out for the cell phone. With each ring Colt actually believed someone was tightening a vise over his temples. Finding the phone, he flipped it open and was almost blinded by the glow of the screen.

"Hello?" he mumbled.

"Hey, Colt, you better get down here. Thompson

was dispatched to a check-the-welfare this morning and found the woman murdered." He recognized the voice as that of the chief of police Dale Montgomery.

"Ah, shit. No problem, Chief, I'll be right in."

"Okay, swing by the office first and pick up Nick. The two of you can meet up with White when you get on scene."

"Sounds good. I should be down there within the hour."

"Thanks, Colt."

"No problem, see you soon." Colt closed the cell phone and sat up in bed. Murders in town were rare, but they had been happening at an increasing rate over the last decade.

Colt had been a police officer in Frontier for five years and had been selected to the investigations division a little over a year ago. It was the fastest any officer had ever made it to full-time investigations, and he had taken a lot of flak for it. Most of his patrol buddies still made fun of him for becoming a "day lady" or "desk jockey." He took it all with a grain of salt, knowing that the world of law enforcement has a niche for everyone.

The officer who found the dead body, Kevin Thompson, was one of Colt's good friends both on and off duty. He'd never aspired to do anything other than patrol the streets and spend the majority of his time conducting traffic stops.

He was very good at stopping cars full of criminals and at taking drugs, guns, and drunks off the street. If someone were to put him behind a desk he would rot away and hate every minute of it. Colt, on the other hand, had put in his time at patrol, not enjoying it but not hating the dynamic nature of the position. His real passion was for outsmarting major criminals, and the best place to do that was as a detective.

Turning thirty-five this year, Colt was one of the most enthusiastic detectives in the department. He had grown up in the era of computers, television, and the Internet. As a result he had been groomed upon entrance to the investigations division with classes in computer forensics and modern crime-scene analysis, as well as various interrogation schools and forensic psychology training.

Learning came very easy to Colt. He never failed to surprise anyone, including himself, with his ability to pick up new skills, learn new techniques, and read and even speak new languages. He had a near-perfect memory while conscious, which made it even more astounding that he never remembered his dreams.

A crashing sound downstairs jolted him out of his thoughts. Colt lived alone in a small house nestled into the mountains on the outskirts of the city. Opening a drawer in the nightstand next to the bed, he took out his off-duty handgun.

Colt had picked a Glock 30 because the small black pistol fit a lot of firepower into its compact frame. The double-stacked magazine held ten .45-caliber rounds, but those rounds in addition to the one in the chamber were more than he would ever need for a single intruder. He was an expert marksman with both pistols and rifles, a talent that had seemed almost second nature after joining the police force.

Not wanting to confront a would-be attacker in just a pair of boxer shorts, Colt slipped on a pair of sweatpants and a sweatshirt before silently moving to the bedroom door.

The house was a three-bedroom, two-bath home split into four levels. His bedroom was on the uppermost floor of the house, sharing the level with a walk-through bathroom, a second bedroom, and a living room.

Colt quickly peeked around the corner, then withdrew back into the room in anticipation of an ambusher's shot. He replayed his mental picture of the hallway he had just observed. Confident that it was clear of any gun-toting intruders, he moved quickly and silently into the hallway. Leading with his weapon, he cleared all the rooms on the top level of the house.

The sound had come from the level below him, so he took extra time clearing the rooms situated just down the stairs. The main floor of the house was much more open, and Colt had a decent view of the entire level from the living-room loft. He visually cleared most of the kitchen, dining room, and foyer, leaving very few areas to physically clear. Moving to the kitchen, he found no evidence pointing toward the origin of the noise.

Quickly sweeping the rest of the house, Colt found no signs of any intruders. *I could have sworn I heard something*, Colt thought. *The doors and windows are locked and the alarm is on. Weird.* The adrenaline slowly drained from his body, and before the fatigue could set in too deeply he returned to the bedroom.

Opposite the bed was a large walk-in closet. Each wall of the closet hosted a different type of attire for his life. Walking into the closet, he faced the wall holding his work clothing.

A small portion of the rack was taken up by uniforms he had worn while working as a patrol officer. Uniform pants, short- and long-sleeved shirts, and jackets, all in dark navy blue, hung in clear plastic bags. The majority of the hangers consisted of slacks, dress shirts, blazers, and suits. The department offered him a meager uniform allowance to help cover the cost of the required dress clothing, and Colt had purchased several more out of his own pocket.

The day was going to be filled with interviews and camera shots, so he decided on one of his best suits. A subliminal portion of police work is maintaining a good public image. Human nature puts a great deal of emphasis on appearance, and people have the tendency to use prejudice when looking at a public official's dress.

"Time to look good, Colt," he said. "You don't want to pull a wrinkle wrap."

Officer Melvin Wrap had retired a few years ago with a reputation for being the sloppiest-looking employee in the department. *I can't imagine what people thought when old Wrap showed up at their door.* And today Colt was not going to just show up at one citizen's door: the media was going to ensure that his image was seen by as many people as possible.

Colt's good looks and athletic physique, coupled with his friendly and witty personality, had earned him a spot as one of the department's public information officers. Whenever a criminal event demanded media attention, the department sent PIOs to deal with the news media. Too many departments had been burned by putting officers that were too new, nervous, or politically incorrect in front of news cameras and hard-question-wielding reporters. Having mastered the ability to work with the media, Colt now handled most of the press conferences.

Colt gathered his best suit, tie, shirt, and shoes and laid the clothing on the bed before walking into the bathroom. He turned on the shower and stripped out of his makeshift tactical outfit as the water warmed. Throwing the sweatpants, sweatshirt, and boxers into his laundry hamper, he stuck his hand into the stream of hot water to test the temperature and found it to be just about perfect.

Stepping into the shower, he let the hot chute of water fall onto his head and down his body. The warm ribbons of water fell over his shoulders and rolled down his back and chest. Setting his head under the flow, he felt the heat slowly steal away the pain in his head and begin relaxing the muscles in his neck.

A quick five-minute shower was all he needed most days, and he could already feel the energy returning to his body. A look in the mirror confirmed he was even starting to look more awake. After drying off and shaving, Colt returned to the bedroom.

The suit he had chosen was a dark, almost charcoal gray with very subtle lighter gray pinstripes. On an initial glance someone might think that the suit was actually black, and that would be fitting for today's events. However, the longer someone looked at the suit, the more the pinstriping made the suit seem lighter. He fancied that the suit instilled confidence that from dark would come light and, in the case of the murder, from death would come justice.

He complemented the suit with a gray shirt, a tie that appeared to be made of tarnished silver, and a pair of ordinary, comfortable, and highly polished black dress shoes. "Looking good," he said to the mirror. "I look emotionally neutral but empathetically strong. It's perfect."

This would not be the first homicide he had worked. He had been present on the crime scenes for the last two homicides that had occurred in the city. Colt had also recently helped sheriff's deputies in an investigation of two bizarre homicides in a small town twenty minutes away. Colt prided himself on not becoming emotionally attached to any case and using self-discipline to follow the evidence to the true killer.

Taking one last look in the mirror, Colt could have sworn he was once again looking at a stranger. Blinking a few times, he focused on the mirror and saw the correct image. "What the hell?" he asked himself before heading down to the kitchen for breakfast.

By the end of the day he would know exactly who it was he was seeing in the mirror: the man who would end his career . . . and possibly his life.

4

The Vault
0730

Samuel Mitchell missed his good friend, Dean Knight. Reaching into his drawer he pulled out two small objects, remembering the day Dean gave them to him. It was the day of Dean's escape.

"Sam," Dean had said, "you have been more than a coworker to me, you have been a good friend."

"'Have been?'"

"I'm getting out of here today."

Sam lowered his voice, "Are you crazy? Do you want to get killed? They had to have heard that. They are probably on their way down here to grab you right now."

"Have some confidence in me, Sam. I shut down the mics in this room. The cameras are still running, but all they're getting for the next one hundred seconds is static. So I have to make this quick."

"Okay, I'm listening." Sam was dumbfounded.

"Everything is in place for my escape. I wanted to get you out too, but I couldn't talk to you about it until today. Here is everything you need if you want to get out of here," Dean said, surreptitiously dropping two items into Sam's open desk drawer, out of view of the cameras.

"What are they?" Sam questioned without looking down.

"There is a CD full of computer programs and viruses and a small USB flash drive. The flash drive is, in fact, the world's smallest satellite phone. You can use it to stay in touch with me."

"How does it work?"

"For the purpose of passing security checks it actually is a flash drive, but I've hidden jacks inside the unit allowing you to bridge the handset of any phone. Plug one end into the phone itself and the other end into the jack from the headset. The device then overrides the hard line and activates a tiny satellite transmitter, allowing you to call anywhere in the world."

"What if the guards try to listen in?"

"We know the guards routinely check outgoing calls, but the device masks the call and makes it look internal. If they do get curious and pick up the line, a tone only we can hear will alert us."

"You said it works on satellite? From down here?"

"Don't worry. I overcame that problem by utilizing the base's wireless information relay network. The device taps into available wireless network hubs and utilizes their connection to place the call. The call is then bounced through a random series of encrypted satellites so fast that no one can track it."

"And the CD?"

"I call that one the nuclear bomb. It has every program you need to defeat the base security. Once you put the disk into the computer, you need to hit Control plus D plus K. That will open the hidden programs."

"What do these programs do?"

"The main program masks the remote computer access capabilities that allow the guards to monitor real-time activities on the computer. It also falsifies the keystroke capture devices, covering any back checks they run on your computer."

"So I can work on the computer without Harrison or his goons having any idea what I am up to? How did you pull this off?"

"A few years back, Harrison came to me and asked me to update the base's security programs, including the computer software. Like any smart programmer, I built invisible back doors that only I know how to access. From that point on I had full run on the base's computers."

"I can't believe he let you do that!"

"Why wouldn't he trust me? I've created some of the most technologically advanced machines here, not to mention the software programs for the agents and Connelly."

"I guess. So what am I supposed to do with this disc?"

"There are two very important programs on there. The first one: If you want to, say, use someone to sneak information off the base, you can create a disc with deeply hidden data that they guards won't be able to detect."

"You're talking about Walter . . . I don't know."

"I'm not saying you have to do it. It's an option.

"The other program is called Doomsday. If you

decide you want to leave the base, Doomsday is a virus that will launch the equivalent of a full-scale nuclear attack on the base's security. Once the virus has launched, all communication and tracking capabilities will grind to a halt for a period of a few hours. That should give you time to clear the base."

"How do I get out?"

"There is a file in there containing blueprints and possible escape routes. I don't know what they will do after I get out of here . . . If I get out of here."

"Time's up, Dean. Are you sure you want to get out of here?"

"Absolutely. They will come here after I leave. I won't tell you anything about how I am getting out of here or where I am going, so they can't extract that information from you. Just keep the items hidden. I'll hack into security from the outside and let you know how to get ahold of me."

"I will. Good luck, Dean. You're a braver man than I."

"Brave and stupid often go together. Have a good life, Sam."

"You too."

And with that Dean walked out the door and out of Sam's life.

Later that day, the security staff tore apart and searched Sam's lab and living quarters. They took and checked all of his CDs and scanned all of his notebooks; even his garbage was emptied and meticulously checked piece by piece. Eventually Harrison decided that Sam had nothing related to Dean's escape and everything was returned to him.

Before that day Sam hadn't even fostered the idea of getting out. Then things started to happen. The general, infuriated by the escape, tightened down an already oppressive regime. Sam started to think about his talks with Dean about family and life on the outside. He was fifty-six years old, but there was still enough time left in his life to enjoy freedom if he could get it.

Since the escape Sam had used the phone to stay in contact with his fugitive friend on an irregular basis. It had taken months of planning to set up his own escape, and when they initially picked today's date it had seemed years away.

Sam looked at the clock and realized those figurative years were now down to hours, and they felt like minutes. The plan was in motion.

5

Freedom Springs, Colorado
0730

Unlike Sam, who had worked for his knowledge, Dean was basically a mechanical genius, able to work with just about anything electrical found on the planet. After his recruitment he was kept busy developing some of the most advanced machines the military had ever seen.

At first Dean had been delighted by the program. At the age of nineteen he had developed twenty-four projects ranging from new weapon systems to faster computer chips. The thrill of it all had started to wear out after the better part of a decade spent inside the base. He suddenly realized he had no future other than making machines in his prison. When he had signed up for the program he was just sixteen years old; thoughts of marriage and children had been far from the top of his mind.

It took Dean six months to secretly develop a plethora

of devices to aid in his escape. His arsenal ranged from computer viruses to bug-scrambling devices. In order to defeat the base security he had needed skill, determination, and a hell of a lot of luck.

Dean used an air ventilation shaft to climb several hundred feet to an escape hatch built to allow egress from the Vault if the main doors were damaged or lost power. Once outside, he happened upon a roadway and was picked up as a hitchhiker.

"You looking for a ride, son?" the old man had said.

"I'd appreciate it, sir. I just need to get to the next town. My girlfriend and I got into a fight, and she took off in my truck."

"I've had a few of those days too. Hop on in."

Climbing into the truck, Dean knew he was putting this man's life at risk. "I feel your pain. Thank you again, this really saves me a lot of walking."

"No problem. My truck broke down during a snowstorm last winter. A nice young man stopped and stood out in the snow with me for more than an hour trying to fix it. When this piece of shit, pardon my French, refused to turn over, he gave me a ride into town. I figure I owe lady luck one for that day."

"I'll have to remember that and pay it forward too," Dean replied.

"That's how the good in this world works. You from around here?"

"No. I was born and raised in a suburb of Minneapolis. Moved out here from Minnesota for college and couldn't bring myself to go back."

"Minnesota, huh? I've never been there."

"It's flat, has a lot of lakes, and is colder than hell in

the winter. The people are nice, but it takes a certain type of person to live there year-round."

"I can imagine. What's your name?"

"Mike," Dean lied. "And yours?"

"Nice to meet you, Mike. I'm Dave." His tone changed, and Dean wondered if he suspected that his passenger had lied.

"Nice to meet you, Dave. Thanks again. Where are you headed?"

"Las Vegas. I just got divorced, and I figure what better place to celebrate than Vegas?"

"Alone?"

"I lost all my friends while I was with my ex-wife. Now I've got nothing but this truck and a pipe dream of hitting it big in Vegas."

"I hope you do, Dave."

The drive to the closest town was fifteen minutes, and the two men filled it with every piece of small talk they could muster. Dean tried to appear relaxed as he secretly wondered when the vehicle would be stopped by black sedans and a helicopter.

He was surprised as they arrived without interference. "Here you are, Mike," Dave said, pulling into a gas station. "They have a pay phone inside. Here's some change."

"I don't have any money to pay you back or give you for gas."

"Don't worry about it. Just pay it forward."

"I will. Thank you, Dave." After the truck left, Dean retreated to the woods. He lived off the land for a few days until he guessed that the initial search would have died down and he could risk the open road. Stealing an old car, he drove until he found a small town close enough to the Vault to aid Sam, but far enough to avoid a run-in with any offsite base personnel.

The place he chose was Freedom Springs, a small town in the mountains of Colorado. The locals shared a certain distaste for government and, although skeptical of outsiders, they took a liking to the young stranger. An elderly couple had invited him onto their farm, and he was plenty content fixing up their vehicles and tractors, using the story that he had recently gotten out of the military and was trying to find his place in life.

With the help of the farmer, Dean had built an apartment inside the barn complete with a makeshift kitchen, working bathroom, and rugged but clean living quarters. The room gave him plenty of privacy, and the farmer left him alone unless he needed some help or something fixed.

In his living quarters he had discovered a trap door that led to an old, long-abandoned cellar. It was just a twelve-by-twelve-foot dirt-floored room that Dean suspected had been used for making bootleg liquor during the Prohibition days.

Upon contacting Sam for the first time, Dean learned that Sam now wished to escape the base. To support Sam's escape as well as their endgame, Dean had turned his basement into an electrical and computer engineer's workshop.

The alarm went off and Dean reached up, tempted to hit the snooze button but immediately aware of the significance of the day that lay ahead of him. There was a lot of work to be done, and it all needed to be perfect. He had been rehearsing for weeks. If everything went right, today Lady Justice would swing her sword and balance a world of rights and wrongs on her scale.

Dean got out of his bed and staggered over to the bathroom. As he emptied his bladder, it dawned on him once more how significant the day's events would be. It was up to him and Sam to stop a research program gone horrifically wrong. It was time for them to atone for their sins.

Dean had escaped the Vault, but the life he wanted was still too dangerous to pursue. A single traffic stop for speeding could put his life in jeopardy. There was no chance of him meeting a woman and starting a family when he was living in a barn and avoiding almost all contact with the outside world. Harrison had to go down, and Dean needed Sam's help. It was a giant gamble: If he played all his cards right and won, he had a chance at a normal life. If he lost he would find himself in a different type of secret room: one with a dirt ceiling and very little breathing room.

6

Frontier, Colorado
0745

Colt's rushed breakfast consisted of a couple of English muffins with peanut butter, a handful of blueberries, and a glass of orange juice. Colt threw some snack food into his work bag and entered his three-car garage. All three stalls were occupied, but he usually only drove his department-issue Chevy Impala. The other vehicles were his personal car, an Audi A4 Quattro, and his winter vehicle, an old Ford Bronco, kept in decent condition and ready for the first snowfall.

Past the vehicles Colt noticed something out of the ordinary. A small wedge of light penetrated the relative darkness of the garage. The service door to the garage was slightly ajar and Colt wondered if the door opening or closing had anything to do with the crashing sound he had heard during the overnight hours. He shut the door, ensured it was locked, and sat down in his Impala.

His ten-minute commute was nothing short of breathtaking. Colt's house sat at 7,800 feet, a full thousand feet higher than the city of Frontier. The city had been built as a resupply and rest town for travelers heading west over the Rocky Mountains. Knife's Edge Pass was roughly three thousand feet above Frontier and still served as a major passage through the mountains. Over the past twenty years the town had experienced a growth in popularity—and population—as a commuter city for people working in Denver.

As Colt drove down toward the city he took in the beautiful surroundings. To his left, past the opposing lane of traffic, a ravine led to a valley formed by the Frontier River, which fittingly ran through the middle of the town of Frontier. To his right was a sheer cliff. It was approximately two hundred feet tall and had been formed as part of the road's construction. What had been a single-track wagon trail one hundred and fifty years ago was now a four-lane highway. First paved in the late 1940s as part of the interstate highway system, it had been expanded in the early 1990s to handle the increasing traffic load presented by the ever-growing population.

Although the views to his right and left were obstructed, the view in front of his car was something from the front of a postcard. To the southeast he could see the plains of Colorado ending their journey out of the fertile fields of Kansas and meeting the imposing giants known as the Rocky Mountains. To the southwest the first amazing ranks of the mountains appeared before him as giant guardians of the West.

Colt wondered what went through the minds of Lewis

and Clark as they traversed across the Rocky Mountains in Montana. *Hell,* Colt mused, *even modern-day travelers get bowled over by the sheer vision of the great snow-covered behemoths rising out of the earth.*

A couple of mountain bends later, the city of Frontier came into view. Only fifty years ago it had been a town of a couple thousand people. Tourists, campers, hikers, and other adventurers had always created a steady bump in the population, but the current city of just under seventy thousand was a sprawling metropolis in comparison to its former skeleton.

One of the first characteristics people noticed is the town's near-perfect symmetry. The river had once been much wider, serving as a drainage channel for snow and glacial melt into the plains of Colorado. The wide flood-plain created both fertile lands and easy development for housing. Agriculture had once helped support the small town, but those farms had since been turned into massive housing developments and city parks.

Frontier's citizens hardly noticed the mass influx of people into the city. The local government purchased hundreds of acres of untouched land and created dozens of parks, large and small, throughout the city. Some parks, kept in their pristine condition, offered families municipal campsites for weekends of camping without leaving the city. Smaller parks were developed into sports fields, picnic areas, playgrounds, and other recreational facilities. Bike paths and walking trails connected all the city parks and large housing developments, allowing people to bike to work, walk to parks, and run around the city at will. Colt's favorites were the several smaller city lakes encircled by paved running trails. He used them to squeeze in a quick three-mile run on busy days.

Only five minutes after entering the outskirts of town, Colt was parking his squad in a stall and walking into the police station, a two-story building nestled into the downtown area. The original police station had been a part of city hall, but as the city had grown, the size of the police force had followed. A few years ago, the city council had approved this state-of-the-art building. The lot had previously housed the historic county jail, which a freak windstorm had leveled several years ago. The county historical society, lacking the money and desire to rebuild the ugly turn-of-the-century building, handed the property over to a public vote. The removal of the police department from city hall opened new space for the other departments within the city, so in the end everyone was happy.

Entering through the non-public door at the rear of the station, Colt scaled the red rock stairwell. The second floor housed the investigations, clerical, and administration units. Because it was a Saturday, the clerical staff and most of the administrators had been scheduled off. Colt knew that the homicide would change that, as the chief, deputy chief, and lieutenants would come in to oversee the investigation. The clerical staff would trickle in during the afternoon hours to handle the influx of reports that would accompany the morning's investigation. The office was not fully awake, but it was only a matter of time before this relative calm turned into a hurricane.

Arriving at his office, Colt sat behind his oversized desk. He had asked for a more normal sized desk at first, but after finding out how much room he needed for his computer forensics tools and how handy the large surface was for laying out files, he changed his tune. Firing up his computer, he checked his e-mail box. It was full of requests for interviews from local news stations. "You know the world has fallen deep into a chasm of laziness when bloodthirsty reporters do not even make the effort to call you anymore," Colt muttered to himself.

"I think you will get some calls about this one," Nick Lawson stated as he entered the room. "This one has psycho written all over it."

"I can't wait. Have the crime scene techs been on-scene yet?"

"They have been working the scene for two hours now. They said it could be a while. Our suspect is good; they claim they haven't found a single piece of evidence. No prints, no tool marks on the door, no DNA, nothing. We are looking at a pro."

"Well, after the Cold Creek killing we were due for a challenge." Three years ago, while Colt was still on the street, Bob Yates, well-known drunk and frequent arrestee, had gotten into a bar fight with someone from Wyoming at closing time. Yates followed the guy to a family-run campground off of Cold Creek, just outside of Frontier. He waited until the guy climbed into his pop-up camper before taking a .38 Special out of his glove box, kicking in the door to the camper, and firing three shots to the victim's chest.

The family who owned the campground called in the sound of the gunshots, and Yates was stopped two miles away for weaving all over the road. He was arrested on scene for DWI, and during an inventory search of his vehicle they found the gun loaded with the spent shell casings in the cylinder. Yates had left his fingerprints all over the gun and the pop-up camper and had gunshot residue all over his hands at the time of the arrest. The prosecutors did not offer a plea bargain, and Yates was found guilty of second-degree murder and sentenced to twenty years in prison. It was the easiest and fastest murder case in the history of Frontier.

"Good point. You ready to go?"

"In a little bit. I'll meet you downstairs in a couple. My stomach has been acting up, gotta hit the head before I get to the scene."

"Sounds good, see you there," Nick said as he exited Colt's office. Colt deleted the e-mails. Chances were he wouldn't even make it to the scene without getting a camera and a microphone shoved into his face.

Another wave of sudden nausea hit him, and he grabbed the wastebasket from next to his desk and fell to his knees. Just before he vomited he felt a familiar pounding inside his head. His English muffins and blueberries made a second appearance, and he hovered over the trash bin to ensure his digestive system was not holding back any more surprises.

After the nausea subsided he felt an odd tingling inside his head. He began to feel lightheaded, as if he was going to pass out. He teetered on the brink of unconsciousness for a few seconds. Then just as fast as it came on, it went away and his mind was clear.

Colt rubbed his forehead and carried the trash can out of his office. Thankfully the night janitor had remembered to place a garbage bag in the bin. He disposed of his formerly delicious breakfast in the bathroom and replaced the garbage can, minus the bag, back in his office. He would have to remember to get a new bag in case the

Olympics continued inside his stomach.

Grabbing his equipment bag, laptop, and cell phone, he headed back to the parking lot. He couldn't see Nick anywhere. As he threw his stuff into the car, Colt felt the familiar tingling in his brain. The lightheadedness returned, and this time he could not hold it back. The colors drained out of the world around him as he closed his eyes and allowed the darkness to overtake his mind.

The window was open, ever so slightly, but enough to tell him it could not be locked. He had anticipated the window being wide open, and when he initially saw it closed on this cold night he had started to panic. He had watched her for several nights and knew that she always left this window open. The urge to kill had been rising ever so slightly. He could hardly hold back the excitement now overtaking him. Slipping his gloved hands under the windowsill, he slowly lifted the wooden frame.

While stalking his victim, he had noticed on the nights when she had closed the window that it did not make a single squeak or shudder. Tonight the window opened the entire way without emitting a single sound. He stood outside and listened for a few seconds; no sounds come out of the room. From his surveillance he was fairly certain she did not own a dog, but to be on the safe side he pulled out and blew a high-pitched whistle. There was no answer to his call, and he breathed a sigh of relief. Pets are notorious for ruining the perfect crime.

After weeks of planning he wanted to make sure that nothing ruined this night. His target was a beautiful widow of a war veteran. Her husband had been shot and killed in one of the recent "peacekeeping" operations.

She lived alone and did not appear to spend a lot of time outside of the house.

She woke up at 5:30 a.m. every day and went for a run. Lately she had been running with a female friend who left as soon as they finished. With luck her body would be discovered soon and his plan could move to the next step.

After her run, she showered and left for work at 7:00 a.m. on the dot, Monday through Friday. She arrived home at 4:30 p.m. and made dinner, then read books until she went to bed. In the few nights that he had been watching, he had not witnessed a single visitor to her house.

The killer entered through the window carefully and quietly. He found himself in a guest room that had obviously not been used in a while. One wall was littered with framed pictures of a man in military attire. He was shown both alone and with other soldiers. Some of the pictures showed him in typical battle uniform, and in others he was wearing civilian clothing but still carrying weapons. Moving silently closer to the pictures, the killer felt a sudden closeness to the soldier. He knew who the soldier was but he had never seen him like this before.

As he turned away from the photos, a small smile broke out across his face. Walking lightly across the remainder of the room, he opened the closed door a crack and peeked through into the hallway. No lights were on and no sounds could be heard.

Slowly opening the door, he entered the hallway and stopped outside the door to her bedroom. He was too smart to leave a calling card and too controlled to make a mistake. He was there to do one thing, and that was to kill the wife of a man he hated. He opened the door just a crack and saw her sleeping on the bed.

Laid across the bed in boxers and a tank top, with her blonde hair streaming down over her shoulders, she looked very like an angel. He entered the room and took out his suppressed Glock 23. Stepping soundlessly toward her, he stopped at the foot of the bed, lifted the pistol, and fired two shots into her forehead.

She felt no pain as the slugs tunneled through her skull and fragmented into her brain. Death was instantaneous, her heart shutting down and limiting the blood flow. After retrieving the shell casings, the bringer of death exited the room. He followed the same path, leaving through the same window and closing it as best he could. The interior lock would have to stay disengaged. It was a small clue that would yield nothing for the investigators other than a possible point of entry and egress.

He carefully extracted himself from the property and then from the neighborhood. He stayed to the shadows until he arrived at his car, parked several blocks away. A couple dogs had barked, but he saw not a single blind raised or light turned on. At the beginning of the night he had felt rusty. Arriving at his car and driving away, he felt confident again. His plan was in motion, and soon he would be free to kill at will.

The opening of the passenger door brought Colt back to reality. "Okay, let's go solve a homicide," Nick said as he slid into the seat next to Colt. He took one look at him and asked, "You okay, man?"

"I'm fine, let's go," Colt answered as he started the car.

"You sure? Because you look like shit."

"Your point? You look like shit every day, and I don't say anything."

"Touché. You're okay all right, and still the same old cranky bastard as always."

"I'd like to remind you that you are actually older than me, my mother and father were married, and the crankiness is only because I haven't slept well in weeks," Colt joked back.

"Damn. That sucks, man. Just get married, and I guarantee you that the boredom brought on by the lack of sex will put you to sleep like a baby."

"Good plan," Colt replied sarcastically. He contemplated whether or not to tell Nick about the blackouts, then decided to keep them to himself. With a murder to investigate he didn't need to be forced to take sick time while the killer was running free. "Let's go get you a collar for homicide."

"Sounds good. I better get some credit when we arrest the guy. I'm gonna catch plenty of hell from Melissa for getting called in on a Saturday. I was supposed to go with her and the kids to the mall for the day."

"Maybe I'll come over and play some ball with the boys and give her some time off. She can't be mad forever."

"You don't know Melissa as well as you think."

"You're right. Consider yourself screwed, and not in the good way," Colt joked as he shifted the car out of park and exited the parking lot en route to the crime scene.

The two of them had formed a friendship after Colt's arrival five years ago. Nick was currently being groomed through investigations to see if he had what it takes to become a detective. Their friendship usually meant that Nick was assigned to cases where Colt was not the lead investigator. The fact that this could be the only murder of the year and Colt was in line for lead on the next homicide made this case an exception.

Colt and Nick started the drive to the murder scene, hell bent on solving the case. Elsewhere two different friends had all the answers the detectives needed, but getting the information to Colt could prove to be a deadly adventure.

7

The Vault
0830

The room was a comfortable seventy degrees, but Sam was sweating profusely. He had been working at a feverish pace to convert the top-secret research documents before his self-scheduled exit from the Vault. Although he was employing almost every security program Dean had provided, he still could feel the steel-cold eyes of the general watching him. While in the middle of converting a file on nerve damage regrowth, he heard footsteps coming down the hallway.

Sam quickly shuffled some papers and started reading through them and jotting notes down on a steno pad. Heavy breathing from the area of the door told him Harrison had arrived. Doubling his efforts, he furrowed his brow and gave a section of a lab report a long look before quickly scribbling some gibberish onto the pad of paper.

The writing would make no sense to any scientist; equations from physics, chemistry, and biology were all that Sam could recall on the spot. But Harrison was not a scientist, and Sam was sure he could convince him that they were relevant brain electro-activity formulas. The general would not know any better.

The encounter, or lack thereof, was wasting his time. Sam wished Harrison would either just come in to ask him what he was doing or leave. Letting go of the same breath he had held for the last minute, Sam looked in the direction of the door. The hallway was empty, and there was no sound of a retreat down the hallway. Wondering whether his mind was playing tricks on him, Sam wiped a bead of sweat from his brow and went back to work.

Reaching under his desk, Sam's fingers found the small ledge that housed his gift from Dean. He always kept it close but not on his body, as all employees were subject to random searches. Walking over to the door, he looked up and down the hallway. Seeing no one there, Sam grabbed a couple safety placards from a cabinet on the wall and slid them into the slots on the door.

The first one said "Experiment in progress. Do not disturb." The second listed a series of dangerous chemicals and warned of possible radiation. The combination would be enough to keep the guards out of the room and probably even give his door a wide berth while on their rounds.

Trying not to look at the cameras and arouse suspicion, Sam sat at his desk and discreetly disconnected the phone handset before connecting the satellite phone relay. Plugging the new clip into the jack as nonchalantly as he could, he raised the handset to his ear. The relay required a code in order to activate the device. He dialed a predetermined number sequence on the keypad.

The code activated the software stored on the device and gave Sam a dial tone. He punched in Dean's number and heard two rings before a familiar voice answered the phone.

"Hey, Sam, how are you doing?" Dean asked.

"I'm ready to get out of here."

"Okay, now you're talking. Let's go over the plan."

"I have all the files on the disc and a nine o'clock appointment with Walter. All I have to do is build the escape sequence and then start the timer for Fat Boy."

"Okay . . . what time are you going to make your break?"

"I told Harrison I would have the files on his desk by noon today. If I leave any earlier than eleven there is a chance that he will come looking for me and lock down the base when he can't find me. If I wait too close to noon I won't have enough time. I am going to aim for eleven, and if all goes well I will be off base by eleven thirty."

"You have the directions, right?"

"Yeah, but let's go over them one more time."

"Take the dirt road until you come to the highway. You will need to secure a vehicle at some point. A lot of people around here leave their keys in their cars. Head west until you are almost out of the mountains. Watch the clock; five minutes before noon find a place to ditch the vehicle. I am sure the general had some backup programs installed after my escape, and in case they can come back online sooner than anticipated you need to be far from the Vault. After ditching the vehicle you will need to hurry up and get to the closest town."

"Dammit, I didn't plan on hoofing it cross-country."

"You'll be fine. If need be, ditch the vehicle early while you are driving through a town. Find some transportation and get to Freedom Springs. I am on a farm on the western edge of town. Harrison will most likely keep the local law enforcement out of the loop for a while, so they won't be looking for you. But try to keep a low profile anyway. The people around here will look out for you; all you have to do is get here."

"Sounds like a piece of cake," Sam replied with obvious anxiety.

"Relax. Harrison and his goons are overly confident in the base's security. As long as we stay one step ahead we'll be fine."

"I trust you. I can't wait to breathe the open air again."

"By tomorrow you'll be breathing the fresh air of freedom, Sam."

"Thanks, Dean, I owe you."

"Don't worry about it, man. Take care, and don't do anything stupid."

"Like break out of a fortified secret military base and bring down a top-secret research program run by a ruthless military general?" Sam joked.

"Okay, do all those things, but nothing else stupid," Dean replied with a laugh. "Good luck."

"Thanks. See you later," Sam said, and hung up the phone. Nervousness was giving way to excitement, and he almost forgot to remove the relay. With the cameras in mind he cautiously removed the relay and stuck it in his pocket. Sam knew Dean would cringe if he saw what he was going to do next. Taking the relay over to a workbench, Sam made sure his back blocked the camera view.

After a few blows from a wrench, the relay shattered into pieces. Scooping up the pieces, he carried them over to a wastebasket and threw them away. There was no going back now. With one of his two ties to the outside world gone, his escape had to be now or never.

After running a quick experiment to make the guards a little less inquisitive, Sam looked at the clock and realized it was almost nine. He quickly tested the CD he had made, tucked it into the sleeve of his white lab coat, and walked to the cafeteria. He had purposely pushed his breakfast back to nine o'clock on his agenda. While this was slightly out of norm for Sam, he doubted either Anna or Harrison would notice.

Arriving in time to choose between two stale donuts or a cold sausage, egg, and biscuit sandwich, Sam grabbed one of each plus a brown sandwich bag. He placed the donut inside the bag and then sat down and took a bite of the cold breakfast sandwich.

He made a disgusted face and lowered the bag into his lap. He pulled the donut from the bag and replaced it with the partially eaten sandwich. He allowed the CD to slip out from his sleeve and into the bag. Removing a pen from his lab coat, he set the bag on the table and wrote the word "nasty" on it. The act was done in plain view of the camera with the assumption the guards would see his behavior as nothing more than more quirky antics out of yet another odd scientist.

Standing up, he carried the bag over to the trash and deposited it on top of the rest of the breakfast refuse. As he walked out of the room, Walter the janitor was heading in. No one saw the small smiles the two exchanged.

8

Frontier, Colorado
0900

It was a starter house, small, but one with everything a young couple could need. Colt and Nick approached the outer perimeter, where a thin line of onlookers had formed along a line of crime scene tape patrolled by a few rookie officers.

The media were there too, their vans parked haphazardly in the street. The antennas fought for air space and the satellite dishes sat ready to beam the information live to Denver. A young cop, straight out of the academy, waved them through a hastily erected checkpoint. Colt parked the black Impala among the marked squads and the Criminal Response and Search Team van.

The CRST was an experimental unit. Led by Colt and a few other detectives, it was a versatile response team capable of performing a multitude of functions.

Their missions included anything from gathering evidence at crime scenes to finding and rescuing lost hikers in the mountains.

Funded by the state of Colorado and the FBI, the team had a large budget and so far the results had been outstanding. They had the highest arrest ratio in the nation and had rescued numerous hikers and climbers from the mountains outside Frontier. Colt had complete faith in the evidence technicians who made up the crime scene portion of the team. He had trained the team leaders, who in turn trained the remainder of the team. Colt still spent a fair amount of time nose-deep in fingerprint dust, working side by side with the team members to keep his skills in form.

"Morning, Colt. I don't like the looks of this," Sergeant Harold Branson bellowed from his position at the front door. It was his task to restrict access to the scene. "One victim. A young woman with two bullets to the head. No sign of struggle, no preliminary signs of sexual assault, no signs of robbery, just looks like she was shot in her sleep."

Branson was one of the oldest guys in the department. His aged bronze skin and white hair added a few years to his true age. He had been the training sergeant in the department for many years. Having a special gift for working with young officers, the sergeant had turned many new officers into well-rounded professionals.

Colt took the sign-in roster from Branson. "Well, there's always a motive; it's just our challenge to find it." Colt signed his name, logging in his time and reason for being on the scene. A crime scene, especially a homicide, is a vacuum for people. In an effort to satisfy their own curiosity, unneeded personnel can inadvertently destroy evidence and interrupt the work of the crime scene techs. The sign-in process tracked those entering the scene and required a follow-up report on what that officer did at the scene. Most officers did all they could to avoid doing reports, so the idea of writing a report stating that they entered the crime scene just to look at a dead body discouraged the vast majority of unnecessary personnel from entering the scene.

Colt opened the front door, instantly recognizing the organized chaos that was underway. Crime scene techs were dusting for prints, looking for trace evidence, and taking pictures of anything and everything. Among the pandemonium, Colt singled out Angela White.

The thirty-eight-year-old detective was gorgeous. Her tight-fitting business shirt and slacks did little to hide her hourglass figure. Her shoulder-length brown hair had been pulled up into a bun. A stylish pair of glasses drew attention to the sky-blue eyes that had won over many a male companion.

Colt had resisted her charm many times, ensuring that their relationship stayed professional. It had not been easy, and Colt feared it was only a matter of time before his temptation to accept overtook him.

"Hey, Colt," she said in her slightly raspy voice. "Looks like a hot one. What do you think?"

"From what Branson told me, we have nothing," Colt replied. His words had come out a little too fast. Having caught Colt checking her out, she wanted to catch him off guard as well. As a smile grew across her lips, he quickly recovered. "What *do* we have?"

"Nothing," she stated, allowing the smile to just

break out of the corner of her lips before retracting it with a wink.

"Great," Nick chimed in.

"I never said it was going to be easy," Colt remarked. Suddenly a pain grew in his head, causing him shut to his eyes and his knees to buckle slightly.

"You okay?" Angela questioned, looking concerned.

"He's fine. I'm guessing a few too many drinks while he was out hitting on the ladies."

"Whatever, Nick. Stop living vicariously through him."

"I'm fine," Colt said with a little sharpness in his voice. Looking at both of the detectives and their now-inquisitive faces, he quickly apologized. "Sorry, I haven't been feeling well lately. Just some lingering effects I guess."

"No offense, Colt, I've had my share of those days, I think everyone here can attest to that," Angela confessed.

"I'll second that," a young voice came from the next room. They shared a quick laugh while Angela rolled her eyes. "Let's get on with this," she said and led the way to the bedroom.

"I left Kosliski in charge of the door," Sergeant Branson stated as he walked up behind Colt. "Let me know what else I can do to help."

"Thanks, Harold. We should be good for now." Branson smiled, nodded, and left the hallway.

"Meet Abigail Connelly," Angela stated. "Thirty-four years old. Resident of Frontier for the last six years. We are still getting information on her, but she sounds like the typical middle-thirties businesswoman, other than the fact that she was a widow. Based on the pictures in the second bedroom, her husband was a soldier. There is a flag that is folded, encased, and mounted on the wall. Under the flag there is a plaque, noting his dates of service and the date he was killed in action. It looks like she may have never gotten over him."

"We aren't looking at a suicide, are we?" Colt quickly asked.

"Can't rule it out, but it looks pretty unlikely considering we didn't find the gun or the shell casings, and it is pretty hard to fire a second shot to your own forehead," Angela offered.

"Yeah, unless someone happened upon the body, shot it again, removed the gun and casings to make it look like a murder," Nick suggested.

"Again, possible but unlikely; this was called in as a check-welfare. She usually meets a friend to go running in the morning, and when she didn't show up, O'Grady got dispatched to check on her. The place was locked up tight; we are still looking at how anyone got in here."

"Well, someone came in here and left. I highly doubt she shot herself and then gave someone the key to come remove the gun and casings. Nick, we need someone to check on her finances, see if she was in debt and see if she had a life insurance policy."

"Copy," Nick said as he pulled out a small notebook and began making notes.

"What did she do after she lost her husband?" Colt asked as he surveyed the scene. His focus was on the blonde woman on the bed. A sense of déjà vu overcame him as he looked past the bullet wounds to her head and the blood-soaked pillows.

"We are attempting to get ahold of her family, but it looks like all she has is very distant relatives. We've talked to her neighbors briefly; they told us she was a pleasant young lady. They did say she always looked sad, not that anyone would blame her." Colt was listening, but he couldn't break the feeling that he knew the young woman.

"When was Thompson dispatched?" Colt questioned. There were signs of livor mortis on the dorsal side of her legs. The pull of gravity drew her blood to the lowest points in her body, marking the time of death as at least a couple hours prior. If they moved the body and blood stayed stagnant, they would be sure she had been dead at least six hours.

"He arrived on scene at five thirty, made entry at five forty-five, and discovered the body almost immediately. He didn't move the body, just checked her pulse out of habit and called for Branson and backup right away," Angela answered.

"What was her body temperature and what time was it taken?" Colt asked, hoping it had already been taken.

"Right around ninety-one degrees at seven thirty. At one and a half degrees an hour, that gives us a time of death sometime around three o'clock this morning."

"Okay, so we have the start of a timeline." Colt stated. As he ran through the answers provided, he felt he was getting a better picture of what happened to the victim. "Do we have anything for physical evidence yet? And I mean anything."

"Nothing. No forced entry, no shell casings, no fingerprints, we have nothing," Angela sighed.

"Well, we always have Locard's principle," Colt stated with confidence.

"No one can ever leave an area without leaving something of themselves behind," Nick piped up.

"Yeah," Angela replied, "I know the rule, and the bitch of it is trying to find what they left behind."

"But we have the best people we can at work on it. Give them some time, they'll find something." Colt moved his eyes from the bed and scanned the rest of the room. The floor was carpeted, creating the possibility of lifting shoe prints using static electricity. He called over a crime scene team member and asked them to dust for prints from the area at the foot of the bed. Turning back to Angela he asked, "Was the bedroom door open or closed when the first units arrived?"

"Closed," Angela replied with a smile on her face. "And I know your next question: We have checked the bedroom windows, and they are all locked from the inside."

"Wow, maybe I should leave Nick with you so he can learn something," Colt said with a smile.

"I don't think he can handle me," Angela replied with a wink.

"My wife would kill me," Nick replied quickly, getting a laugh out of Colt and Angela. "Okay, I see where you are going. So the killer had to enter the house from another room."

"Exactly, Nick. Hopefully we can retrace his or her steps." Colt went over to the window and examined it. "Since the windows only lock from the inside, the killer would have had to exit through one that was unlocked, or they had a key to lock the deadbolts on the exterior doors. If we don't find a window unlocked, then he or she had a key."

"We looked at the windows in the guest room and found one unlocked."

"Okay, I'll check that out, you run Nick through the coroner's notes. I'll come back after looking at the room."

"Sounds good. It'll take me a few minutes to explain all the parts of the notes."

Colt gave them the nod and entered the guest room. He found himself drawn to the pictures of the victim's dead husband.

The soldier had been a handsome young man. In almost every picture he was smiling and had a look of confidence and purpose. Walking from picture to picture, Colt admired the young man for the sacrifices he had made, including the ultimate sacrifice. Abruptly Colt felt the room start to spin; then, as quickly as it started, it stopped. Shaking his head, he moved to the wall with the flag. The Stars and Stripes were framed in a shadow box and hung on the wall. Inside the box and centered underneath the flag he read the inscription:

This flag was flown at the U.S. Capitol in recognition of the life work and ultimate sacrifice of Master Sergeant William E. Connelly.

Service Record:
Enlisted—January 14, 1993
3/75th Ranger Batt., August 1993—Sept 1997
1st Special Forces Operational Detachment-Delta
(SFOD-D) Combat Applications Group (CAG),
Sept 1997—Sept 2006
KIA—Southwest Asia—Sept 30, 2006

After reading the last line, flashes of light filled the

room. Colt felt like a strobe light was going off inside his head, and he fell to the ground, curling up in a ball.

Connelly continued toward the bright white light. Though he was at peace, something was not right. No matter how hard he tried, he never got closer to the light. He tried running, but his legs locked up. A sensation of falling came over him, and suddenly noises filled his head. Sounding distant at first, they soon grew louder, as if they were approaching him. The light remained bright, but as the noises moved closer the glow appeared to move farther away. In an instant he felt painful tongues of fire raking his skin. He began screaming, attempting to flail his arms, but he found they were locked down.

Dark shapes started to form around his head. They were talking, but he could not make out the words, as if they were talking in a foreign language. Slowly his eyes began to focus, and he saw their faces covered in what he realized were surgical masks, goggles, and hairnets. He was still screaming when they gave him his own mask, and he felt the fire leave his body. The light was still there, but he now knew it was a surgical lamp. He couldn't see, move, or hear anything. Feeling the full effects of the gas, Connelly gave in and let his mind drift away, thankful to have the pain gone once again. He would awake thousands of miles away to a new type of pain.

"Colt!" Angela yelled as she entered the room. "Are you okay?" Colt waited to answer because he wasn't sure what to say. Initially he could not remember what had transpired; then, slowly, bits and pieces of the past few moments started coming back to him. He could remember looking at the flag, and then his mind was blank. "Colt, is everything okay?"

Angela was kneeling next to him, her soft hand holding his. Nick stood off to the side, a worried expression on his face. "Yeah, like I said, I haven't been feeling so good," Colt answered honestly.

"Well you look like shit; you want someone to check you out?"

"No, I'm fine, just bad headaches. They come and go." Colt rose to his feet, feeling his face flush with embarrassment. "You finished with the report?"

"Yeah, nothing too surprising. The official report will have to wait for autopsy, but unless the tox labs or internals show others, the likely cause of death will be the first gunshot wound to the head. The external exam showed no sign of any other pre-existing injuries at this time," Nick recited.

"Okay, then let's get some guys to concentrate on this window and pull up anything they can. I doubt we'll find prints, but maybe a tool mark or some bodily fluids, anything that will give us something to work with," Colt said as he stared at the window. "Come on, Nick, let's go talk with a couple of the neighbors, and see if they have anything more."

Angela opened her mouth, but Nick beat her to it, saying, "You sure you don't want to call it a day, Colt? You're not going to get much information passed out on someone's floor."

"I'm fine," Colt protested. "Look, we'll talk to the neighbors, get what we can while it's fresh, and then I'll go back to bed."

"It's your head," Angela declared, looking dubious.

"I'm going to stick around a little longer and see if anything comes up on the window."

"Great, give me a call if you get anything. I'll call you if we learn anything from the neighbors."

"Copy. Take it easy, and if those headaches don't get any better, I would get them checked out," Angela said with genuine concern. "It would be a shame to not get to see your gorgeous face around." With that last comment she shot him one of her wicked smiles and turned back toward the window.

"Okay, Angela, talk to you later," Colt stuttered out. He had never handled compliments from women well. He and Nick left the room and headed out, stopping to see the progress of a few of the CRT members along the way. As they left the house, Colt and Nick signed out on the log and compared notes on what they had so far.

"Well, the most likely point of entry was the unsecured window into the guest room. The fact that no fingerprints, shell casings, et cetera were left behind shows that the killer was on his or her game. If they were good enough to leave little to no evidence behind, then they probably had some prior knowledge of the victim's residence. We'll confirm this, but I am assuming she is a bit of a recluse, so any information about her will best be obtained by someone who lives close to her. My guess is the suspect is a coworker or a stalker."

"Well, we can figure that out with some good old footwork and interviewing," Nick volunteered. "It should be easy to eliminate neighbors and coworkers once we talk to them."

"Exactly what I was thinking. I just hope we are both wrong, because finding a stalker could be a problem."

Mitch Wilson, a property crimes detective called in to help with the murder, was standing near his squad, jotting down some notes. "Hey, Mitch," Colt asked as they approached, "which neighbors did you interview?"

"Umm . . . I got the ones next to the house and the ones across the street. They're all older folks. They said they would be home for the rest of the day and would be happy to answer any further questions."

"Great, I have a few questions for them. The scene hasn't given us anything to work with, so hopefully they can help us out."

"Okay, good luck, guys," Wilson replied.

With Nick in tow, Colt turned off the sidewalk and headed toward the house to the left of the victim's. The news that the neighbors were elderly was a small stroke of luck. Colt had found that older people tended to have higher rates of cooperation with police and were more apt to be observant of their surroundings. They might have noticed a stranger hanging around the area or someone coming to visit the victim recently.

The first house had both stairs and a wheelchair ramp. Nick walked up the stairs and rang the doorbell, which sounded an abnormally loud buzz on the other side of the door. They could both hear the whir of an electric wheelchair as it approached the door. Colt noticed that the peephole was halfway up the door, not in its normal location. There was a pause as the owner of the house more than likely looked through it at his or her future guests before the door swung open.

A man in his early eighties gave them a quizzical look as he asked, "Can I help you?"

Colt took out his badge and ID and showed them,

saying, "I am Detective Colt Sullivan with Frontier police, and this is my partner, Nick Lawson. We'd like to ask you a few questions, if that's okay with you."

The old man's face lit as he ushered the men inside, "Why sure, detectives, come in and sit down. I was worried you were one of those bozos from the news." The old man turned his wheelchair around and zipped off into the living room. "Have a seat. Would you like anything to drink?"

"No, thank you, we're fine," Colt replied for the both of them. "This is a beautiful house you have here."

"Thank you, my wife keeps it up. I try to help out, but she tells me I am just getting in the way."

"I know how that goes. Is your wife around?" Nick asked.

"No, she ran into town to get some groceries. Saturday is grocery day. The grandkids come over on Sunday, and I swear they can each eat a whole cow."

"I have two kids of my own, but thankfully they are still small."

The old man smiled, "I'm sorry, I must have left my manners in my seventies. I'm Edward Meyer." He extended his hand toward Colt.

"It's nice to meet you Mr. Meyer. I just—"

"Please call me, Ed. 'Mr. Meyer' makes me feel old," he said with a whimsical smile.

"Sure thing, Ed. I know you have already been questioned by the police, but we just have a few more questions about your neighbor, Mrs. Connelly."

"Oh, she is or, sadly, was a sweet young thing. When she moved in she was so sad. We got to talking one day and found out about William. I remember what it was like for all the widows in my generation. War is such a travesty. She was too young to be filled with so much pain. It did seem like she was starting to smile more and more over the last year. Oh, I'm sorry. You haven't even asked a question yet."

"That's quite alright. Feel free to talk away, you may give us some information we can't get through questions. In fact my first question was going to be 'what do you know about her?' and you were right on track. Keep going," Colt reassured the man with a smile. Nick jotted down notes while Colt stored the information in his head.

"Okay. Like I said, the past year she had started to do better. We had her over for a dinner last month and she was full of smiles. My wife and I thought she was getting ready to move on with her life. Not in a romantic way; her heart still belonged to William. She told me once that she kept the guest-room window unlocked, just in case he ever found her and needed to get in. We tried to tell her that he was gone, but she kept insisting that there was a chance he was alive. She never explained why, but she believed it with her heart."

Colt had heard exactly what he needed. This further confirmed the probability that the killer had entered through the window. "You say she was moving on with her life. Did she appear to be going out more or meeting new friends, stuff like that?" Colt asked.

"She did say she was meeting some friends at work, but she never came home with anyone, if that's what you mean. She kept the same schedule, running in the morning, going to work, and then watching TV or reading at night. Lately she had been running with a female friend of hers that we hadn't seen before. We assumed it was a coworker."

"Thank you for all that, it really helps our investigation. Could you describe her friend?" Nick chimed in.

"Sure thing. She was about the same age as Abby, but a little shorter. You know, she was a real cute, petite woman. Curly red hair I believe. I think Abby told me her name once, but at eighty-two years young, I can't seem to recall it."

"That's okay, we should be able to find her," Colt replied. "My final question is sort of open-ended. I want you to think of anything that would answer this question. Don't think anything is stupid; just answer with whatever comes to mind. Have you noticed anything out of the ordinary in the neighborhood lately? Could be a strange vehicle, person, flashes of light, anything that caught you as strange." Colt had taken out his fishing rod. He just hoped the old man had something to bite with.

"As a matter of fact, now that I think of it, there was something one night. I can't believe I didn't tell the officer this earlier. I must be getting old or something." Colt watched Nick lean forward, listening intently. "The other night, this must have been a week or so ago, I woke up in the middle of the night with pains in my legs. It's common for me. I took some shrapnel in the war and it is still affecting me. Some nights it is just unbearable. I got up to get some painkillers. My wife normally gets them for me, but she was sleeping so soundly, I didn't want to wake her. I got into my chair and got the medications from the kitchen. I took them and realized I was suddenly very awake. I came into the living room to watch some television, and when I looked out the window I saw a young man standing between the houses. It was dark, and he was staying to the shadows, so I couldn't see his face. But he definitely was not from around here. The way he was dressed, in all black, caught my eye too. I thought he might be a burglar or something, but without seeing him do anything wrong, I didn't think to call the police. Maybe I should have."

"We could have talked with him, but chances are he would have been gone by the time we could get someone here. It's no big deal." Colt was lying now. He knew it was a big deal, and they could have had a chance to identify the guy before the murder ever occurred. He couldn't hold it against the old man; it is often the misconception of the public that they are wasting police resources by calling in strange things. In reality, a lot of in-progress crimes are stopped by citizens calling in suspicious activity. "Have you seen this man since then?"

"No, I haven't been up at night since then. I didn't hear of any burglaries or anything, so it went to the back of my mind until you asked just now."

"I know you said you didn't see his face, but could you describe him to me to the best of your ability?"

"Sure, he was about six feet tall and did not appear to be too skinny or overweight. He did have some size to him, a good amount of muscle. Your build type," he replied, pointing to Colt.

"Okay, and what kind of clothes was he wearing?"

"Dark sweatpants and a dark shirt. He had a baseball cap on, it was dark too."

"Okay, and was he white, Hispanic, African-American?"

"Couldn't tell for sure, I just saw the corner of his face, but he looked white to me."

"And nothing else has been out of the ordinary?"

"No, just him that I can think of."

"How long ago did this happen?"

"A week ago."

"Okay, Ed, you have been a great help. Could you do me a favor and ask your wife when she gets home if she has seen anything? Especially anybody matching the description you gave me. If so, could one of you give me a call?" Colt said, standing up and handing Ed his business card. "Thank you very much."

"Not a problem, detectives, swing by anytime. We love visitors. Let me show you to the door." Edward wheeled over to the door and shook Colt and Nick's hands. "Let me know if I can be of any more help."

"I will. Take care, Ed."

"Good-bye detectives. Make sure you catch the bastard that killed Abby."

"Don't worry, sir, we'll get him," Nick assured him. "Good-bye."

They stepped out of the house feeling much better. They had a lead. It wasn't a great lead, but it was a lead nonetheless. They split up to save time and canvassed the other houses but came up with no new information. Nobody had seen anything at night, although one elderly woman had told him that her cat had been hacking up more hairballs lately. Colt laughed as he left her house. It wasn't her fault; he had asked for anything out of the ordinary.

Re-entering the victim's home, he located White and filled her in on his new discovery. "So that gives us an unknown suspect, but we need something to locate him with," Colt stated as he watched the techs work the window.

"Yeah, so far no luck, the window is completely clean as far as we can tell. And that leaves us with nothing." She sighed. "I don't like where this case is going, Colt."

"Don't worry, we'll catch him. I just hope it's before he strikes again."

"The town is going to be in an uproar if we don't catch him soon," Nick stated. "The people are not going to like to hear that a random killing occurred and we have no suspects and no motive."

"I'll handle the press," Colt said with a sigh. "I'll just choose my words carefully. Which reminds me: I'd better get ready for the press conference. You want to come with, Nick?"

"I'll hitch a ride back to the department and start looking at any contacts we have with the victim. Maybe she reported something that we just haven't found yet."

"Sounds good, Nick. Once I am done feeding the press monster I'll come find you. When everything is wrapped up here we'll head to her office and talk with the coworkers. The friend who called in the check-welfare might know something."

"Okay, you guys head out. I am going to stay here and work with the techs. If we get anything I'll call you right away," Angela acknowledged.

"Great. Hopefully by noon we'll have something to work with," Colt said as he started walking toward the press. He would have to give a quick statement and answer some very limited questions. As he thought about the media he could feel another headache coming on, but this one made sense. The media always had a way of bringing out the worst in an already bad situation.

9

The Vault
1000

The Vault gained its nickname from the fact it was dug into the side of a small mountain. The entire facility existed underground, buried beneath hundreds of feet of solid rock. From the highway the only evidence of the base's existence was a small gate situated along a side road. A few signs warned of severe criminal consequences for trespassing on federal property. The few people who dared drive down the road never made it more than a quarter mile before they were met at gunpoint by Harrison's base security.

The facility had been built during the Cold War to provide shelter for high-ranking military officials and to house a logistical support base in the event of a nuclear attack. In the mid-1980s, with the Eastern Bloc crumbling, the underground city had been transformed into a top-secret research facility. What resulted was a secure site for the nation's most classified projects, impenetrable to everything but espionage.

The first and still most important area of research for the base was the human brain. The Cold War had taught the United States that there were more ways to fight a war than with bombs and bullets alone. The psychological effects on the human brain of the mere threat of nuclear war were amazing.

The scientists at the base were given the mission of studying how the human brain really works. They focused their efforts on cracking the code that controlled cognitive thought and memory. They found that the brain was nothing more than a highly complicated machine. Once they understood how the machine worked—"the code," they called it—they discovered several methods to manipulate and modify it.

Within the walls of The Vault, an elderly janitor pushed a garbage cart through the cavernous hallways.

"I didn't storm the beaches at Normandy for this," Walter Brown said quietly. "And if Frank's father could see him now . . ."

Walter had shared a foxhole with General Harrison's father throughout most of Europe. Young Frank had spent hours listening to the two men swap war stories and speak of their fallen brothers. Chosen to be Frank's godfather, Walter took the appointment seriously. He attended the general's graduations and promotion ceremonies, and eventually helped to bury Harrison's father.

When Walter lost his wife to leukemia several years back, Harrison had offered him a job. Walter accepted it to avoid the loneliness of old age and to stay close to his godson. He was the only staff member on the base who could come and go as he pleased. Although Harrison was a harsh man, Walter believed the general had a soft spot that convinced him not to make Walter a prisoner for the last years of his life.

Walter's first encounter with Sam had taken place in the Vault's cafeteria. The elderly janitor had been eating by himself, as he always did, when Sam sat down next to him. "Don't mind if I join you, do you?" Sam had asked.

"No sir, have a seat." That was all it took for the friendship to form. Walter had been impressed by the younger man. Sam was a brilliant scientist, and Walter appreciated his dedication. However, it was no surprise to Walter when Sam finally confessed his true feelings about the program. Although Walter loved General Harrison like a son, he was far from ignorant about the madness in his godson's behavior.

The initial group of scientists recruited to work at the base had been hard-working and fun-loving. They made scientific breakthroughs in their respective fields on an almost weekly basis. Many of them confided in Walter that they thought they were building resumes that they could take to major private companies and make a fortune.

Eventually they realized their work was so secret that they would never be allowed to speak of it again. They couldn't use any of their accomplishments to better their careers. Their displeasure was so great that many started turning in resignation letters, only to find that they landed in the general's shredder. The base security staff that they had thought was there to keep intruders out ultimately became prison guards.

All outgoing communications were monitored and edited. Harrison had specifically chosen scientists with no spouses or children. Some of them had parents, but the ones who had been hired had been screened and shown to have poor family contact. The vast majority of them had not talked to family members in years.

Walter had been on the general's side in the beginning. Sometimes sacrifices needed to be made, freedoms taken away, for the good of the country. Gradually, however, he came to empathize with the scientists. Although Walter had the freedom to come and go from the facility, he was subject to intense searches and more than once found himself being tailed or under surveillance by agents outside the base.

The first time he saw the gray panel van outside his house he thought nothing of it. A week later the same van was parked down the street at an odd hour, and it raised his curiosity. Deciding to take a midnight walk, Walter found that the van followed him. Eventually he walked to a park and sat on a bench. The same van drove by the park no less than ten times in the five minutes he was at the park. He returned to the house and found the van parked in the same spot it was prior to his midnight stroll. Two thoughts had crossed his mind: They were either very inept in their ability to be subtle, or they wanted him to know he was being followed. The latter made more sense, and it enraged him.

In all the years Walter had spent with the Harrison family, he had never once given Frank a reason to distrust him. Walter realized Frank Harrison was out of control and needed to be brought down.

Walter knew that notifying the Pentagon would not

work. Harrison had far too many connections high up in the chain of command. Any attempt to talk to the press would result in the government saying that the old man had dementia. It didn't matter what he did. Alone, he would fail and the general's punishment would be swift and brutal. Walter now believed his godson—his boss—was capable of having him murdered to keep the base's secrets. Walter had watched Frank grow up and become a monster. There was only one way to stop him.

One day while eating lunch, Walter saw Sam approaching.

"Hey, what do you have today?" Sam asked.

"Peanut butter and jelly sandwich, same as always."

"Of all the things in the outside world, you choose to eat PBJ sandwiches?"

"Hey! They are mighty tasty. Besides, I was never much of a cook. That was Gloria's specialty."

"I remember. Every time you talk about her lavish meals you leave me drooling. Anything can beat the slop they call food around here."

"Why do you think I bring PBJ sandwiches?"

"I don't blame you," Sam replied, looking at his watch. "Walter, I have shut off the microphones in this room. Do you trust me?"

Walter didn't hesitate. "Yes, Sam."

"I only have sixty seconds before the system resets, so please listen. I am going to try to escape like Dean did."

"You'll be killed!"

"That's a possibility. That's why I am asking you to be my backup plan. I need you to sneak a disc filled with classified documents off the base."

"Damn it, Sam. I don't know."

"Walter, you know what this place has become. You know what *Harrison* has become. This is no longer for love of country. This is about doing what is right."

"You're right," Walter admitted, letting out a big sigh. "I've known for awhile that this place is evil. Harrison was like a son to me, but he's gone too far and someone needs to bring a stop to it. What is the rest of the plan?"

"You get the disc off the base and deliver it to a location I will discuss with you later. Then it is up to you. You can risk coming back and lying about your involvement, or you can join us."

"I'm not coming back. Harrison has dug his own grave, and I'm not laying down in it with him."

"I can only shut down the mics a couple more times before security gets suspicious. We'll talk about the rest of the plan later, our time is up. Hey . . . how about them Rockies?"

"They put the balls in a humidor, and Kaslow still hits them four hundred and fifty feet."

"No kidding. Always good to talk baseball with you Walter. Have a good day."

"You too, Sam. Good-bye."

At the time the plan was concocted, Walter was not allowed to bring anything on or off the base. Over the course of a few weeks he began hinting to Harrison that he wanted to bring a CD player so he could listen to music while performing the monotonous tasks of mopping floors and emptying garbage cans. Harrison reluctantly agreed, on the condition that the player and any CDs going in and out of the base would be searched both physically and electronically. Walter had grudgingly agreed to the deal, acting as if the additional intrusion on his privacy almost outweighed the benefit of the music. He had brought the CD player for over a month now, and while the daily inspections were annoying, his patience would pay off.

"Here goes nothing," Walter whispered as he focused back at his task at hand. Pushing his cart full of garbage toward the incinerator, he stopped in the hallway and fumbled with his CD player. He pressed a few buttons and then took off his headphones. Opening the case, he removed the CD to look it over. While doing so he made sure it slipped out of his hands and into the garbage can on his cart. Showing a not entirely false expression of surprise and disgust, he reached into the garbage to grab his CD. The bag marked "nasty" was on top of the garbage he had gathered from the dining room. Quickly reaching into the brown paper bag, he pulled out the CD. He looked it over, checking for any garbage, wiped it off on his shirt before putting it in the player.

Walter closed the player's lid and pressed play, a smile breaking out across his face as the player functioned perfectly. He then resumed his normal routine, pushing the cart toward the incineration room.

The black orb of a nearby security camera had recorded the entire event. The security guard in charge of that camera made a note in his log. While he had not seen the actual switch, the guards had been told to be suspicious of any activity outside normal limits. Before Walter left, additional checks would be run on the CD player and compact disc.

Pushing the cart to the shredding and incineration room, Walker offloaded his cart, parked it as usual at the end of his shift, and gave the security camera a wave as he made his way to his vehicle.

Walter had little difficulty in locating his car under a dim security light in the base's underground parking garage. The large lot only contained a few vehicles, Walter's car sharing the space with a few security trucks and some dark-colored sedans. The government gave him a new car every two years. Walter was sure it was full of the latest bugs and gizmos to track his location. He had no doubt that if he decided to take off one day and attempt to disappear, the agents would find him in short order as long as he remained in his vehicle. Normally Walter had nothing to fear from their tracking. He drove from work to home and back, stopping occasionally at stores for basic supplies. Walter had never given them any reason to be suspicious, and he tried to keep it that way.

The electronic chirp from his wireless remote confirmed that he had disengaged the locks. After opening the door, Walter removed the CD player from his fanny pack. In the month he had been wearing the device he had already formed the habit of getting it ready for inspection. He set the player and the fanny pack on the front passenger seat and shut the door.

He turned the key in the ignition, and the car started with a soft purr. The government spared no expense, and although he did not need it they always gave him the best package available for whatever car he was getting. This one had an upgraded engine, a state-of-the-art navigation system, and a premium stereo, along with all the other options a car owner could want. Walter backed out of his spot and drove through the poorly illuminated garage to the exit.

Approaching the dark side of a large door, Walter hit

one of the custom-installed buttons on his dashboard and waited. After the base had been fully converted, a small service door had been cut into the massive blast doors. Sluggishly the blinding light of the outside world flooded the dark cavern as the door opened. The sunglasses that he slid onto his face were a requirement for anyone leaving the base. Although the sterile white walls did reflect a large amount of light, the dark corridors of the base could do little to prepare someone for the full onslaught of the sun.

Even with the sunglasses it was often hard for Walter's eyes to adjust. He left the base at a crawl, letting the light penetrate his corneas slowly. Once he was able to see the guard shack on the outside of the blast doors, he tapped the gas and drove toward the structure. As the vehicle approached, a guard got out and waved him to a stop.

The afternoon-shift security guard had been a linebacker in the NFL. Walter had gotten to know him over their hundreds of daily interactions and inspections. While there were other guards who worked the front gate, Mike was Walter's favorite.

Mike approached the Stratus as Walter lowered the window for him. Mike's massive forearms rested on the driver's side windowsill as he leaned down to begin their ritual. "Good afternoon, Walter. How's your day? I didn't expect you to leave until later this afternoon."

"Stomach issues. I fear I might be coming down with a touch of the flu."

"That's no good. Let's get you through this as quick and painless as possible."

"All right. I had tickets to the ballgame tonight, but I guess I'm not going anymore."

"At least you can watch the game. I've been begging someone for months to get us a TV out here so we can watch sports."

"Good luck with that. I thought Harrison was going to have my head for lunch when I asked him for this CD player."

"About that. Word is I need to do an additional search on that today. Probably just some new software they want to run."

"No problem, Mike."

"I just need you to step out for the normal body and vehicle search, and then I'll check the disc."

"Sure thing," Walter replied as he opened the door and got out of the car. "Do whatever you need, but go easy on the cavity search."

"Not that tight of security, Walter," Mike replied with a laugh. He ran a quick physical search of Walter and found nothing on him. Mike popped both the hood and the trunk and found nothing that hadn't been bolted down in the factory. On the passenger seat was Walter's fanny pack, containing the CD player. "Like I said, I gotta take a look at this."

"Go ahead, just a little Beethoven today," Walter said with a smile. He watched as Mike looked over the pack, removed the CD player, and opened it up. Walter stood by as Mike walked back to his guard shack and put the CD into a machine. In all of the searches he had gone through, Walter had never seen that particular machine in operation. His heart started to beat rapidly. If the machine broke the encryption, everything was ruined.

Mike's large frame blocked Walter's view. He tried to think of an excuse if the true identity of the disc was discovered. He could say that he found the CD when cleaning up some trash. That could work for a few minutes, but eventually they would review tapes and understand the big picture.

Through all of their lunch meetings they would link the CD to Sam, and they would both crack under interrogation. Suddenly Mike turned around and time stood still for Walter. Mike's hand reached for his gun, his massive thumb fumbling with the snap on his hostler. Mike spoke, but Walter's mind was somewhere else.

Walter fell to his knees and hit the pavement with enough force to expel the air from his lungs. He was as good as dead.

10

Freedom Springs, CO
10:18

Brian Cill awoke, well rested. It had been a long time since he slept so well. The drive back from the widow's house was a distant memory as he felt the energy flowing through him.

He considered himself the greatest serial killer of all-time. He hoped that one day his name would appear next to Jack the Ripper and the Zodiac Killer. The only difference is that while those murderers were only known by a code name, Cill had been indentified, arrested, tried, and put on death row for his crimes. The American public was going to be shocked when they discovered he had struck again.

They would ask questions about his escape and the government would have no answers. In reality he had willed himself from captivity and was now free to kill again. There were still a few barriers to total freedom but last night's killing had given him the opportunity to break free for good. Today would be one of the greatest days of his life and his heart raced in anticipation.

He reached over to his nightstand and flipped open his cell phone. The phone rang three times before he heard, "Hello, Freeman."

"Hunter Liberty. How the hell are you today?"

"Living the free life and loving it. What can I do for you?"

"I need that address you promised me."

"I have it. Do you have the sniper rifle I need?"

"You give me the address and I'll give you the sniper rifle. It'll be slightly used."

"As long as it can reach out and touch somebody, I'll take it how I get it."

"With all the modifications I've done, that won't be an issue."

"Excellent. The guys in FFR have been talking about this guy living up on the Anderson farm. The guy is younger and has been working some computer jobs for people for cash and equipment."

"Sounds like the guy I need to talk to. Where would I find this farm?"

"Take highway 41 south from town about four miles. It will be on your left side after the narrow bridge that spans the small creek that runs under the road."

"I know where that is. If your information pans out, I'll call you and get you that rifle."

"Okay, bud. Have a good one."

"You too." Cill shut down his phone. He loathed having to work with anyone. He was much more comfortable working alone. But his short time with the Freedom Fighters of the Rockies had taught him that associates could be useful.

Cill contemplated the rifle on the table in front of him. Gaining trust among the lower-level members of the FFR hadn't been difficult. He recalled his first conversation with the FFR's charismatic leader, L.A. Citizen.

"What's your name?" The former army drill sergeant still carried his voice as if he was talking to eighteen-year-old recruits.

"Michael Thomas," Cill lied.

"What's your story?"

"Same as most around here. Joined the Army, did my time. I did two tours in Iraq. Last year I came back and got discharged."

"What makes you want to join the FFR?"

"Army life was nice. You got paid . . . most of the time. And as long as you were in the sandbox, it was tax free. Back on native soil I found I couldn't take a piss without paying a goddamn tax."

"I agree. But for all I know, you're a cop."

"A cop? Fuck that! I got enough problems with cops. I'd rather shoot a pig than look at him."

"Well, we can't have any of that. We can't afford anymore bad publicity."

"You're talking about your man going nuts in that courtroom last year?"

"G.M. Liberty was driven to madness by the feds. He was an armourer in Afghanistan. They gave him everything from handguns to shoulder-fired anti-tank missiles. Then he comes home and gets arrested for trying to sell a sawed-off shotgun to an undercover fed. The bastard asked him to do it, but they didn't call it entrapment."

"That shit is messed up. I have my issues with the law, but I can stay clean for a bit."

"What can you do for the organization?"

"Damn near anything. I can fix anything that rolls on four wheels and I majored in accounting before I joined the military."

"Sounds like you might be of some value. Work with Freeman, he'll show you the ropes and get you squared away."

Cill wanted to use the FFR to his advantage but he had a few loose ends to tie up first. Needing to create some space, he had claimed he was still wanted by police for some bullshit criminal charges and didn't want to draw extra attention to fellow freedom fighters.

His ruse had allowed him to stay in good standing with the group and take advantage of certain resources. Thanks to documents gained through the Freedom of Information Act, the FFR had data on a lot of government agents and activities. Cill had used this information and his personal connections to track down his targets, including last night's victim.

Cill gathered his equipment and left the hotel room. It didn't take him long to find a car to steal. He could hardly contain his need to kill. In short time he would slake that lust with the murder of Dean Knight.

11

Frontier PD
1030

The microphones reached out toward Colt's face like the arms of a mutated octopus. He had spent the past few minutes giving the standard, dry textbook statement before facing a barrage of questions from reporters. Most of the media members were locals writing for the town papers, but a half dozen or so had made the drive from Denver to report the news for their syndicates.

"Do you have any indication that the killer is from the town?" a local newspaper reporter shouted.

"As I said before, we are following leads that will hopefully result in the arrest of the individual or individuals responsible for this crime," Colt replied.

"What is the name of the victim?" another one shouted.

"We will release the victim's name after their family

is notified and gives us permission to do so."

"Is it possible that there is a serial killer loose in the town?" a rather young reporter yelled out.

"In order for there to be a serial killer, there has to be a *series* of killings. One murder does not count. There is no indication that any previous murders are linked to this killing, so I believe it is safe to answer a resounding NO to that question."

"When did the murder occur?" the same reporter asked.

"As I said in my earlier statement, we are not releasing any details of the investigation at this time. I can only tell you that it appears that a homicide occurred within this residence sometime during the overnight hours, and it involved a single victim. That's all the time I have for questions, we will let you know when we obtain any further information for release." Colt stepped down from the podium amid a storm of frantic queries.

"I'd be up there all day answering their ridiculous questions if they had their way," Colt mumbled to himself as he walked away toward his car. His mind drifted back to the case. It was often easiest for him to break down an investigation like this one based on what they actually knew.

An outline of the crime formed in Colt's thoughts. The cold hard facts were few, but Colt had solved cases in the past that presented a similar dearth of information. The first fact was that the killing had occurred during the night. There were no defensive wounds, suggesting that there had been little to no struggle leading up to the killing. That meant the victim would have been taken by surprise, and if her tox results came back clean, with no date-rape drugs in her system, she was most likely shot while in a natural state of slumber.

Second, the victim was a widowed female in her early thirties. Although she had reason to commit suicide, the neighbor stated he had witnessed a turnaround in her depression. A quick mood swing before suicide is common, but the neighbor genuinely believed she had been feeling better and for an extended period of time.

The home-invasion burglary style of murder could be linked to a jealous ex-lover, a soon-to-be or already divorced husband, or a robbery/burglary gone bad. However there were no initial signs of a lover, her husband had been killed in action, and there were no signs that anything had been disturbed or taken from the home.

Colt fell back on the stalker theory, recalling the statements the neighbor had given about the man in black. However, most stalkers would try to take some form of satisfaction from their kill. The victim would likely be raped, and according to the initial report there were no signs of a sexual assault.

Going back to his mental outline, Colt moved down to the next fact: method of killing. The victim's most likely cause of death was the two gunshots to the forehead. The lack of soot on, in, or around the wound and the lack of tattooing or stippling of powder around the wound meant the shots had been fired at some distance away from the body. Therefore the killer was skilled with a handgun, with possible military or law-enforcement training. Chances were this was not the killer's first murder, as unsteady hands would have made two such precise shots impossible. He or she also wanted to ensure that the victim would be dead and unable to identify the attacker.

Finally, the attacker wanted to ensure that death was

instantaneous. While this could be the result of sympathy for the victim, Colt figured the suspect just wanted to make sure there was no chance of survival and no screams for help.

Colt began forming a picture of the killer. Based on the neighbor's description, he would be a white male, tall, with normal to muscular stature. The level of intelligence as well as the discipline on the crime scene indicated he might be dealing with a highly organized, nonsocial offender. More commonly known as a sociopath or someone suffering from antisocial personality disorder, the killer was likely intelligent, clean cut, and appeared normal at first glance. Although the killer had shown some asocial tendencies, like leaving the body at the scene, leaving the body intact, and performing activity at night, most of the crime scene pointed toward a nonsocial offender.

Sitting down in his car, Colt turned the key in the ignition. His phone rang as he pulled on his seatbelt. Mental fatigue made it surprisingly hard to decide whether to answer the phone first or finish putting on his seatbelt. Shaking the cobwebs from his brain, he realized the order in which he performed the tasks did not matter. Colt clicked his seat belt closed before fishing his phone out of his pocket.

Normally he would have looked at the number or name that came up before he answered. In the pseudo-rush caused by his brain's earlier hiccup, however, he snapped open the phone and answered with his customary "Sullivan here."

"Is this Detective Colt Sullivan?" a strangely electronic voice asked through the cell phone speaker.

"Yes, can I help you with something?"

"I have information vital to the Connelly homicide within your city. I need you to follow my instructions very carefully. Start by . . ."

"Hold on a minute, if you want to give me information, just give it to me over the phone, starting with your name. I don't have time to play games," Colt interrupted. Having dealt with this situation before, he figured it was some nutjob who had seen him on television. It wasn't unusual for some mentally ill person to call him and tell him that the real murderers were aliens that controlled Bigfoot and made him commit the crime in order to bring balance to the universe.

"You are right: you don't have time to play games, and neither do I. Unfortunately, for our protection, we must not speak about the matter over the phones."

"Listen, either give me information that will help my case or hang up. I really don't have time for this."

The caller's hesitation was obvious, but just before Colt snapped his phone shut the caller proved his value. "The dead woman is Abigail Connelly, and she was killed with two gunshots to the forehead. The killer left little evidence, and her husband's name is William Connelly."

Colt was shocked and interested all at once. There are many reasons limited information is released to the public at the onset of an investigation. One of these reasons is to separate the prank leads from real leads as they are called in. Only the killer or someone with intimate knowledge of the killing would be able to provide this information. Colt regretted not being able to record the conversation. Grabbing his portable digital recorder, he attempted to record as much of the conversation as he could by placing the call on speakerphone. "Okay, you have my attention. Are you willing to come down to the police department to give a statement?"

"As I said earlier, Detective Sullivan, if you want to know all that I know, you need to follow my directions very carefully."

"What do you need me to do?"

"Drive to Boyd Lake State Park."

"Boyd Lake?"

"Yes. Meet me there at eleven thirty sharp, not a minute early, not a minute late. Park by the map board at Parker's Gulch, and I will provide you with further information."

"It would be a lot easier if you came down to the station. I can meet you there at eleven sharp." Colt didn't trust this guy in the least. *Why meet at a secluded location? What did he have to fear about coming down to the station? Was this the killer himself?* A million questions raced through his mind.

"You'll understand why after I fill you in on what I know. And one more thing . . . come alone. I will be watching you, and any attempt to bring backup will result in me disappearing and withholding information vital to solving your case."

"Okay, eleven thirty sharp, by the map board, Parker's Gulch, come alone, and is that it?"

"If you feel like you are being followed, abort the plan. I will know when you don't show up. See you at eleven thirty." Colt started to ask another question and found the line was dead. He checked the screen for the caller information and did a double take: the information was missing. There was no number, no restricted, unknown or private listing, the line was simply blank. Shaking his head, he shut off his recorder and stuffed it and the phone in his pocket.

A quick check of his watch showed a time of 10:42 a.m. Colt would need close to an hour to get to the park, leaving him no time to waste. He started the car and headed north toward Parker's Gulch. While en route he called Nick and told him he was following up on a lead and did not need any help. Although he felt foolish about doing so, he checked for tailing vehicles and noticed nothing out of the ordinary.

At a stoplight Colt made one final preparation for the meeting. He drew his sidearm and double checked that it was loaded and ready for action.

12

The Vault
1040

"Walter . . . you okay?" Walter's world came spinning back in a flash of light. "Do you want me to call the medics?" Mike's strong hands were vises against Walter's body. "Don't get up . . . let me call the medics."

"No, Mike, I'm okay," Walter replied.

"Are you sure? You went as white as a ghost there for a second, and then you hit the ground pretty hard."

"Well, I saw you reaching for your gun . . . just a little war flashback, I guess."

"I'm sorry, Walter. I just wanted to show you the new sidearm they issued us last week."

"Oh, really?" Walter replied, trying not to show too much relief. "Do you like it?"

"It's not bad for one of these fancy new composite guns . . . still too light, if you ask me. I like the feel of a heavy handgun."

"Yeah, nothing will beat the weight of the old Colt 1911."

"Now you are talking my language. You know, you still owe me that day at the range."

"Any day you want, Mike. Just let me know."

"Are you sure you don't want me to have the medics check you out?"

"No, I'm fine. I'm sure it has something to do with this flu," Walter said, sitting back in his car.

"Okay, I hope you feel better. And here's your CD back. Drive safe."

"Thanks, Mike. Have a nice afternoon."

"You too, Walter," Mike replied with a wave good-bye. Walter's heart was beating out of his chest, but he mustered a casual wave before putting the car into drive. The pounding in his chest did not slow down until Mike and the guard shack were nothing but a small dot in his rearview mirror.

Once at the highway, Walter turned left and followed his normal routine in exact detail. Although he had been too afraid to look, he was sure that the car was loaded with cameras, audio recording devices, and electronic override controls. If Harrison's men decided to put an end to his commute, they could do so.

Walter's largest fear was that the car was nothing more than a 1:1 scale remote-controlled car. If Harrison deemed it necessary, someone from the command room could probably just drive the car off a cliff. He cursed himself for letting Harrison take so much control over his life. He should have stayed retired, avoiding the high stress that accompanied working at the Vault.

After ten minutes of driving, he took the first of many gambles and altered his course ever so slightly. To his right, a small, run-down liquor store sat slightly off the highway.

As part of the plan, Walter had frequented the store the past few months. Although he was a light drinker at best, he managed to find a rare brand of Irish whiskey that he enjoyed and bought a small bottle every couple of weeks. His last visit had been fifteen days ago. The stop today would look like any other time he hit the bottom of the bottle and needed a refill.

Parking the car in the gravel lot, he stepped out into the suddenly stale air. All of his senses kicked into overdrive. From his time in combat he recognized the hypersensitivity as his body's response to stress. His vision narrowed, and while he could see the individual cracks in the faded tan paint of the liquor store door, he hardly saw anything to his right or left.

Suddenly he felt himself breathing deeply. The air went in for four seconds, stayed for four seconds, and released for four seconds. His peripheral sight returned, and the aroma in the air dissipated. Reaching back into the car, Walter grabbed the CD player. He fumbled it open and almost dropped the CD into the gravel while attempting to slide it into his pocket. Throwing the player back in the car, he walked into the store.

The eighteen-year-old clerk failed to say anything or even look at Walter, preferring to keep his nose buried deep in the same fantasy novel he had been reading during Walter's previous visit. In his five or six trips to the store Walter had yet to engage the clerk in a single conversation, and he favored that level of relationship. The less the clerk knew the better.

Walter strolled to the whiskey section and found his brand. He wasted no time sliding the CD out of his pocket and into an envelope that was taped under the shelf. Having been in the store for thirty seconds, Walter realized he had been holding his breath the entire time. Letting go of the air in his chest, he drew in a new breath and walked toward the checkout.

The clerk let out a sigh as Walter approached with his purchase. The slanted name tag loosely pinned to his stained rock-concert T-shirt read "Tim." The teenager managed to punch the exact price for the bottle into the ancient register and then asked for $18.75 without making any eye contact with Walter.

Walter placed a crisp twenty-dollar bill on the register and advised the clerk to keep the change before walking out of the store. He started up the car and left the lot in a small cloud of dust.

On his way home, Walter took a second gamble and headed to an old overlook he had been to many times with his wife before she died. The fifteen-minute drive felt like fifteen hours as he worried he would never make it to the overlook. Arriving at his destination, surprised to see that they had not shut off his car, Walter pulled into the empty lot.

He exited the vehicle, leaving the engine running, and walked to the edge of the overlook. The view was grand, and his heart warmed as thoughts of holding his wife close with her head upon his shoulder came rushing into his mind.

He was in a meditative state when he heard his car engine die and the doors lock. Knowing he had twenty minutes before the goon squad showed up and started asking questions, Walter weighed his options. Sam had warned him about the choice he would have to make.

To his right there was a walking trail that started from the overlook lot and traversed three miles through dense forest, eventually ending near a small lake. The body of water was only accessible by other walking trails and a small maintenance road. If Walter could make it over those three miles in less than thirty minutes, there would be a vehicle waiting to take him to relative safety. If he failed to make it in the thirty minutes, a backpack would be left for him containing food, shelter, and a pistol.

The food and shelter would last him a week, buying time for the plan to come to fruition. The pistol would be there in case he was discovered and decided he needed to make the ultimate self-sacrifice. Walter's only other option was to commit suicide from the overlook, throwing his body over the five-hundred-foot cliff and into the forest below.

Capture was not an option. Sam had explained that no matter how strong Walter thought he was, hours of brutal torture and finally a truth serum would be used to extract all the information Walter had about Sam's plan. Although Walter knew little of the plan, after his rendezvous with the truck he knew he didn't want to spend his last hours on earth being tortured to a slow and painful death.

He missed his wife. Although he was an older man and might not make it to the vehicle waiting for him by the lake, Walter was born a fighter and would die as one. He set off at a light jog down the walking trail, using adrenaline to override the pain in his joints and lungs as he forced his legs to push him along at a ten-minute-mile pace.

He was now one of the hunted, and while he did not regret his decision to help Sam, he did fear the uncertainty of the future. Two and a half miles into his journey he heard the helicopter. The beating of the rotors sounded like the flapping wings of a dozen fallen angels, coming to deliver him to Satan himself.

Checking his watch, Walter saw he had five minutes before the escape vehicle left. The glimmer of the sun off the mountain lake punched through the trees as he rounded a corner of the trail. He was close, but as he came to a halt in the small field where the rendezvous was meant to take place, he found only a backpack. Looking at his watch, he saw he was three minutes late. Had he been even a few years younger he might have made it in time, but he knew he was now down to a single option.

Picking up the backpack, Walter set off down a different trail. The dense vegetation above his head would make it difficult, if not impossible, for the chopper to track him. The paths were dry, and he was careful not to leave many tracks.

Once he was deep enough into the woods he walked off the trail and opened the backpack. It contained a small tent for shelter, thermal blankets, food, water, matches, and a handgun with a couple magazines of ammunition. Opening a small pocket at the top of the backpack Walter found a satellite phone and a hand-written note:

Walter,

Sorry I couldn't meet up with you. I need you to lay low for a couple days so I can take care of Sam and finish the plan. Sam or I will call you when this is over and it is safe for you to meet us. If more than two days go by and you do not hear anything, assume we have been killed and then you must decide what to do. Stay safe and thank you for your service to your country.

Sincerely,
Dean Knight

Walter put the phone back into the pocket. He burned the letter with one of the matches and stamped out the smoldering ashes. In forty-eight hours he would either be a hero or a villain. Walking deeper into the woods he looked to the sky. "Lord, please protect Sam and Dean. I leave them in your hands."

Walter had no idea what lay in store for his friend Sam. Walter's part in the betrayal was over and he disappeared into the brush.

13

Vault 15
11:00

The base security alarm sounded at exactly eleven o'clock. A smile crept across Sam's face as he realized that Walter had successfully removed the data from the base and alerted the security personnel to the breach. The chaos of Walter's defection was his own opportunity to escape.

Finding a weakness within the base had not been an easy task. It had been built and constantly modified with security in mind. Sam had spent hours poring through hundreds of classified blueprints, trying to find a way past the laser, heat, and audio-detection alarms.

Sam recalled his conversation with Dean about his escape. "How did you get out?"

"When they built the Vault, they needed a backup plan for oxygen. The architects knew that breathing potentially contaminated air was a risk, but having no oxygen guaranteed death for everyone inside the walls, so they drilled air shafts into the mountain."

"How many shafts are there?"

"They bored eight shafts into the rock. Each one is large enough to accommodate a small car. They travel outward from the center of the base. It wasn't easy. Harrison rigged them with several traps and alarms. I damn near set off a couple alarms and almost fell to my death at one point."

"Aren't the doors to the shafts alarmed?"

"Yeah, but lucky for us, I designed the software that controls those alarms. I installed a virus that shut down the alarms until I could make my escape."

"Don't they test the alarms?"

"Yes. The virus remained dormant during the time leading up to my escape. It passed dozens of tests."

"And you are sure the virus will still work?"

"I can't be one hundred percent sure, but I timed the virus to go dormant again immediately after my escape. When they ran the tests after my escape it should have looked like it vanished into thin air."

Sam drew in a deep breath. His fingers flew across the keyboard as he opened the doors to a half dozen of Dean's hidden and dormant viruses. The timing of the bugs had to be perfect or he wouldn't make it out of his office, let alone out of the base.

As a necessary step he uploaded a virus that rewrote the code controlling the oxygenation system. This in turn opened the physical doors to the ventilation shafts as well as the vent covers at the surface. It would take a while for the technicians to find the faulty code, and it would take longer for them to realize the code had been altered.

With the vent shafts open, Sam activated the alarm virus and prayed that Dean hadn't made any mistakes. The closest accessible vent shaft was a quarter mile away, and he needed to get moving. Grabbing the discs he had burned, Sam left his office and walked as fast as he could. Months of planning almost gave way when he ran into Denise just a few hallways from the vent shaft.

"Oh, Sam . . . this is crazy . . . they say someone took data off the base," Denise exclaimed after almost running him over with an electric golf cart.

"Oh . . . yeah. I didn't think that was possible," Sam stammered as he tried to think of all he wanted to say to her.

"I didn't think a lot of things were possible. Then Dean got out and now . . . you're leaving . . . aren't you?" Her voice was filled with concern and a little hint of pain.

"Denise, I don't have much time. I can't tell you anything. You know that."

"I know, Sam. But please, if they find you they will kill you!"

"Then I just have to make sure they don't find me. Now please get out of here."

"Sam . . . good luck and take care."

"Thanks. Keep smiling . . . one of these days will be a better day, I promise." Sam walked away from Denise without looking back.

The ventilation shaft was hidden behind a maze of pipes in an electrical room. Sam managed to navigate the obstacles and found himself staring up at what appeared to be a two-hundred-foot elevator shaft that was missing its elevator. His only way up was a steel ladder fastened to the side of the oversized concrete tube.

Slowly ascending, he cursed himself for skipping out on all the fitness opportunities inside the base. To compensate for the lack of time outside, a full gym with health-club quality treadmills, elliptical machines, and stationary bikes had been made available. Free weights, pull-up bars, and even a rock-climbing wall kept the guards in top physical form—and their intimidating physiques kept most scientists away.

Sam preferred a good book or movie to the gym, and after only fifty feet of climbing he found every muscle in his body aching. In that short amount of time he already discovered two mechanical booby traps on the ladder. The first one had been a small trip wire strung across one rung of the ladder. It was designed to break and trigger an alarm when a person put their weight on the step. The second trap was a rung made of a lightweight material and painted to look like metal. Once enough weight was put on it, it would shatter, tripping an alarm as well as potentially causing a deadly fall.

Exhausted, Sam looked at his watch and realized he was making good time. While he assumed Dean's alarm virus was working, he could not help but imagine a group of armed guards storming into the bottom of the shaft and shooting him off the ladder. With that thought pushed to the back of his mind, Sam neared the top of the shaft. The relative darkness gave way to a dull glow.

The blueprints showed a simple hatch, disguised as a rock and made to blend in with the mountain. Sam's heart sank as he realized the shaft had been updated since his version of the blueprint. The hatch he needed was now beyond a steel grate that was locked from both sides.

Suspended two hundred feet in the air, Sam was at

a complete loss. The freedom he longed for was so close, but for all the fancy computer viruses that had gotten him this far, he lacked the simple key that would grant him his liberty. With no other choice, he slowly began his descent back into the darkness and formulated a new plan.

With limited time, resources, and options, Sam was still hell-bent on escaping. The next hour would find him breathing fresh air or no air at all.

14

Highway 15
11:20

Dean cursed himself for lying to Sam. He had promised to take care of Walter but he didn't have the time or resources to protect the old man. The backpack of supplies and the note would have to do for now. Still, the thought of Walter being forced to hide in the woods was not sitting well with him.

Letting go of his emotions, he focused on the task at hand. Every minute he stayed in the area of the rendezvous point increased his chance of being caught by Harrison's agents. He needed to increase his distance from the search area as fast as possible.

The beat-up pickup truck groaned with every bump of the maintenance road. Dean began to wonder if the aged vehicle would hold together. Reducing his speed, he heard the squeaks lessen and felt more in control behind the wheel. The heavy tree cover above the windshield hid his movement from the air and dissipated the dust cloud left behind as he bounced along the gravel.

Dean relaxed into the drive as much as he could and prepared for the riskiest portion of the plan. The next ten minutes represented, literally, the difference between life and death for himself and his friends.

As his mind raced through the itinerary, he almost failed to see a large rock protruding from the trail. Swerving at the last second, he felt the truck began to fishtail, and with every slip of the back wheels his heart skipped a beat. Not wanting to overcorrect, he let up on the gas, straightened out the truck, and managed to regain control.

"Shit. That was close," Dean said aloud. "Come on, Dean, keep it together. Looking in the rearview mirror he grimaced. He knew the consequences, had he failed to recover the steering. If the truck had crashed, his plan did not allow time for walking to his next destination.

Bringing his breathing back under control, Dean lowered the gas pedal and focused on the last half mile of service road. He arrived at the highway at precisely 11:30. Without traffic delays, and maintaining the speed limit, the drive to the state park would take no more than ten minutes.

Once on the firm pavement of the highway Dean relaxed enough to run through his upcoming speech. Growing up as a child prodigy had not allowed him a lot of social time, and therefore his personal communication skills were highly unpolished. The task of revealing information to a police detective, who would most likely be adept at controlling a conversation, was not an easy one for Dean to attempt.

He needed to get his target's attention and make sure to say what he had to say with as little interruption as possible. It would be up to Colt to believe what Dean had to say, and they both needed to hope it wasn't too late.

Dean's heart began to race as he exited the highway and noticed a blue sedan following him up the ramp. The car had first appeared a minute after he left the service road, and it had kept the same distance for the past few miles. To complicate matters, the sun's reflection off of the windshield prevented Dean from seeing who was driving or how many people were in the trailing vehicle.

If aerial reconnaissance had spotted him leaving the service road, Harrison would send a car full of agents to follow him and attempt to take him and any other people he met into custody.

Stopping at the top of the ramp, Dean found himself tapping the steering wheel nervously as the blue sedan came to a rest behind him. The glare from the sun still hindered his view into the suspect car. Dean reached under his seat and pulled out a toolbox. The rusty-red sheet-metal box held two handguns, several magazines, and some spare boxes of ammunition.

He set the toolbox on the bench seat next to him and blindly fumbled around with the latch as he took a right onto a county road. The mechanism gave way and he flipped open the top, retrieving a Glock 27 from the tray.

The Glock had no external safety, and with a round in the chamber the gun was ready to fire. The sedan hesitated at the sign before following Dean's truck.

"Damn it! What the hell do I do?" Talking himself up, he ran through his options. "Okay. If I stop, I might miss my meeting with Sullivan. If I don't stop I could be leading them straight to myself and Sullivan. Either way, if that car is full of agents I am going to find myself on the losing end of a shootout."

Dean realized that putting Colt in danger was too risky, and he applied the brakes as he moved onto the gravel shoulder. The sedan's driver abruptly pulled in behind the truck. Tempted to jump out and start putting gunshots through the windshield, Dean raced through his options as he watched the driver's door open.

The portly man in a stock-car racing T-shirt who exited the vehicle looked far from a highly trained federal agent. Then Dean saw a flash in the man's hands, but the reflected sunlight vanished as quickly as it appeared. The man was now ten feet from his truck. Dean told his arm to reach for the door and open it, but he just sat there, his body paralyzed by fear. The portly man stepped up to Dean's window.

"Excuse me, sir. My family and I are lost, and you look like you might be from the area," the man said.

Quickly concealing the firearm, Dean stammered, "Oh uh uh . . . yeah. I can try and help you out."

"Golly, thanks. We are looking for Boyd State Park. Any idea if we are on the right track?"

"As a matter of fact, yes you are. It's only a few minutes down this road on your left. You can't miss it."

"Thank goodness. My kids are driving me crazy, and my wife told me to ask you for directions, but . . . you know how it is."

"Yeah," Dean replied with a forced chuckle. "You have yourself a good day, sir."

"You too, thanks again." The man retreated to the

blue sedan and drove off, the car passing Dean's truck on its way back onto the road. Dean could now clearly see two small children in the rear of the car and the wife in the passenger seat.

Happy that he had not shot an innocent man in front of his wife and children, Dean was nonetheless mortified by his inability to perform under intense circumstances. The next time he failed to pull the trigger it could be a fatal mistake.

After placing the gun back in the toolbox, Dean drove toward the park and went over the final contingency for the plan, figuring that talking to himself was probably the least crazy thing he'd done today. "I asked Sullivan to come alone, but he might have brought backup units. I might be facing just Sullivan or an entire SWAT team. Either way, I have to try and make the meet."

Boyd State Park had several entrances to its hiking and camping areas. The blue sedan containing the unknowingly lucky man and his family continued down the highway toward the campground. Dean found the entrance to Parker's Gulch. The lot served as a parking area for hikers setting out for a day's trek on the mountain. Arriving two minutes early, he was pleased to see that there were no other cars. Dean parked his truck and walked to the map of the hiking trails.

Glancing over the trails, he saw several trails that offered escape. His finger traced the path of one trail until he heard the sound of a car approaching on the highway and briskly walked back to his truck. As the car came into view, Dean recognized the driver. He took a deep breath and prepared to tell his tale. He only hoped that Detective Sullivan would believe him.

15

Vault 15
1130

Sam could barely lift his arms. He had made it back to the floor of the ventilation shaft after five agonizing minutes. After re-navigating the maze of pipes, he stepped back into the electrical room. During his descent he had come up with a new escape plan. It was riskier than the ventilation shaft, but his options were limited.

He returned to his office and found that a half hour had gone by since the original alarm. Harrison's guards were performing sweeps of the building, so he needed to stay one step ahead of them. He used his computer to manipulate the alarm system and set off an alert on several of the ventilation-shaft tamper devices.

With the agents focused on checking each vent, Sam could use one of the two remaining exits. The front gate was heavily watched under normal conditions and would undoubtedly be under increased surveillance. Sam knew the only other exit was an old mineshaft that had been uncovered during the excavation for the Vault. Old blueprints showed it had been modified into an emergency escape tunnel.

While walking out of the old mineshaft was easier than climbing a two-hundred-foot vertical tube, it was much more dangerous. The entrance to the tunnel was located near Harrison's office and monitored by multiple cameras.

Droplets of sweat fell from Sam's forehead as he frantically worked the keyboard to manipulate the necessary cameras. He created massive errors in the video feeds while setting the cameras covering the mine entrance to run on a three-minute live loop. "With all of the chaos, the guards should be too distracted to notice anything unusual with those particular cameras," Sam told himself.

Setting off fire and front-gate alarms further depleted the guards' manpower, allowing him a small window for escape. The white walls of the Vault appeared to collapse in on him as he left his office. He told himself it was just nerves and adrenaline, but he began to have problems breathing. His pulse raced as he turned corner after corner, just waiting to run into a group of guards on the prowl.

Sam made it to the last hallway without incident. He stopped and froze, looking up at a small black dome camera that was situated halfway down the hallway. He couldn't remember if he looped that specific camera and felt exposed. It was too late to turn back, so Sam took a deep breath and walked directly under the dome.

Arriving at the red door just to the left of Harrison's

office, he read a metal sign in front of him:

Emergency escape tunnel.

Any personnel using this tunnel except under authorization by General Harrison will be detained. Failure to comply with detention requests will result in use of deadly force.

Under normal conditions the door would be magnetically locked to prevent accidental opening, but Sam had overridden the electronic lock and with a simple push the door opened. The virus he had planted for the vent-shaft alarms had also shut down the mineshaft tamper devices. Although confident he would not set off any alarms, Sam still had to be on the lookout for deadly booby traps, and there was still the possibility of running into a guard.

Finding several more security doors in the shaft, Sam opened each one without problem thanks to Dean's software. The doors varied in thickness, with a few of them heavy enough to convince Sam they had lead cores and were designed to withstand radiation. Each door he opened increased his chances of coming face-to-face with a guard or worse, an agent. Luck was on his side. He saw no one, and each new hallway's air smelled a little fresher.

Sam tried to soften his steps, but the sound of his feet hitting the solid floor and reverberating against the narrow walls was like a bass drum in his ears. The faintly illuminated hall ended at a T intersection with a darkened drop-off that almost cost Sam a few broken bones.

His vision depleted, Sam found a crude steel ladder and climbed down the five-foot drop into the original mine. The pitch-black tunnel was larger than Sam had imagined. He estimated that it averaged over eight feet in height and six feet in width. Like a pinball he bounced from wall to wall. After a painful run-in with a ninety-degree turn he never saw, he discovered an old broken rail line on the floor. It was easy for him to follow it with his feet in the dark abyss.

After traveling several hundred feet down the tunnel, he arrived at another T. Both offshoots were pitch black, and the ground felt fairly level in either direction. Relying solely on luck, Sam turned left.

The rails in the side tunnel protruded farther from the ground, and Sam found himself trying to decipher the easiest walking path. The dirt floor was far from smooth. It was filled with small potholes that threatened to twist or break his ankle. Larger holes threw his balance off, and he often fell to the ground and took a mouthful of dirt.

His other choice was walking on the railway itself. It was composed of bent metal rails with loose and broken rail ties and half-exposed spikes. The rails and beams endangered his shins and ankles, but it was the spikes that kept stubbing his toes. "Shit!" he cursed under his breath. "Man, does that hurt!"

Sam was about to give up and turn around when he noticed that the tunnel had become brighter and the air wasn't as thick with dust and mold. A small amount of light now allowed him to see most of the potholes. He picked up the pace. The tunnel was getting brighter, and he could almost jog safely among the pitfalls.

The helpful brightness soon forced Sam to slow his pace and allow his eyes to adjust. He now faced the opposite problem: too much light. Blinded and moving at a good pace, he tripped over a bent rail and fell hard. In addition to eating dirt he now had the wind knocked out of him.

Struggling to regain his breath, Sam forced himself to keep moving toward the light. "Son of a bitch. I better not make it out of here in one piece just to get captured on the other side," he wheezed. Some of the dust he had swallowed made it into his lungs. Sam forced himself to hold back a couple coughs as he approached the tunnel's mouth.

The interior of the old mine entrance was bathed in light. Sam located a simple sign reading:

Warning:
Abandoned mine. Do not enter.

- **This site was used for nuclear waste storage and contains high levels of deadly radiation; trespass will result in radiation poisoning.**

- **This site is monitored by audio and video surveillance, and trespass will result in detention and prosecution under federal law.**

The sign alone would be enough to deter any spelunkers or adventure seekers from entering the mine. Anyone curious enough to make it to the inner portion of the escape tunnel would trigger an alarm, dispatching guards that would quickly detain the trespasser.

Sam opened the rusty chain-link door that separated the mine entrance from the outside world. Breathing deeply, his lungs absorbed their first fresh air in decades.

The birds and the chatter of squirrels in the trees made him realize how precious life and freedom truly are.

The old rail tracks continued through the mouth of the mine and ran alongside a gravel road that traveled out of sight, past a crest in the mountain. Fresh truck tracks in the gravel indicated the area was patrolled. Sam quickly hid behind some boulders, angry at himself for not using more caution while exiting the mine.

A survey of the surrounding area revealed no signs of movement. Sam doubted the guards watched the mine exit at all times but reckoned they had a guard post somewhere nearby. Working his way through the rocks and trees parallel to the path, Sam quickly discovered he had been correct.

A small gravel parking lot with a semi-trailer–style guard shack was situated just down the mountainside. Outside the guardhouse sat a four-wheel-drive pickup with some hard-to-read markings.

Sam could clearly see one person inside the shack. The man was sitting on the other side of a small window on the near side of the trailer. Well above average size, the guard had large, broad shoulders and a thick neck. Sam could not see any additional personnel through the other windows on the trailer.

The truck would be ideal for his escape. It would allow him to put additional distance between him and the Vault, but he needed a plan to steal the vehicle. He couldn't alert the guard or guards inside the trailer, and Sam knew the major flaw in the plan was that the vehicle's engine turning over would surely alarm anyone inside the trailer.

Moving between areas of concealment, Sam picked a

semi-circular path around the trailer, scanning the windows for any additional guards. The truck was marked with a badge identifying the vehicle as property of the Department of Homeland Security.

The guard had to be assigned to oversee the mine exit. To anyone approaching the mine from the outside, he would appear to be an overpaid security guard at a nuclear waste disposal site. To Sam, the guard was the last thing standing between him and freedom.

Sam knew the odds were stacked against him. The guard most likely had access to a firearm and a panic button inside the trailer. A single push of the button would be all he needed to call in the cavalry.

Any effort to overpower the armed agent without setting off any alarms seemed futile, but Sam weighed his options. He had no weapons and no training in hand-to-hand fighting. The guard would have a handgun, submachine gun, or compact assault rifle, and would be an expert in unarmed combat. Sam knew the scales were tipped heavily in favor of the man inside the trailer.

Conversely, Sam could also walk off into the woods. From there he could hope to find the highway, flag someone down, and secure a ride, all without being seen by undercover agents. While the latter seemed to be the safer choice, he would be leaving a lot up to chance.

Deciding to control his own fate and take out the guard, Sam put a small amount of faith in his own intelligence and the element of surprise. The truck was out of view from inside the trailer. Sam moved to it and looked in the windows. A metal box had been installed between the two front seats as an aftermarket modification. It was black and had a small key lock on the top. Opening the passenger door, slowly and quietly, Sam anticipated an alarm. Instead he was greeted with the sweet sound of silence.

Reaching for the lockbox, he found it to be predictably locked. "There's no way," Sam whispered as he reached up and flipped down the driver's side visor. Three keys on a metal ring slid down the visor and into his waiting hand. "All right!"

Sam recognized two of the three keys. The truck was older and required separate door and ignition keys. Moving those aside, he examined the third key, which was clipped to the others but could also be separated. He inserted it into the lockbox and gave it a twist.

The lock disengaged, and the open box exposed a small handheld radio, two electronic switches to control hidden lights, and two full magazines for a handgun. Sam removed the portable radio and gently turned it on, keeping the volume low. He heard status checks and information being relayed over the channel. The guards were still looking for the cause of the false alarms, but there was no indication they were actively searching for Sam.

Still lacking any weapons, Sam reached under the passenger seat and found a tire iron. "Never bring a tire iron to a gun fight," he quietly joked with himself. Now he had to get to the guard. The trailer doors were likely alarmed, so Sam would never get within striking range before the guard recognized the threat.

He had to draw the agent outside. Searching the ground, he found a good-sized rock. Sam moved to the corner of the trailer and underhanded the rock onto the roof. The resounding thud was louder than anticipated, and he worried that he had overdone the distraction.

Listening for a call for help or any report of suspicious activity on the radio, Sam held his breath. If he heard the guard request backup, Sam would jump into the truck and drive away. It would not take long to get outside the effective range of the guard's weapon, but he would lose the element of surprise and due to the vehicle's GPS tracker he could expect unwelcome company on the highway. Fortunately for Sam, there was no call for help before he heard the exterior trailer door opening.

The man who stepped out would have easily fit into a carnival freak show as living proof of giants. Just shy of seven feet and no less than three hundred pounds of muscle, the brute almost froze Sam in his tracks. Sam immediately regretted his decision to not just jump in the truck and leave.

While the weapon in the guard's hand would be considered a cannon in any normal-sized hand, in his it looked like a toy pistol. The behemoth swung the gun toward Sam's corner with unexpected speed. Having ducked behind the corner at the first sign of movement, Sam prayed that the guard hadn't seen anything. He froze and waited for a few seconds before the sound of heavy footsteps grew closer. Sam held his breath and began to shake.

The air coming from his adversary's nostrils sounded like that of a large draft horse. Audible from over five feet away, the rhythmic snorting entranced Sam as he let the air out of his lungs, trying to control the volume of his own exhalations. Just before the large man reached the trailer's corner, Sam heard the man pivot and walk away. Using the guard's heavy footsteps as cover, Sam snuck up behind the sentry.

Just as Sam was about to swing the tire iron, the ogre turned his head. In slow motion Sam arched the tool toward his target's cranium. Sam used all of his extended arm reach, in addition to the foot-long tire iron, to land the bludgeon square on the guard's skull.

The sickening thud of metal on bone preceded the sentry's collapse at Sam's feet. Not knowing whether he had killed the man or just rendered him unconscious, Sam picked up the dropped firearm and pointed it at the unmoving body.

There was no more heavy breathing or movement from the titan with the caved-in skull, so Sam retreated into the trailer. The main room was equipped with a card table, microwave, coffee pot, desk, and phone. Sam made sure no one occupied a small restroom in the back before returning to the main room. During a search of a desk he found a map of the area.

A quick glance of the topographical chart showed the mining road intersecting a county road on the back side of the mountain. Sam estimated the straight-line distance between him and the county road at ten miles. With the winding road and its poor condition, it was more likely a thirty-minute drive.

Afraid that the massive man outside would recover from his injuries or miss a timed radio check, Sam left the trailer. He started the truck and began his drive down the mining road.

For the first time in a long time, Sam cried. Tears of joy streamed down his face as the rocky mountainside gave way to a lush evergreen forest. The mining road ahead was steep and rock-strewn. Sam wiped away the tears as he paid attention to the sharp curves and the fallen stones that had tumbled through the forest and come to rest in the roadway.

He laughed as he thought about the definitions of a rocky road. There was rocky-road flavored ice cream. Then there was the road on which he was driving, with plenty of sharp rocks threatening to puncture his tires. Finally there was the metaphorical definition, a period in life when times are tough. Having escaped the Vault, Sam thought the worst of his rocky road was over. In truth it was only beginning.

16

Boyd State Park
11:45

Colt Sullivan studied the old truck and its owner. The man's hair was ragged, and he had a short, scruffy beard that added a few years to his age. *Mid-twenties, posture straight, body tall, no fat but hardly any muscle. He's a computer nerd or some type of engineer,* Colt told himself. Either way, he did not look like the type of person who would drive an old Ford pickup or meet with detectives in remote locations to discuss a homicide investigation.

The man's nervous energy did nothing to settle Colt's own worries as he drew his sidearm and placed it firmly atop his right thigh. Slowing his vehicle, Colt parked with the engine block of the squad between the male party and himself. He stepped out of the squad, stood with the firearm out of the man's sight, and calmly but assertively introduced himself.

"I'm Detective Colt Sullivan with Frontier Police. Are you the man who called me?"

"Yes I am, Detective. My name is Dean Knight, and I have important information for your investigation."

"I appreciate the call, Mr. Knight, but understand that you asked me to meet you under very unorthodox circumstances." Colt raised his sidearm and pointed it at Dean. "I need you to walk toward my car slowly with your hands in the air. Do not make any sudden movements or you will be shot. Do you understand?"

Dean immediately put his hands in the air. "Yes, Detective. I understand. I am not here to hurt you, I simply want to help."

"I appreciate that. I just need to make sure you don't have any weapons. Then we can talk."

"I don't have a gun on me, but I have a gun in the truck. It is loaded and ready to fire. It is for my protection."

"Do not move toward the truck. Walk toward me." Dean complied, keeping his hands in the air. When Dean was a few feet away, Colt ordered him to stop. "Turn around slowly, leaving your hands in the air. After two turns, stop and face away from me."

Dean performed the movements and came to a stop. "Now, place your hands behind your back," Colt ordered. As soon as Dean complied he felt cold steel against his wrists. He tried to protest, but he found himself locked into handcuffs.

"I apologize Mr. Knight. This is the safest way for us to talk."

"I understand. My life is now in your hands. What I have to tell you will be hard to believe. And please, call me Dean."

"Be that as it may, I'll listen with open ears, Dean. I just need to pat you down for any weapons." Colt ran his hands over Dean's body. "Okay, you are clean. Do you want to sit in the back of the squad or stay out here?"

"We can stay out here."

"I want you to know that you are not under arrest. You are in handcuffs for my safety, and you are free to go whenever you wish." Colt pulled out his recorder and switched it on. "I'm going to record this conversation as well. You can watch me destroy it later if it comes to that."

"Okay, Detective. I'll let you know if that time comes, but for now I need you to listen to what I have to say. Feel free to ask questions when you feel it necessary."

"I can live with that. Go ahead."

"I know I am going to sound like a crazy conspiracy theorist, but please hear me out. There is no easy way to tell you this . . . the killer you are looking for is a participant in a government experiment gone wrong, and—"

"I told you, Dean, I don't have time for games! I am in the middle of a homicide investigation!"

"Detective, please don't interrupt. It will sound crazy at first, but I promise to explain it and answer your questions when I am done."

"Okay . . . just tell me one thing to prove you are not just jerking me around."

"The victim you found today is the widow of an American serviceman. Her husband was alleged to have been killed in action on September 30th, 2006, in Southwest Asia."

"Well, Dean . . . you have my attention. Proceed." Colt realized he was dealing with someone who either knew the victim or the killer, or both.

"In order for you to understand, you need to know how this all began. William Connelly was not killed in action—well, not entirely. His team was wiped out in a raid on a terrorist cell, and he was mortally wounded. The army had spent a small fortune on his training and did not want to let it go to waste. They were able to keep his brain alive on a heart-lung machine until a donor body could be located.

"When the donor body was ready, Connelly's brain was fused with its new host, and he was brought back from the brink of death.

"The main problem we ran into was dealing with the fragility of the human psyche. Although millions around the world believe in reincarnation, the idea that the brain could be unplugged from one body and placed into another in machine-like fashion is almost unfathomable, especially if the patient is an unaware and unwilling participant. So instead we chose to program a new life into the donor brain."

"And you expect me to believe all this?" Colt said. He made no effort to hide his frustration.

"Please, let me finish. The original tests were a success, and Connelly was placed into society and closely monitored. The initial decision was to employ him in the real world on a five-year experiment. This gave us the ability to monitor both his physiological and psychological functions.

"The physiological dangers were great. Just like with any other organ, the host body could reject the brain, causing instant death. The subjects of this procedure were also prone to a host of chemical imbalances and coordination issues.

"As I mentioned earlier, the psychological dangers were even greater. When a subject realized who he or she was, in body or mind, the lack of true identity tended to cause massive anxiety and depression. There was also the danger of multiple personalities forming as a result of the implantation of false memories.

The killer you are looking for is part of one of our projects. I can help you stop him, but you have to play by my rules."

Colt furrowed his brow. Years of interrogating criminals had exposed him to everything from a half-assed truth to complete bullshit stories. While he didn't believe Dean, he wasn't ready to completely dismiss the man's story.

"You don't have to act like you believe me; I don't expect you to at first. But hopefully after I answer all your questions you'll realize that this is the truth. I haven't told you everything yet because before you believe it all, you need to understand that it's possible."

"Okay, Dean, you're right, I don't believe you. I need more than a crazy story to convince me you are telling the truth. What is your background?"

"I was recruited to work for the government straight out of college. I'm smart—genius smart—and I have a background in nearly every field of engineering, and one day I came to the conclusion that the human brain is no different from a computer. It uses electronic signals to operate on the true or false checks of the binary system. When someone remembers something they access stored memory and utilize energy to transport the signals.

"My mission was to find a way to plug into the brain and force newer, stronger memories that would travel more easily though the brain while blocking older ones. After an extensive trial run we succeeded in creating false memories and suppressing real, experience-based memories. The key was a microchip we implanted in the brain. The microchip acted as a translator and allowed us to remotely control and download information. It was as simple as logging into a computer and telling it what to do and when to do it—"

Colt interjected, "But a human brain has to be too complex to just transplant it from one body to another. Spinal cord injuries are often non-repairable because we don't know how to reanimate the nerve impulses." Colt had enough of an understanding of the human body to know that what Dean was implying was decades, if not centuries away.

"It was . . . when we thought of it as the supreme organic mass that comprises the various parts of your brain. But in reality it is no different than any other complex of cells in the body. It requires basic supplements via the circulatory system. Consider that to be the power cord for the computer. The first thing that needs to be done in the transplant is to ensure the brain is constantly provided power—"

"So you simply plugged this war hero's brain into a host body?"

"In a manner of speaking, yes."

Colt shifted his weight and accidently dropped his recorder. As he lunged for the falling device, the silence of the parking lot was broken by a single gunshot.

A second shot rang out. He felt the world go dark around him, and the cold settled into his bones.

17

Hwy 44
Noon

Sam knew he was driving the truck on borrowed time. The truck had a GPS tracking unit installed, but every mile driven was one more mile the agents had to drive before they could catch him. So Sam ran the truck with the gas pedal kissing the floorboards as much as possible. Once he was on the county road he passed cars with reckless abandon. He was willing to risk a run-in with law enforcement. It wasn't on the top of his to-do list, but it was preferable to a run-in with Harrison's agents.

Narrowly missing a few bumpers of fellow motorists, Sam found himself dissecting his next move. It would have been ideal to escape with at least a half hour's head start, but he figured he had already lost a lot of time by taking out the guard.

A few miles after turning onto the highway Sam

spotted a gas station. He parked the truck near a pay phone on the exterior wall of the convenience store, conveniently placed so he could talk on the phone and watch the customers as they entered and exited the store.

Sam jumped out of the truck and walked up to the phone, mimed feeding in coins and dialing a number, and made conversation with the dead air. Fortuitously for him, the station was busy, and within a minute he watched a man on a cell phone park in front of the store.

The car was nondescript: a domestic-made sedan, dark red in color, with Colorado plates. Sam looked for, and failed to see, any children in the car. Most importantly, the driver left the vehicle without shutting off the engine.

Sam watched the driver enter the store and walk toward the back. Dropping the receiver, Sam briskly walked to the car, opened the door, and sat down. Once again he confirmed that there were no children in the car before backing out and leaving the station without drawing any attention.

At best he had two minutes before the owner called the police. The owner would then wait for an officer to call him or come to the scene and take the stolen-car report. Finally the car would be registered with the National Crime Information Center as stolen. By the time the ordeal was over, Sam would be far enough away to lessen his chances of being found by local law enforcement.

Most importantly, Sam had created a cushion of time and distance between himself and the agents. They would track him to the gas station, arrive, figure out rather quickly what happened, and then wait. Without GPS tracking or eyes in the sky, the agents would have to rely on law enforcement or dumb luck to find Sam.

Breathing a sigh of relief, Sam kept to the speed limit and signaled all his turns and lane changes. To everyone on the road he looked like an older, middle-class man out for a drive. Five minutes later he pulled into Mountain Lake Liquors.

Sam's mind wandered to Walter as he parked the car. He wondered what had become of his elderly friend. He took a deep breath and hoped Walter hadn't had a change of heart.

Sam realized there was a small chance that the agents had already traced Walter's stop at the store and he was walking into an ambush. A glance toward the parking lot and local roads revealed no additional vehicles. *If agents were around, they are doing a damn good job of hiding,* Sam thought as he entered the store.

Looking at the signs above the aisles, he found the one identifying whiskey. Sam located Walter's brand halfway down the aisle and reached past the bottles to the underside of the shelf, way at the back, and found it was empty.

Sam's heart skipped a beat as he withdrew his hand. *Was it an ambush? Did Dean make it here first? Did Walter have a change of heart?* Sam began to walk away, and then it hit him: Walter had not just said he had a favorite brand of whiskey, he liked a specific age of that whiskey, twelve years to be exact. Returning to the middle of the whiskey aisle, Sam located the twelve-year-old bottle in a section dedicated to more expensive liquors and felt along the underside of the shelf. "Got you," Sam said, pulling the envelope from behind the bottles.

Pocketing the envelope and disc, Sam approached

the register. “Hey, Tim. Do you guys carry Middleton’s?”

“Never heard of it,” the clerk replied without looking up from his book.

“No worries. I’ll check somewhere else, have a good day,” Sam turned to leave the store, content he had not raised the clerk’s attention. But as he looked through the front glass doors he froze. A police car was parked in front of the doors, and the officer had his radio mic in his hand. The patrolman was wearing sunglasses, but Sam could swear he was staring right through his soul.

18

Miner's Gulch Park
12:10

It did not matter how tightly MSG Connelly kept his mouth shut, the sand always found a way in. He hated the feeling of it gritting between his teeth and sticking to the roof of his mouth. They were under fire for the third time this week. His team took refuge behind a four-foot wall made of mud and stone. The wall ran along the outskirts of a Taliban compound. Intelligence had been wrong again. Their target had been a small building in the back of the compound that was used for the production of improvised explosive devices. American IED casualties in the area were becoming an issue in Washington, and Connelly's men had been tasked with taking out the factory.

Intel indicated a small, squad-sized element of eight to ten Taliban fighters staying in the compound. They also reported several women and children living in the homes within the walls. Knowing full well that a successful surgical missile strike would kill Taliban and wipe out the IED site, the Pentagon did not want to deal with another global media storm surrounding the killing of Afghan civilians. Connelly was confident that within minutes of such a strike, local media would have images and videos of the bodies streaming on the World Wide Web to be picked up and reported by the BBC, CNN, and MSNBC.

The media would conveniently not report that the target compound was directly linked to the killing of two dozen U.S. soldiers and countless innocent civilians. When Connelly received the order to go in and shut it down, he understood why his team was picked. They could be in and out in minutes, selectively killing or capturing enemy combatants.

He didn't understand how the intelligence information could have been so far off, mainly in the strength of resistance. Connelly and his team had expected a ten-minute operation. Their only foreseeable obstacle was the discovery of a large amount of explosive material that, if destroyed in place, would cause too much damage. In case of such a stockpile, several armored vehicles were waiting to come in and provide security while the munitions were moved to and detonated at a safe and secure location.

The drop had gone according to plan. Connelly and his men jumped from a C-130 flying dark at twenty thousand feet. Landing in the sandy plains, they had moved across the desert for several miles until they arrived unseen at the compound. As part of the effort to minimize confusion and prevent civilian casualties, an Afghan spy had thrown an infrared beacon onto the roof of the target building.

Locating the beacon and ensuring they had the correct cluster of buildings, Connelly radioed to his superiors that his unit was on site and ready to conduct the raid. The compound was too large to storm with ten men, so they breached the rear wall using a lightweight portable ladder. Once over the wall, they stacked along the rear wall of the target building.

Connelly ordered one of his men to recon the building through an open window. The operator reported that he could see four males sleeping on the floor of the room, surrounded by weapons, ordinance, and tools. The building was twenty feet by thirty feet, with an opening in the front large enough to hold a vehicle for the purpose of making car bombs.

Ordering half of his team to enter the building and eliminate the sleeping men, Connelly radioed to command that the attack was about to begin. A seasoned operator knows there is no easy, quiet way to kill a man. The Delta operators opted for the most silent weapon in their arsenal, their knives. Four operators stood by and then simultaneously slit the throats of the sleeping men.

Once, after a mission, Connelly had contemplated what a normal citizen would think of their actions. Most likely they would deem it cruel and unnecessary, claiming that the men who lay there, bleeding to death, unable to yell due to their severed windpipes, deserved a second chance.

Connelly and his Delta brethren knew differently. They had all seen the bodies of the soldiers killed while walking down the street. Just last week he had learned of a nineteen-year-old former high-school baseball star who had turned down a full-ride scholarship for the chance to serve his country and protect innocent people around the world. His life was taken as a coward remotely detonated a device that also killed the young soldier's squad leader. The latter was a husband and the father of three children. His youngest child never got to meet her father.

After dispatching the sleeping men, the operators gathered in the IED building. Connelly was amazed at the scope of the munitions within the room. There were grenades, RPGs, Claymores, mortars, and even some 155mm Howitzer rounds. The walls were covered with electrical tools, wiring, circuit boards, sheets of metal, and large cases of shrapnel devices including marbles, jacks, nails, and screws. They would shut down this factory of death if it was the last thing they did.

The remainder of the compound needed to be searched and secured so the ordinance could be removed and detonated. Connelly ordered a building-by-building search in complete silence. If further enemy combatants were located, the operators were to kill without hesitation or secure the area for transport operations.

There is a moment in many battles where the plan starts to get fuzzy. True leaders can see through the blur and complete the mission, while others will fail, often at the cost of many soldiers' lives. The first building Connelly's men began to search created that moment of distortion in the strategy.

The single-story mud house had a wooden door that opened to a small entryway. From there it split, leading to a small, empty kitchen on the left and on the right a living room that held six Taliban fighters. Four of them were sleeping on the floor, but two were awake, apparently on guard duty. They were sitting at a small table, smoking and talking, when they noticed the operators. There was a split second of recognition between the forces before the two closest members of the Delta Team opened fire. Their weapons were suppressed, but the bullets were not fast or deadly enough to stem the scream that erupted from one of the guards.

In an instant the compound came to life. Delta dispatched all six Taliban fighters in the first building, but as the team members reloaded their weapons, terrorists flooded out of the six other buildings in the compound, armed with AK-47s, AKS-74s, PKMs, and RPG launchers. There was not a woman or child in sight as the Delta Team took cover and concealment within the first building.

Connelly knew they needed help and needed it fast. They were outnumbered, at a conservative estimate, by five to one. It would take ten minutes for armored reinforcements to arrive. He radioed for help and then dug in inside the home, hoping his team could survive until the cavalry arrived. The Taliban fighters initially ran across the open courtyard, allowing the Delta Team to make short work of ten to fifteen enemy soldiers with well-placed and controlled bursts of lead from their weapons.

The enemy troops quickly took refuge inside nearby buildings as the firefight reached maximum lethality. Within a minute two Delta operators were down, injured and unable to continue to fight. An RPG exploded on the outside wall of the home, sending a shockwave into the building. Particles of dust and chunks of mud flew in every direction.

Connelly knew they were very susceptible to being surrounded; he deployed one team member to the rear and two to the sides of the house, ordering them to hold their ground and advise if the enemy tried to flank the building. That left Connelly and four uninjured soldiers to hold the front of the building. Connelly watched the smoke trail from an RPG and ordered his grenadier to fire a 40mm explosive round from an M203.

The grenade scored a direct hit through an open doorway across the courtyard. The shot was perfectly timed, and the projectile, armed at 25 meters, exploded with a flash of light, producing a roomful of screams. For two minutes Delta took no RPG fire.

It was at that moment he heard his rear security start to yell. "Colt, Colt, we are under fire . . ."

Colt awoke to Dean screaming as he dragged Colt's semiconscious body out of the center of the parking lot. "Colt, we are under fire, we need to get out of here!"

It came to Colt in an instant. The sound of gunshot, the whine of the bullet, the cold, the dream, and the screams sobered his confused mind instantly. "Keep your head down!" Colt yelled. Finding himself at the driver's door of his squad, he crawled into the seat and started up the car.

"What the hell are we going to do?" Dean shouted as a bullet entered the car through an open window and buried itself in the front passenger airbag.

"Get in back! I am going to call for backup," Colt reached for his radio and noticed the bullet hole in the LED screen. "There goes that idea . . ." Grabbing for his cell phone, he realized it had fallen off the center console and out of sight.

"You can't call for backup! These guys will kill you and anyone else who comes to help you. We need to get out of here!"

"Those shots are coming from the only exit out of this park. The only reason we are still alive is the shooter has a bad angle."

"What about the trails?" Dean suggested.

"They start out wide and get pretty narrow. I don't know how far we could make it."

"Far enough to get out of his sight for a minute or two?" Dean asked.

"Maybe . . . hell, it's worth a shot. I have a rifle and some body armor in my trunk." Colt slid down until he was almost sitting on the floor, able to work the pedals and steer without exposing his head or body—or, unfortunately, see where he was going. Risking a quick glance at the closest trail opening, he put the car into drive and punched the gas. He would steer blind and hope he hit the wide part of the trail. Once he felt the gravel he would look up and get them into cover. If he missed the opening it would only hurt a little while before they were both dead.

19

Mountain Lake Liquors
12:15

Sam had very few options. He could retreat through the back of the liquor store, arousing the suspicion of the clerk. He could turn himself in and hope that the police could protect him long enough to get to Colt. Or he could act casual and hope the officer had not run his license plate.

The latter option seemed his best choice, as his vehicle was parked on the side of the store, out of the officer's view. Sam stepped out the front door and watched as the officer stepped out of the squad car. Sam noted that the officer kept his eyes on him, and a sudden tightness in Sam's chest left him breathless and paralyzed.

"Hello," the officer said as he walked past Sam and into the store. Sam could not muster a breath to answer. He simply nodded his head and walked swiftly to the stolen car.

Sam started up the car, backed out of his spot, and drove past the parked cruiser. Looking in the rearview mirror, Sam saw that the officer remained in the store. "Too close of a call," Sam told himself.

Back on the highway, Sam reached into his pocket and pulled out the envelope and disc. They had all gone through a lot of trouble to get the disc off the base, and Sam and Dean had run almost obsessively through all their options.

"Why don't I at least make two copies?" Sam recalled asking Dean. "I can carry out one and Walter can bring out the other."

"Because if they catch you and find the disc they will know you made a backup copy. They will hunt Walter down to the end."

"And if they catch me without the disc? What happens then?"

"They assume you had a late midlife crisis and decided to make a run for it. The truth may come out during interrogation, but by then I hope to use Walter to gain Detective Sullivan's trust. Once Sullivan is on our side we will retrieve the disc."

"Why don't you just get the disc from Walter?"

"We have no assurance that Walter can ditch his vehicle and get to me. If they catch him with the disc we'll have no evidence. You need to get to the store and get that disc, and then meet me in Frontier."

"How will you know I didn't make it?"

"Sullivan and I will head back to my place. You need to get to the Frontier PD by whatever means necessary. Once there, advise them that you need to speak with Detective Sullivan. We'll know you are safe and have the disc. If we don't hear from you within a couple hours, we'll assume you were captured and take matters into our own hands."

"It sounds just crazy enough to work," Sam had said, only half-joking.

"We'll need a hell of a lot of luck, but it's our only shot," Dean had replied, his voice devoid of humor.

Sam snapped back to reality. He needed to get to Frontier and establish contact with Dean and Sullivan. Once that was complete, the second phase of their operation would commence.

Distributing the evidence would not be an easy process. The data incriminated everyone from Harrison and his agents through senior members of the U.S. government and even the president. It was not as simple as giving the disk to a local media station and spreading the word. The medical information would need to be confirmed by nongovernment doctors, and the whole idea of robotic brainwashed killers would not be easy for the public to grasp.

Of course, none of the data that Sam and Dean had selected carried the president's or any senior official's signature. It was bad enough that they would be tarnishing America's reputation by releasing one of its ugliest and best-kept secrets. They had decided to give the president a chance to wipe his hands clean of the incident and enact punishment on Harrison in order to restore at least some image of justice served with the people of America and the world.

Breathing deeply, Sam looked at the open road before him and then up toward the sky. The glowing blue hue filled his vision as he once again considered how simply beautiful the world outside the Vault really was.

Sam watched as a minivan passed him. It contained a young mother with a scowl on her face. She was yelling at two children in car seats behind her for some unseen act. Sam couldn't help but think she would see things differently if she lost her children or could never have had them in the first place.

A sign in front of him indicated that Frontier was only five miles ahead. The highway began sloping downward and Sam could see the glistening Frontier River as it came alongside the highway before continuing into Frontier and bisecting the city.

Sam braked and glanced into his rearview mirror. A police car was directly behind him, and it showed no signs of speeding up or changing lanes. The car he was driving had likely been reported stolen, and the officer had found him.

Continually checking on the squad car in his rearview mirror Sam realized he had no idea when the officer had begun following his car. A minute passed, and still the officer had not taken any action. They were entering the outskirts of the town, still on the highway but leaving the mountains and forests behind.

A second squad car sped down an entrance ramp, and Sam realized what the officer had been waiting for. The backup unit merged into traffic behind Sam and the first police car. Within seconds both cars activated their light bars and sirens. Three miles from the downtown exit, Sam pulled over.

He twisted the key in the ignition, turning the car off, and watched in his side-view mirror as the officers exited their vehicles with their sidearms drawn. They ordered Sam to throw the keys out the window and keep his hands in the air. Once he was ordered out of the car, he was told to face away from it with his hands high in the air.

As he followed their orders to turn around, showing his waistband area, Sam felt like he doing some absurd version of the Hokey Pokey. The officer ordered him to walk backwards and quickly Sam felt cold metal on his wrist.

"You have the right to remain silent—" the arresting officer began.

"I understand my rights, and I will remain silent for now. I wish to be taken to the police department for questioning," Sam replied as coolly and respectfully as he could.

"I have to do a pat-down search, and then you can have a seat in the back of my car."

"I understand. Do what you need to do, but please get me to the station as quickly as you can."

"No problem, sir. We'll be on our way shortly." The officer completed the pat-down and found the envelope and disc in Sam's pocket. "What is this?"

"Evidence. You'll want to hang onto that."

"Whatever you say. Here, have a seat. We should be at the station in a few minutes."

"Understood, officer. I don't mean to be any trouble. I just need to get to a safe place." At that, the officer gave him a strange look and shut the door.

"Wow, this guy is a real nutcase," the officer said to his backup. "Why steal a car and then beg to be brought to the police station as soon as possible?"

"Probably some mental-health case."

"Either way, he was one hell of an easy arrest. You taking care of the tow?"

"Yup. I got it. Have a good ride to the PD. At least you get to dump him on the detectives."

"I'll be glad to. Thanks for the backup and calling the tow. I thought we'd have ourselves a midday pursuit."

"I thought so too. Oh well, have a good trip."

Sam watched as his arresting officer climbed into the driver's seat. He volunteered, "By the way, my name is Sam."

"Sam. I am Officer Richland. You have invoked Miranda, so I can't ask you any questions about the crime you committed. Do you understand?"

"I understand. I just want to thank you for a job well done, Officer Richland."

"A job well done? Are you high on something?"

"Not at all. Just make sure Colt Sullivan is there to interview me when we arrive."

"Whatever you say, Sam." Officer Richland radioed in his transport and drove the squad toward downtown.

20

Miner's Gulch
12:20

Colt blindly raced the unmarked car toward the trail opening. He tried to listen over the engine noise for any indication they were still under fire. "Hold on!" he yelled to Dean in the backseat.

The Impala cleared the gate at the trail opening with inches to spare. A quick glance told Colt that the path opened up before taking a sharp turn. After clearing the curve, he saw he was out of room and stopped the car. He estimated he had put an additional three hundred yards between himself and the shooter. The trees would provide cover and give him time to develop a plan of action.

"Who was that?" Colt asked in a quiet but stern voice.

"A government agent. He most likely had orders to kill us both on sight."

"There is no way they would kill a cop in broad

daylight."

"Look around. Do you see any witnesses? They don't care that you are a cop."

Colt undid Dean's handcuffs and opened the squad's trunk. His suit would be cumbersome, so he removed his coat, tie, and dress shirt. The squad always carried a raid kit consisting of a tactical vest, body armor, and his carbine rifle.

Colt's AR-15 rifle held a M68 red-dot sight, a popular target-acquisition device used heavily in the war on terror. While the iron sights that came standard with the AR-15 were accurate in ideal lighting conditions, they did poorly in low light.

"Damn. You guys don't mess around," Dean remarked. "Do you guys always carry that much firepower?"

"Sadly, yes," Colt replied. "You know the saying, you don't bring a knife to a gunfight? In the early nineties, cops armed with revolvers were getting into shootouts with punks carrying semi-auto handguns, fully automatic machine pistols, and assault rifles."

"So you one-upped them?"

"A lot of departments tried falling back on twelve-gauge shotguns. They loaded them with double-odd buck or slugs, but seven pump-action shotgun rounds still didn't level the playing field."

"That gun looks like it leveled the playing field."

Colt shrugged on the tactical vest. "After the North Hollywood shootout, a lot of departments turned to the military for the answer. The army was downsizing, and police officers were able to throw surplus rifles in their squads."

"You think it will be enough?"

"It's all we have." Colt loaded up with ammunition and readied his weapon. As he slid one of the magazines into the rifle, he felt the world start spinning.

"Detective Sullivan!" Dean reached over and shook Colt by the shoulders. "Snap the hell out of it!"

"I'm okay," Colt replied. "You stay here. There is less chance of him seeing us if I move alone."

"I won't argue with you there. How are you going to find him?"

"He started shooting from the area beyond the entrance to this trail. My guess is he will be somewhere on the hill on the opposite side of the highway, in front of the park entrance."

"They will have backup here in anywhere between ten and twenty minutes. You need to hurry," Dean said as Colt ran from the vehicle.

If Dean was telling the truth, then he had less than ten minutes to take out the threat.

It took him less than two minutes to navigate the quarter mile of thick forest and arrive at the highway. Staying low to the ground, he moved parallel to the road until he could see the park entrance. Colt's plan was to flank the sniper and try to take him into custody. If he could interrogate the sniper, he might have a chance to figure out what the hell was going on and see if this attack was tied to the murder of Abigail Connelly.

Scanning the ridgeline opposite the park entrance, Colt located three areas providing good sectors of fire. The two-lane highway in front of him was the biggest obstacle. Such a linear danger area, as it was known in military circles, would leave Colt visible and susceptible to enemy fire throughout the crossing.

Assuming that the sniper would keep his eyes on the entrance to the park, Colt doubted the suspect would have time to bring his gun sights over to the road before his quarry reached the trees on the other side.

The sprint across the road took less than eight seconds, but to Colt it felt like an eternity. Releasing his breath on the opposite side of the road, Colt hunkered down behind a large tree and double checked his rifle. He pulled the charging handle back and witnessed the live round in the chamber before silently sliding the bolt back into place.

After slapping the magazine to ensure it was fully seated, Colt moved low and fast, zigzagging his way toward the suspect. Four minutes had passed since he left the car. His brain ticked, counting down like a time bomb as he pushed himself faster. Traveling farther up the ridgeline, he noted that the area was more open. He found himself sprinting between bushes and small rock outcrops that barely hid his frame.

Colt could see the first target area approximately two hundred yards in front of him. He needed to move close enough to gain the element of surprise and still have verbal control of the suspect. Closing to within fifty yards took another minute off his clock, and he cursed himself for the spent time.

He ended at an advantageous position overlooking the first possible sniper nest. The rocky shelf was covered with small shrubs, providing muzzle-flash suppression as well as concealment. The flat shelf would have been the perfect place for a sniper to lie down and stay concealed. Colt observed the lack of disturbance in the dirt under the shrubs and knew the sniper had not been here.

The next target area was only thirty yards away, but it was blocked by a massive stone outcropping. Slinging the rifle on his back, Colt muscled his way through the boulders. At the top he crawled forward and glanced over the edge. He found himself looking down at a man dressed in black fatigues, laid out among some shrubs, and holding a sniper rifle. The long-range weapon was still aimed at the entrance to the park.

Placing his adversary in his gun sights, Colt shouted down, "We have you surrounded. Put down your rifle and stand up with your hands in the air. If you make any sudden movements we will kill you." The enemy did not move a muscle—clearly debating his next step or deliberately wasting time. "Move now, or we will shoot!"

The agent lowered the rifle and stood up with his hands in the air. "Go ahead and shoot. You are already dead. My backup will be here in minutes."

"I don't want to kill you." Colt saw the man had a sidearm holstered on his hip. "I want you to remove your sidearm slowly. Throw it on the ground and move toward me."

"I can't do that. My mission is to kill you and Dean Knight."

"Who gave you that mission?"

"I am not at liberty to tell you. I can only tell you that the program has been terminated."

"What program?"

"I would have thought Dean would have told you by now. Oh well." The agent's hand flashed toward his sidearm, and Colt reflexively squeezed the trigger three times.

He was no farther than fifteen yards from his target,

and each shot found its mark. The first two shots had been aimed center mass, targeting the vital organs in the chest. Colt saw the suspect's head whip back as the third bullet bored through his skull. It had been the insurance round in case the man was wearing ceramic body armor.

The sound of the gunshots reverberated through the mountains. Colt scanned the woods for any other suspects before making his way down to the suspect. He knew he had to work fast, remembering Dean's warning about the sniper's backup.

Colt dropped down next to the body and examined the effects of his bullets. Two small crimson circles, each smaller than a dime, were positioned in the upper left side of the chest. One of the rounds was positioned to blow out a chamber of the target's heart. The other slightly higher shot likely destroyed his aorta.

While the suspect might have been able to fire a shot or two with a blown-out heart, the third bullet had ensured instant death. The final bullet had turned the sniper's brain to mush and severed his brainstem. Colt quickly searched the area around the dead man.

The sniper's weapon, a military-issue M21 EBR, lay next to the body. Colt noted the rifle was fully equipped with combat modifications. It belonged on the battlefields of the Middle East, not in the mountains of Colorado. The complex scope, modified magazine, and sound suppressor hinted at Special Forces. "Who the hell were you?" Colt asked aloud. The suspect's USP .45 handgun, which Colt retrieved from under the man's back, was highly modified and eclipsed the parameters for self-defense.

The serial numbers had been expertly removed from the weapons or had never existed in the first place. The sniper was wearing a variation of the battle dress uniform worn by military forces around the world. Colt opted to only search a few of the sixteen-odd pockets. He found a few spare magazines but no documents, identification, or easily detected communication device.

Gathering up the weapons, Colt retreated from the sniper's nest, aware that the man's backup could appear at any time.

Risking exposing himself to a second, well-disciplined sniper, Colt descended from the ridgeline and broke into a full sprint across the road and through the parking lot. Burdened only by the weapons, he moved quickly.

He needed to get back to Dean and figure out what was going on. He had found himself in the middle of a murder investigation, an assassination attempt, and an officer-involved shooting. It was turning out to be one hell of a day.

21

Frontier Police Department
12:30

Sam watched out the back window as they pulled into the parking lot of the Frontier police station. The building swallowed up the cruiser as it pulled into the underground garage. Sam felt his heart beating faster. He had worked so hard to escape the confines of Harrison's prison, only to head back underground.

"You're safe now, Sam," Richland said, turning around and speaking through the plastic divider.

"I'll never be safe." Sam's reply was not meant to be as cold and dejected as it came out. He knew safe was a relative term, and just how safe he could be depended on Dean and Colt. "I do want to thank you for being respectful."

"You haven't given me any reason not to be. Keep cooperating and we'll see what we can do about your future. I can't promise much. We don't cut breaks for those who commit felony theft, but I'll make sure you are kept in the loop."

"I appreciate that. The only other thing I ask is that you don't allow anyone to be alone with me. Especially anyone from the government or posing as my lawyer. I don't have a lawyer and I don't request counsel. Make sure everyone understands that."

"I will. I will escort you to a holding cell where you will remain until a detective is free to come interview you. If you need anything, let someone know right away."

"Thank you, Officer Richland, I'm ready to go when you are."

"Okay, Sam. Hold tight a minute." Sam watched the officer get out of the squad and walk over to a gun locker. After securing his weapons in the locker, Richland returned and opened the door for Sam.

"That is one uncomfortable ride back there. Those plastic seats are a pain in the ass, literally."

"We don't make them for comfort, and you should appreciate the cleanliness of the plastic seats. It used to be near impossible to clean out all the vomit from the seams of the old seats. After a month on the streets, most squads started to carry a faint but constant smell of alcohol and greasy bar food. And it may not seem like it, but taking out the padding gives the backseat a little more legroom."

"Makes sense," Sam agreed as they reached the security door. "This holding cell I am going into . . . will I be alone?"

"One hundred percent alone. You have your own toilet, sink, and concrete slab with a small mattress pad. It's not a Hilton, but I have seen people sleep in the cells before. In any case, you should be in and out in a few hours."

"In and out? Where do I go from here?"

"These are temporary cells. The boys from the county have the permanent jail. You'll head down there after your interview and remain there until you can see a judge. The judge will decide whether or not you are allowed to post bail. If you are allowed to post bail there will be plenty of bondsmen there to assist you. Then you will get to enjoy the 'we'll gct to it when we get it' attitude of courts portion of the criminal justice system."

"Okay. As long as I have a few hours alone and an interview with Colt Sullivan everything should be okay."

"I'll see to it that you are left alone, and I'll get ahold of Detective Sullivan ASAP."

"I appreciate that," Sam replied as the metal security door disengaged. Officer Richland stood behind Sam and directed him forward. The holding facility was smaller than Sam had imagined. From the sally port a small hallway, bathed in white, led to a slightly larger hallway with six large metal doors on one side. The other side of the hallway had four less-imposing doors marked as interview rooms A through D. Sam was led to the cell marked number 4.

"Turn around and face the wall, Sam." With his arrestee in the proper position, Richland conducted a more thorough search. Finding nothing additional in his pockets, waistband area, crotch, or mouth, Richland removed Sam's handcuffs. "Take off your belt and shoes, and if you have anything illegal on your or in your person, now is the time to tell me."

"I have nothing else on me," Sam replied while

removing his belt and shoes.

"Thank you. I'll put your CD and envelope into evidence. Any requests before I take off to do some paperwork?"

"Just get ahold of Colt Sullivan as soon as possible. I really need to talk to him."

"Will do. Is there anything I can tell him in order to have him better understand why you want to talk to him?"

"Just tell him it's about Abigail Connelly. That should get his attention."

"I'll pass it along." Officer Richland shut the cell door.

Sam looked around at the white walls and stainless steel sink and toilet. "You've got to be kidding me," he said. "Not white and stainless steel again . . . "

22

The Vault
12:30

"Agent 47 is down," the monotone operator relayed to General Harrison. "Several shots were fired by the agent a few minutes prior to his death. He advised command that he had visuals on both Knight and Sullivan and was taking the shots. The vehicle they were in fled into a wooded area. The agent felt his high-ground position still gave him the best chance to inflict a kill shot. Approximately six minutes later we intercepted communication between 47 and Sullivan. The agent was advised he was surrounded and ordered to surrender. Sullivan attempted to extract information from the agent. Seconds later three gunshots were fired and 47's heart monitor stopped. Sullivan searched the agent's body and fled."

"Goddammit. Was there any truth to the agent being surrounded? Did Sullivan bring police backup?"

"Our scanners emplaced within Frontier PD dispatch software did not pick up any communications with or about any units working in the area. It appears to have been a bluff on Sullivan's part."

"Have we intercepted any radio traffic to indicate Sullivan reported the firefight and death of the agent?"

"Not yet. We have his cell-phone trace activated now. He has not made any calls and has not left the area."

"How long until additional agents are on scene to clean this up?"

"Ten minutes, sir. One helo is inbound with four agents to neutralize the targets and a second helo has a medical team and extraction equipment for the body."

"Why the hell is it going to take ten minutes?"

"Mitchell damaged the vast majority of our software during his escape. Knight must have provided Mitchell with every back door he ever built into this system. We are trying to rebuild from the ground up. Our internal communications are back to one hundred percent, but our external communications are spotty at best. Knight knew he had this window to work with, which is why he risked a meeting with Sullivan via cell phone. He knew we would be reduced to using old technology.

"For now, Sullivan's cell phone trace is being done using triangulation and cell-tower communication interruption. When we first got a hit on his location, Agent 47 just happened to be in the area looking for Mitchell. We were still a few miles from his exact location, but the park lots were the only feasible spot for a meeting. We can't stay with Sullivan full time until we get the GPS and third-party software back online. If he heads back into the city before we are up and running, we are as good as blind for at least the next hour."

"What about Mitchell? Are there any updates?"

"Frontier PD stopped a stolen vehicle on the highway. From the information we gathered, it appears Mitchell was driving. He was taken into custody and transported to Frontier PD for booking. He arrived a few minutes ago."

"Send in a couple agents to take care of Mitchell. Make sure they go in clean and come back clean, or they don't come back at all."

"Understood, sir. Any direct orders on the kill method?"

"No kill method; extract him using a federal warrant. I want him back here and alive to tell us where to find Knight. Mitchell is a scared rat; he won't survive twenty seconds with me in the interrogation room."

"Understood. What if we run into problems and agents can't remove him?"

"He's in police custody, so any death is going to be put under a microscope. They'll do a chemical screen as part of the autopsy, but we've gotten around that before. Tell the boys to use the Aconitum napellus. It worked well in the Middle East, and their best scientists never found it. I doubt the local medical examiner will be looking for it."

"Will do, sir. I'll update you with any breaking news."

"Roger." Harrison slammed down his phone and stood up. There was still a chance to contain the situation, but he was walking a fine line. He could call Washington and advise them of the situation. Confident they would give him every asset available to plug the leaks, Harrison's only fear was of repercussions for losing control in the first place. Once everything settled down he would be out of a job, sent somewhere to rot for the remainder of his years.

To avoid that outcome he decided to contain the issue by himself. He would report the losses of his assets, but through clever and careful testimony he was sure he could downplay the significance of the deaths of a couple of his scientists.

The greatest loss was going to be William Connelly. He was out there somewhere, and Harrison needed to find him. Harrison's men could capture Connelly and bring him back alive, and in turn he could be used to hunt down the loose ends.

Harrison found his confidence, drawing in a deep breath to puff out his chest. The helos would be on site in five minutes to round up Sullivan and Knight. Mitchell was in police custody with agents en route to secure him. Harrison had everything under control, but just to be sure he picked up the phone and dialed in a favor.

"Hello," a familiar voice answered on the other line.

"Joe." Harrison opted for the first name in an effort to keep it casual. "How are you doing?"

"Frank Harrison. I'm doing well. And yourself?" answered Colonel Joe Peterson. He was the commander of the nearest army attack helicopter squadron.

"To be blunt, not good. I need some help."

"Sure thing, bud. What do you need?"

"I need your best two-man chopper crew airborne immediately. Then I then need them to open a secure communication patch with my command and take direct orders from me."

"Frank . . . this is highly unorthodox. I can get you a

crew, but you have to tell me what you are doing."

"Don't worry, Joe. I have the backing of the Pentagon. I just need to borrow them for a training exercise for my men."

"I understand. You want them fully loaded?"

"Now you are speaking my language. What can I expect for an ETA?"

"Well, since I only know your base is somewhere in eastern Colorado, the ballpark figure is twenty minutes."

"That will work. Thanks, Joe. I owe you."

"Send me a twelve-pack and we'll call it even."

"Sounds good. Take care, Joe."

"You too, Frank." Harrison managed a smile as he hung up the phone. He called his command center and relayed some instructions.

A few minutes went by before his phone rang. "Sir, we have the Apache pilots patched in to you," the operator relayed. "Gentlemen. You are on the air with General Harrison."

"Good afternoon, General, Captain Miller here. Happy to be of assistance. How can we help you out today?"

"Captain Miller. Thank you for helping me out. I might need you and your gunner to take care of a problem for me."

"Sure thing, sir. What's the problem?"

"A few minutes ago we had a breach of security at our outer gate. A party dressed in all black took several photos of our highly classified operation. That information in the wrong hands could be disastrous for America. I have agents en route to intercept, but if the target evades them I need you to take him out."

"Roger that, sir. How will the target be identified?"

"I will let my dispatcher handle that with you. Just know that you have the complete backing of the Pentagon to engage this enemy, no matter the circumstances. While you should clearly avoid any collateral damage, just know that we can't afford another 9/11."

"Understood, sir."

His orders given, Harrison turned the logistical aspect back over to his command center. He sat down in his chair, drew in another breath, and reached into his desk drawer. From it he withdrew a bottle of Wild Turkey whiskey and a shot glass.

"God Bless America," he said, pouring a stiff shot. He tipped the glass back and let the warm liquid run through his mouth and down his throat. "Oh, and enjoy hell, Mr. Knight."

23

Miner's Gulch
12:45

Colt used the sprint back to the parking lot to comprehend the last thirty minutes of his life. He was living the proverbial bad dream. Any second he expected to find himself sitting in bed, wondering why the dream seemed so real.

But the nightmare was reality, and he had just killed a man. Colt felt no different after the shootout than if he had stopped at a stop sign or purchased groceries. Killing felt normal, somehow, and it bothered him.

Department policy was clear-cut on officer-involved shootings. He needed to advise dispatch, his supervisor, and his union attorney that he had been involved in a deadly force incident. Arriving back at the car he walked past Dean, fumbled around inside the car, and found his cell phone. He took it and started dialing his dispatch center.

"Whatever you do, Colt, do not call this in!"

"I have to. It's department policy."

"Forget the policy! They have your phone bugged. If you make that call, they are going to know we are still alive. Harrison's men will be here in a few minutes, and this time they will finish the job."

Colt heard the dispatcher pick up the phone. "Dispatch. Sara speaking. How can I help you?"

"Sara. This is Colt calling. How are you today?"

"I'm doing okay Colt, how are you?"

Colt took a look at Dean and saw a combination of fear and strain. Colt's career, not to mention his whole future, hinged on his next sentence. If he chose not to call in the shooting and Dean was lying, he would be fired and indicted on felony charges. However, if Dean was right and more attackers came, Colt's life would be over in a matter of minutes.

"I'm doing well. Say, I was just flagged down by someone on the highway near Miner's Gulch. They said they heard some gunshots coming from the area. Can you send some squads up here to check it out? I'm in the middle of this homicide investigation. I am sure it's just someone doing some target practice."

"Sure thing, Colt, anything else you need?"

"Yeah, start me a call for some follow-up over in Silver Springs. It's just a witness statement, so you can show me code four."

"Will do. Take care, Colt."

"You too, Sara." Colt ended the call and took a deep breath. "You'd better be right, Dean, because if you aren't I just lost my job and we are both going to prison for a long time."

"Thank you for trusting me. I am going to assume that the man you shot up there was wearing tactical gear?"

"Yeah, and he was short on words for why he was trying to kill us."

"He was most likely an agent. We need to get out of here, I'll explain more on the way."

"We will take my car. I don't trust that truck of yours."

"Neither do I. Chances are we aren't going to make it out of here without running into more agents, and my truck won't last long at high speeds. Your vehicle is pursuit-rated. We'll just have to see how it handles being in the front of a chase."

"That still doesn't answer where we are going."

"Step one: ditch the phone. Otherwise they will know where we are at all times."

"And if we need to call someone?"

"Pay phones are our best option. They have access to most of the ones in the area, but I doubt they will be paying much attention to them right now. I also have some safe phones for us to use, but only as a last resort."

"This is nuts," Colt said, tossing his cell phone aside and climbing into his car. "Hop in the front. The back doors only open from the outside."

"Thanks. By my estimation we should be expecting company any second. Let's get out of here."

As Colt sat in the driver's seat he heard the distant thumping of the helicopter's rotors. The all-too-familiar feeling of lightheadedness and nausea started to creep into his body. He was about to lose control when Dean slapped him.

"What the hell was that for?"

"You didn't look good. You sure you can drive?"

"I'll do my best!" Colt started up the engine and threw the car into reverse. Exiting the trail at full speed, he spun the wheel while shifting into drive. The Impala rotated one hundred and eighty degrees, ending the spin pointed at the lot entrance.

"Hold on a second. I need to grab something from my truck." Dean made a short sprint to his truck and retrieved a backpack and a toolbox. He held onto the items as he jumped back into the still-open passenger door. "I have a feeling we are going to need these."

Dean held onto the dash as Colt floored the accelerator and launched the vehicle out of the parking lot. "You have some more explaining to do!" Colt yelled above the groaning engine and squealing tires.

"What do you want to know?"

"Who the hell are these guys? Military? Special forces?"

"The sniper? He was an agent."

"I've heard you say that before. What the hell is he an agent of?"

"In addition to the brain-transplant program, I was part of a government-led assassination program named Project Capitalis. Capitalis is Latin for 'head,' the root of the term *capital punishment*. It was a fitting name, as we took the worst of the worst on death row and reprogrammed them to be near-robotic killers. They were sent on homicidal and suicidal missions around the world to take down political targets. If the agent was captured or killed, their information was impossible to locate for anyone other than the highest-ranking members of the U.S. government."

"So who regulates the agents?"

"Short answer? William Connelly. He was too valuable to use on standard assassination missions, but he was the best-trained killer we had. If one of our assassins failed their mission, we utilized him to track down the agent and clean up the aftermath. Through more than a hundred slayings we had a one hundred percent success rate in untraced kills. Until Brian Cill."

"Wait . . . as in the infamous serial killer, Brian Cill? He was killed on national television!"

"Yes, he was sedated during his public execution and administered potassium chloride. His heart and lungs stopped before he was quickly taken out of sight of the public for revival. Under heavy sedation he was transported to our secure facility for the beginning phases of the rewriting process.

"It was at our base that he met William Connelly. Cill was a classic sociopath. On the surface he was able to hide all outward appearances of his true nature. He was a pathological liar and often murdered people by befriending them, secluding them, and killing them slowly and painfully."

"Why would Connelly befriend him?"

"Connelly and Cill met right after Connelly underwent his brain transplant. To buy time until we could ready his alternate life, we convinced Connelly he was in an army hospital recovering from his wounds. In an effort to make it more believable we introduced Cill as a fellow soldier.

"They became friends, but after they were both brainwashed, neither party recognized the other, and Cill was given his assignment. He was supposed to kill the leader of a domestic terror cell known as the Freedom Fighters of Colorado. The man had recently made underground threats against the First Lady. Cill was to join the militia in order to befriend and eventually kill the leader and several other high-ranking officers."

"What the hell happened?"

"A week into the operation Cill went silent and was never heard from again. We initially believed the militia leader had suspected Cill as a traitor and killed him. However, the GPS locator in Cill's body was shut off somehow, and he was never located. A raid on the militia compound and several brutal interrogations revealed that Cill left unannounced of his own accord."

"Why don't you get to the part where this involves me?" Colt replied. He was trying to compute everything that Dean was telling him, but it was difficult to do while driving at breakneck speed.

"I came here today to tell you that Cill killed Abigail Connelly, and you are the one who needs to stop him before more innocent people are killed."

"Yeah, but why did Cill kill Abigail Connelly?" Suddenly Colt looked in his side-view mirror. "We have company. It would have been nice for you to tell me the back-up would be in the form of an attack helicopter."

"Whatever you do, don't stop! If we stop they will turn this car into scrap metal and then come finish the job hands-on."

"I'll make sure not to stop, but what is going to keep them from shooting us while we are moving?"

"For right now? Nothing. The only difference is that while you are moving we have a slightly smaller chance of being turned to Swiss cheese. Don't worry, I have a plan."

"Is it better than 'meet me at a parking lot where a sniper can take us both out'?"

"Honestly, no. But all you have to do is keep us alive long enough to see if I can hack into the control systems on that helicopter." Dean removed a laptop from his backpack and flipped it open.

"How long will that take?"

"I don't know. I've never tried it before. Hopefully it will take less time than the helicopter's gunner needs to make us a stain on the road."

"Brilliant," Colt replied. Dean's story was getting more believable by the minute.

24

Highway 55
12:50

Colt checked his side-view mirror and saw the helicopter had gained significant ground. Although he had the Impala traveling well over 100 miles per hour, he figured the helicopter was doing closer to 180 and would be within gun or missile range shortly. "Whatever you are doing, you'd better do it fast!"

"On the plus side, we are being stalked by one of the most deadly attack helicopters in the U.S. Army," Dean remarked.

"How can that be a plus?"

"They sent a UH-64 Apache Longbow. It has one of the most advanced target-acquisition platforms in the world."

"I don't think you know what 'on the plus side' means . . ."

"The more advanced a system is, the more reliant it is on computers, thus making it more susceptible to hacking."

"So you can shut down their targeting?"

"In theory, yes. But I have never tried before . . . and in theory, communism works."

"You need to work on more optimistic deliveries. How long will it take?"

"Two minutes if everything goes well."

"I don't think we have two minutes. I'll be surprised if we are still driving on four wheels in one minute."

"I'll buy us another thirty seconds by emitting a friendly RF signal. That will confuse their targeting, but not shut it down. No matter what I do, there is going to be a window in which they can and will shoot at us."

"Okay, no promises on my end," Colt admitted. The road toward Frontier was full of curves, and he lost precious speed around each turn. In the five or so miles they had traveled from the parking lot, Colt noticed, there had been no traffic. "They must have figured out a way to shut down the highway. I don't think they want the general public seeing what is about to happen."

"Okay, RF jamming is in place. That should shut down their Hellfire missiles for a couple minutes. It's up to you to keep the 30mm guns off of us."

"No prob—" Colt's side-view mirror exploded as a single 30mm round, part of a twenty-shot volley, struck the side of the car, missing Colt by inches. "Damn it!"

At eighty miles an hour, Colt could barely turn the wheel without the car responding. Inching the wheel to the left, he punched the accelerator, hoping to complicate the helicopter's shots with the addition of uneven speeds.

The road to the front left of the car exploded before their eyes as the cannon-sized projectiles hit the pavement. Small chunks of asphalt peppered the hood.

"How much longer?" Colt yelled as he swerved the car down the highway. Dean failed to respond as he feverishly worked the laptop's keyboard. A third volley of rounds tore chunks out of the road to the rear and right of the squad. Colt realized they were trying to scare him into pulling over. These were warning shots; no amount of swerving or changing speeds was going to dodge the impending kill shots.

"Hold on!" Colt screamed as he stomped the brake pedal and turned the car down a gravel side road. "This is only going to buy us a few more seconds. You'd better have something soon!"

Colt's turn forced the helicopter to make a wide bank, bleeding off airspeed and forcing them to reacquire their aim point. The gravel road was narrow and lined with trees that created a canopy above him. Colt had chosen a straight tunnel of death, but at least the trees provided a small degree of concealment.

"Just a few more seconds!" Dean's fingers flew across the keyboard. Several small trees splintered to Colt's left as cannon rounds punched through the treetops above them. Mashing the brake pedal, Colt slid the car to a stop on the gravel road. The Apache flew over them and made another wide bank. Colt slammed the car into reverse and watched in horror as the helicopter completed its turn. It was now flying directly at them.

The flashes from the gun barrels were visible as the gravel a hundred yards in front of the car burst into the air. The gunner in the rear of the chopper seemed content with walking the rounds into his slow-moving target. Colt had nowhere to go. In a few seconds the verdant tunnel would be their coffin.

"Got it!" Dean announced. The last round fired by the 30mm cannon was close enough to shower the squad with fragments of gravel.

"Nice work!" Colt screamed. The helicopter flew over them, hovered for a second, and then flew out of view. "I don't get it? Why leave? They are still an eye in the sky."

"I shut down their communications and their GPS beacon. They were just a seventy-million-dollar waste of aviation fuel."

"Good work. What's our next move?"

"Harrison sent backup agents to the sniper site. They are the ones who shut down the highway. They are also most likely on their way here now. We need to get into Frontier as quickly as possible."

"On our way," Colt replied. He put the car back into drive and followed the road. It was little more than a service road for logging trucks, and Colt prayed that it fed onto a highway far from Harrison's agents. Letting out a sigh of relief as the squad's tires found pavement on a lightly used county road, he said, "That was too close."

"Nice driving, Colt. I owe you my life."

"Nice work with the helicopter. How the hell did you manage that?"

"Hacking into the onboard computer was easy. The hard part was trying to type while you drove like a madman. On a less positive note, we need to get rid of this car. Harrison has his hands very deep in the pockets of Frontier PD."

"I don't believe it. How is that possible?"

"Think about all the federal grant money that was pumped into your budget. You think all small cities in America are getting that kind of money when Washington is bankrupt?"

"Shit. Does he have anyone on the inside?"

"No. Harrison has trust issues, so he keeps everyone locked up in his own little prison."

"So my phone was bugged, this car is bugged . . . what else should I be worried about?"

"Not really . . . well, other than the fact that you are being hunted by a small army of some of the best assassins in the world led by a U.S. Army general run mad with power."

"Good. I was starting to get worried."

"Pull over up ahead. I should be able to override the GPS tracker. My virus will have prevented them from tracking us to this point, but they will be back online soon."

"How long do you need? We are about twenty minutes from Frontier."

"I'll have it down in less than five minutes."

"And if they are already tracking us?"

"Then you get to show off your driving skills, version 2.0."

"Fuck my life . . ." Colt stated, gripping the steering wheel. "My life was going great until I met you."

25

Highway 3
12:55

“That could have been a lot worse,” Colt commented. From the outside, the car appeared to have sustained only minor damage during the run from the helicopter. Other than the missing side-view mirror and some major paint damage to the front, the car was running great.

“It somewhat goes without saying, but they have a lot of resources at their disposal. I am guessing Harrison is still playing this one close to the vest, but with time we can expect more coordinated efforts, especially if Washington gets involved.”

“Great. Can I ask you something while you work on that GPS tracker?”

“Sure. I am guessing you want to know why Cill killed Abigail Connelly.”

“And you’d be correct.”

"This is going to be the part where you probably tell me to go to hell."

"Try me."

"I can't tell you outright. You need to understand what we did." Dean popped the hood and went to work on removing the trackers. "Some of the top surgeons in the world were recruited to work for Harrison. Straight out of medical school, they signed on the line and became indentured servants to the Department of Defense. And when I say years, I mean decades. The history of brain-transplant operations began in the fifties, when Stalin ordered his scientists to begin researching the concept of brain removal.

"During the start of the cold war, the Soviet Union announced they had succeeded in placing the head and upper body of a small puppy onto the neck of fully grown dog. While not a complete transplant, the operation did show the ability of a transplanted brain to survive on another body's power supply.

"In the sixties, the pioneer was an American scientist named Robert White. He took the research a step further by removing the brain of a dog and keeping it alive outside the body. A few years later he removed a dog's brain and placed it in the head of a different dog. The blood flowed from the host dog to the brain, but White was unable to prove that the brain was still conscious.

"In the early seventies he did a complete head transplant between two rhesus monkeys. Removing the head from Monkey A, he attached it to the body of Monkey B. The monkey that received the head almost bit Dr. White after it was awoken."

"Damn . . . When did they move to humans?"

"With the surgery ruled a success, the ramifications of a human head transplant became obvious to the U.S. military. Dr. White's notes were obtained, and several young doctors were assigned to the project. They needed to ensure a human brain could be harvested, and they had to find a way to repair the damaged nerve endings to ensure the brain could provide control to the host body."

"And you are going to tell me that this was done and the first test subject is now a widowed hero, living a life he doesn't really know?" Colt watched Dean work on the electronic components of the engine, looking for the expertly buried tracker.

"Yes . . . well, no. There were several test subjects over time. The hardest part of the project ended up being repairing the nerve endings. A nerve cell is different from other cells in the body due to its layout. It is a long, sometimes very long, cell consisting of a single axon. Think of it as a chain of paperclips that you made as a child. If all the paperclips are intact, so is the chain. If a paperclip breaks, then the chain is broken. Most cells in the body could just make a new paperclip, and the problem would be solved.

"But the human body can't make new paperclips."

"Exactly. Therefore a break in the chain creates a permanent injury, oftentimes causing paralysis. So scientists needed to find a way to make new paperclips, and the ever-expanding world of genetics was the answer.

"If nerve cells were truly impossible to grow, then a human body would never exist. An embryo has the ability to make nerve cells. While researching embryo growth scientists discovered a protein, released at the command of an embryo's genetic makeup, that creates nerve cells.

By isolating the protein and the genetic marker scientists were able to over-activate the genetic code at very specific spots in an adult human's body and thus force nerve cell growth and repair."

"But why keep this a secret? Why hasn't everyone in America heard about this? It would cure hundreds of thousands of people who are paralyzed or suffer from certain diseases."

"The findings were too premature to release. Trials, long-term studies, and new training had to take place before it could be made public."

"So how do you go from brain transplant and nerve repair to brainwashing assassins?"

"That is where I came into their equation. My brain doesn't quite work like yours, or I should say, the brain of a normal human being. Where you see a car, I see the parts working in unison and the equation that keeps the engine running. Where you see your watch, I see the programming that tells the watch to keep perfect time. When I look at a brain, I see a computer."

"So you are saying you found an equation that makes the brain work?"

"No, I found hundreds of equations that make it work. The human brain has a hard drive, a CPU, input/output nodes, and many other similarities to a computer. I found that if I treated the human brain like a processor. I could write equations that controlled the most intimate part of the brain, the memory.

"You see, all of our brains function on the same basic level. Our brains must be capable of providing several areas of unconscious or subconscious control. Breathing, heart rate, reproduction, even movement equations can be left alone, because they represent a common function. A transplanted brain does not need to act differently from one body to another on the basic level."

"But it would need to adjust for certain things, like height and weight? Right?"

"Not necessarily. The brain simply tells the organs what to do. They do the physical work, and because the body is not changing in size, the organs don't need different commands. The chemicals secreted by the brain need some adjusting, but the human body is amazingly adaptive to chemical change as long as it is given a proper amount of time.

"The real problem is in the conscious control, recognition, and remembrance functions of the brain. If I took your brain out and put it in my body, you would still feel the same but you could look and see that you were not the same person. You would sense that you are alien to that body, and it would create some major psychological issues. The first true transplant successes were death-row inmates who received each other's brains. They went crazy in a matter of minutes, unable to comprehend the idea that they were in another body. Several attempted suicide. Others reverted to a comatose state. The remaining ones had full-scale organ rejections and died shortly after the surgery."

"And this all took place over the last few decades?"

"Actually, most of the breakthroughs occurred at the turn of the millennium. We began to understand which brain would be compatible with another body; it's not so different from organ matching for hearts, livers, kidneys, and so on."

"So once the match is made, you just wipe the brain clean?"

"When officials realized we needed to reprogram the brains, they turned to me for the technical answers. I knew that the brain receives and stores thoughts and memories using electrical pulses. I concluded that the brain can be formatted using electrical stimuli and then rewired using very carefully controlled stimuli. In simple terms, I developed a way to create and store human memories on a computer and then transmit them to a human brain using electricity and the microchip.

"A new set of trials resulted in constant gains, and eventually we were ready for a real sample, one that could be useful for the government."

"And that was William Connelly."

"Yes."

"How does coming to me help? Why not use your skills to track down Connelly?"

"Connelly's microchip failed a few days ago. We lost the ability to monitor and control him. Prior to his chip failure he was showing signs of breaking down, and they feared his brain may be regressing to his pre-programming state."

"And you think Abigail's death has something to do with it?"

"I know it has something to do with it. Connelly is the only true threat to Cill. If Cill can break Connelly down, he will be free to commit countless murders."

"But why kill Abigail Connelly? If what you are telling me is true, Connelly wouldn't even know his wife exists."

"What if Cill could guarantee that Connelly saw Abigail's body—"

"That's not possible. The crime scene was sealed by the police department." Colt watched as Dean stepped back from the car. Seeing Dean's hesitation, he pressed further. "What am I missing here?"

"Colt . . . Connelly saw the body."

"That's impossible. Only a few cops saw the body. I was there."

"I know you were. And I know about the nightmares that you have. The ones that are so real you feel as if you are there in person. I know about your nausea and unexplained dizziness. Most of all, I know about your memories of fighting in some godforsaken stretch of dirt halfway across the world." Dean looked Colt in the eyes.

"I don't believe you."

"Your brain is William Connelly; your body is that of a serial killer. For your sake, unless you put a gun to my head, I won't tell you which one."

"You're wrong. I've been a cop for years. I wasn't overseas. I've never been married."

"You were programmed to believe your life is real. I don't know what else to say. Why else would they have trackers on your car, try to kill us, and send a goddamn helicopter after us?"

Colt took a second to process the information. "I need more proof."

"I know about the scar on your lower back."

"The one I got skiing seven years ago?"

"And the scar from the gunshot wound on your left shoulder."

"That was an accident at the firing range . . ."

"Finally, I know that you can never remember your dreams because we programmed you that way. Dreams were an area we couldn't control. If you always dreamed about a past you didn't recognize, it would create a hell of a lot of problems. Now how could I know all that if I just met you in the parking lot?"

"Shit." Colt realized he could no longer deny what Dean was telling him. He had just been shot at by a sniper and a state-of-the-art military attack helicopter. Dean would have no way of knowing where his scars were, and no one at all knew about his dream amnesia. "So you programmed me?"

"I wrote a majority of the programs that were uploaded to you. As I said before, we tried our best to leave your weapons training and combat skills intact. I was more responsible for your false memories and law-enforcement training."

"So, why am I breaking down?"

"Firewalls protect computers against attacks, but firewalls can be breached. To protect your brain from itself we filled it with firewalls. We built one around every old memory you had, and it worked great for several years. Somehow we missed something, or one of those firewalls failed, and once the virus is in other walls are going to fall."

"So you are saying that in a matter of time I will be William Connelly again?"

"Yes, mostly. I wanted to build a dump program that would speed up the process. Something that allowed us to unload all the information we loaded onto your head and let you go back to being who you were, but I was denied. I figure they saw it as a waste of time. If something inside you failed and we couldn't fix it, you would be treated like a broken piece of equipment and terminated."

"Holy shit . . ."

"Right. The trackers are down, but we should get out

of the area. I'll explain on the way to my place."

Colt's mind was a mess. He didn't feel like driving, but he knew they had no choice. Pulling back onto the road, he turned to Dean. "Explain my role in your whole operation."

"You were the failsafe. We were putting a lot of agents into the field with minimal testing. By the nature of the beast, some were going to run into issues. Whenever something needed to be cleaned up we called on you."

"You mean you *would* have called on me?"

"No. You were used more than you will ever know. With two well-publicized wars and dozens of covert operations in progress, we were using agents to assassinate terrorist leaders, train rebel troops, and commit politically motivated crimes. We had several agents go off the radar, but we used you to terminate the leaks."

"And I won't remember any of this?"

"It's hard to say. Once your memory fully breaks down, you might be able to recall portions of your memory. We never erased anything. We simply wrote over the existing memories."

"Reassuring. You have no idea what is going to happen to me, do you?"

"No. But natural memory is stronger than implanted memory, so in the end your life as William Connelly will come back in full. How much of the last five years you will remember is the unknown."

"That's great," Colt replied sarcastically as he looked in his rearview mirror. "Should we be worried about a black sedan that has been with us for the past mile?"

"Is it a black Dodge Charger with smoked-out windows?" Dean checked his side-view mirror but couldn't see the vehicle.

"Bingo. He's been riding close to the center line to stay out of your line of sight. They must figure you would make them right away."

"That makes sense, but they should have engaged us by now."

"This is different than the helicopter. With the road open, I've been staying in traffic, hoping to blend in and praying they wouldn't attack us with civilians around."

"Good plan, but what happens if we lose the traffic?"

"We don't have a lot of options. They'll definitely engage if we get too close to Frontier."

"I must not have gotten the trackers down fast enough. They were able to get back online and saw our location. They probably sent multiple cars, knowing we would move as soon as the trackers were down. It was just a matter of finding us."

"Hold on!" Colt waited to the last second. Grabbing the wheel and jamming the brakes, he shot across two lanes of traffic and onto the exit ramp, the tires barely maintaining their grip on the pavement.

"What are you doing?" Dean screamed.

"You wanted to see how this car did at the front of a pursuit. Hold on, you're going to find out." Colt saw the driver of the Charger slam on his brakes, but it was too late. The agent couldn't react in time to make the exit and shot past it. It would only buy Colt a few seconds, but in a pursuit a few seconds is a lot of time.

"Just remember they have excellent driving training and a better car," Dean said sullenly.

"Thanks for the vote of confidence," Colt replied. "I just hope you know how to shoot."

26

The Vault
12:45

General Harrison stared at the file folder lying open across his desk. "Cill," he said aloud. Brian Cill had been a gamble and Harrison had lost. Knight and Mitchell had warned him that Cill's brain was too complex and warped to be a successful agent, but Harrison had ignored them.

Cill was kept on American soil with several safeguards to keep him under control. He was on track with his orders until the day he went off the grid. The raid on his last known location revealed nothing other than a taunting note, written by Cill. The childish scribble simply stated, "Thanks. Catch me if you can."

Harrison had the note in his hand. "Once I deal with Connelly, Knight, and Mitchell . . . you're next." He closed the folder as his phone rang.

"Sir, we have a visual," the voice advised over

the telephone. “Agents are following the vehicle on Highway 3.”

“They already have the green light. What are they waiting for?”

“They advised that the suspects are staying close to civilian traffic. It has been impossible to make a discreet and non-witnessed kill.”

“Understood . . . how far out from Frontier are they?”

“Fifteen minutes.”

“Tell them if they make it within five miles to take action, discreet or not.”

“Will do, sir. Oh, and the preliminary in-flight analysis is back from the Apache’s computer.”

“Let me guess, a Dean Knight special?”

“Affirmative. It appears Knight was able to take the Longbow targeting computer offline with a modified RF signal.”

“I guess that’s what you get when you recruit the best. It doesn’t matter. They’ll be dead in less than ten minutes.”

“I’ll relay your orders to the agents. You will be the first to know when the job is complete, sir.”

“Copy.” Harrison could feel the blood pounding in the veins in his head and neck. He was used to stress, having spent most of his career pushing the limit of lawlessness in order to achieve results. Through Southeast Asia, the Middle East, the Balkans, and south into Africa he had commanded from both the front lines and behind enemy lines. He had ordered hundreds of assassinations and executions, and despite some personnel losses he had never failed a mission.

Learning not to accept failure had come early in his army career. After graduating West Point he had shipped to Fort Benning, GA, for his indoctrination as an infantry officer. He stayed at Benning for both Airborne and Ranger school. After completing his training he had felt he was ready for anything, but that all changed a few months later. Nothing had prepared him for his first real combat drop in Vietnam. He could recall the day as if it were still happening.

The NCOs in his unit reminded him that the life expectancy of a second lieutenant dropped into a hot LZ in Vietnam was approximately sixteen minutes. If he could survive the first contact and establish his men and his mission, then he was going to be good to go.

Sixteen minutes.

It kept running through his head. What could you do in sixteen minutes? Hand wash a car? Run a few miles? Suddenly he realized it didn't matter. He was going to die or he was going to live, and that was as simple as life is when you are in combat.

He suddenly took notice of the blue sky out the open door of the Huey. The wind whipped by his face. It was a warm, muggy wind that had not abated since the day he landed in this hellhole. The lush green jungle below the helicopter gave way to rice paddies and small huts. He could see the people working in the fields; none of them looked up as the choppers flew over.

"You ready, sir?" his platoon sergeant yelled in his ear. Sergeant First Class Mark Benson was the spitting

image of a wartime leader of enlisted men. He kept his head shaved to the standard high and tight, his body toned and lean, and his eyes carried a hardness that came with fighting in three wars.

"Cocked, locked, and ready to rock" was Harrison's response. He could feel the adrenaline flow as his body prepared for combat. His vision narrowed, his heart raced, and his hands shook, not in fear, but in excitement.

"Here we go!" Benson bellowed as the choppers banked and dove toward the earth. Their target was a tiny village at the base of a small mountain. Military Intelligence had advised that the inhabitants of the scattered huts were hiding food and weapons for the North Vietnamese and Vietcong. There was rumor of a company-sized element of one hundred or so soldiers operating out of a hidden base in the area. Their objective was to search the town, secure and destroy any weapons and food caches, and gather further intel on troop strength and movement in the area.

The village came into view as the Huey pilot expertly rotated the chopper into position for a no-touch combat exit. The helicopter would hover a few feet above the ground and release its load of troops as quickly as possible before leaving the combat zone at a high rate of speed.

"GO, GO, GO," Harrison commanded as his men leapt from the helo onto the moist earth at the edge of the rice paddies. The men each dropped to a knee in a circle around the chopper, scanning the area for enemies. Once the chopper was clear they moved quickly and quietly to the outskirts of the village.

Harrison called for his platoon sergeant and squad leaders. "Benson, I want my command post set up here, at the edge of the village. Jackson and Rodriguez, I want you to take your men and move them through the village. First platoon has the left side, second platoon take the right side. Smith, you take third platoon and push through to the far side of the village and provide security for the search. Hemming, take your gun teams and set them up at the edge of Smith's security line. We have thirty minutes before those birds return, let's make Uncle Sam proud."

Without question each NCO set about his assigned task. Ten minutes into the operation they had yet to run into any resistance, and several village members had been brought back to Harrison for interrogation. His interpreter advised him that the farmers claimed to have no knowledge of weapons, food caches, or troops in the area.

Fifteen minutes into the mission his men found the first weapons cache. Several assault rifles, two light machine guns, and thousands of rounds of ammunition and dozens of grenades were found in a room hidden under a residence.

Harrison was about to have his prisoners interrogated a second time when first contact was made. Private Kennedy, an eighteen-year-old draftee, was hit by a sniper round and fell to the ground, screaming. Private Swanson, his best friend and lifetime neighbor, who had enlisted after his friend was drafted, ran out to aid his injured buddy. His head exploded as a 7.62mm round, fired from an old and rusty but reliable Soviet-made Dragunov, passed through skull and brain.

"Contact right!" Smith's security team spread out in a half-moon around the far side of the village and opened fire with a mix of M60 machine gun, M14, and

M16 fire. Smith's team quickly took three casualties as a large but invisible contingent of enemy soldiers opened fire on them.

Harrison quickly ascertained he was losing fire superiority, his primary advantage. He ordered Second Platoon, currently hunkered down among the structures on the right side of the village, to establish a base of fire and augment Third Platoon's security. First Platoon was commanded to return to his position. Upon arrival at the command post they were to flank the enemy by moving two hundred meters east of the town and then turning sharply north to attack the enemy on its side.

Harrison chose to lead the flanking attack and quickly discovered how difficult it was to move in the thick jungle. It took several minutes to get into position, and from the sound of diminishing gunfire from the village, he had lost more men. Once his men were on line he ordered them to move forward. The advance was tough going through thick vines, trees, and undergrowth. Harrison could feel the sweat running off his forehead, and it began to sting his eyes. He wiped his brow before removing a smoke grenade from his harness.

Smoke grenades were useful, and Harrison knew how to employ them. He could use them to conceal his troops, signal battlefield commands, and mark areas such as drop zones or medevac sites. Red smoke was the predetermined signal for his base-of-fire element to shift their guns off of the target area, helping to prevent, or at the least reduce, fratricide.

Harrison pulled the pin and threw with all his might. The light cylinder wobbled through the air, losing velocity as it struck foliage. It ended up a mere fifteen yards from his current position, but that would have to do. The faint puff at detonation was inaudible above the gunfight. The smoke struggled to disperse in the thick jungle, but after fifteen seconds Harrison ordered his men to charge.

Harrison drew his wood-grained 1911 handgun, a weapon commonly carried by infantry officers, and moved toward the cloud of smoke. Running through the small obscuration, he emerged on the other side to find himself ten yards from a young Vietcong soldier. The boy looked no more than fifteen and was wearing badly torn clothing and a straw hat with small leaves. Harrison brought the soldier into his sights and pulled the trigger. His first shot missed the target, and he quickly brought his sights back on-line and fired a second shot. The heavy .45-caliber round struck the boy in the shoulder, spinning him around and knocking him to the ground.

The men to Harrison's left and right had also picked up targets and began to lay down a deadly wall of bullets. Harrison almost forgot to throw the second smoke grenade, but he hastily deployed it as they moved across the objective. This signal advised his base-of-fire element to lift their fire off of the objective completely unless they still had an enemy in their sights.

In less than a minute Harrison's men cleared the objective, having killed or wounded a dozen enemy soldiers. He reformed the lines in anticipation of a counterattack. Grabbing his radio operator, he advised his company commander of the incident and requested further instructions. Ordered to hold his ground, Harrison established a new command post in the village and called in a medevac for his wounded and KIA troops. Of the thirty-eight men he commanded, four were dead and six were badly wounded. The men were shuffled around to make two full squads and two gun teams. The medic was doing his best to plug holes and keep the wounded alive, but he kept advising Harrison they needed to be medevac'd ASAP.

The counterattack came before the medevac chopper was even halfway to the village. It began with mortars raining down death indiscriminately throughout the village. In an instant SSG Jackson and one of his team leaders were killed by a direct hit from an 88mm mortar shell.

Harrison instantly recognized that they were facing a large element. Mortars were traditionally a company-sized asset, and the speed at which they had been deployed meant the attackers were close by and familiar with the area. The shelling continued for five minutes and claimed the lives of two more soldiers before it was done. Harrison had lost a full squad of men, trading it for the squad of enemies he had killed in the jungle.

"Call base and advise we are under heavy indirect fire from somewhere near these coordinates. Advise we need close air and indirect fire support or we won't last much longer."

"Copy that, sir." Private Olson, his RTO, answered. With the hell from above over, Harrison heard what sounded like whistles coming from the mountainside east of the village. Small breaks in the jungle confirmed Harrison's fear; a company of men appeared to be moving toward his platoon. "Advise them we are facing a minimum of a company-sized element that is moving toward our location." Olson nodded and continued to work his field radio.

"Benson, tell the boys to dig in and prepare for hell. Command is aware of our situation and will do what they can to help."

"Roger that, sir," Benson grunted and then moved through the village, advising his squad leaders. "Conserve your ammo and save a bullet for yourself if we get overrun."

Harrison went on to lead his troops to an improbable victory in his first combat mission. He was wounded twice, shot once in the leg and took three large pieces of shrapnel to his shoulder. His small platoon held out against the opposition force through sheer grit and determination, and a lot of help from air support and artillery. After surviving his first sixteen minutes on the ground in combat, he knew there was no battle he couldn't win and no mission he couldn't complete.

Just then the phone rang. "Sir, they exited the highway; our vehicle overshot the exit but is closing the gap."

"Understood. Green light the kill under any condition and report back."

"Copy, sir."

Harrison risked a small smile as he hung up the phone and then rubbed his shoulder. "If a company of battle-hardened Vietcong couldn't defeat me when I was barely out of diapers, these guys don't stand a chance." Patting the same 1911 he had carried into battle that day, now resting in a holster on his hip, Harrison had but a single regret. He wanted to be the agent with Colt Sullivan in his gun sights, and he wanted to pull the trigger.

27

Highway 114
12:50

"Do you know how to shoot?" Colt asked again. The lack of response from Dean was disheartening

"I know how to shoot. You know, I was kidding about getting into a pursuit with these guys. It's practically suicide."

"I drive up here all the time to mountain bike. If we stay to the right, the road takes us through a mountain pass. The path is filled with switchbacks and hairpin turns. We can't outrun their vehicle on the open road, but my car is more maneuverable. We should be able to gain some distance, and with luck we can lose them. They'll run us down in a heartbeat if we stay on the straight highway. So if you could pull anything out of that bag of tricks, I'd appreciate it."

"I'll bring up some maps and see if I can help navigate

these turns. If I think of anything else I'll let you know."

"Copy that." They reached the top of the exit ramp and Colt blew the stop sign as he turned onto the new road. He jammed the accelerator and listened as the engine answered the call.

"They are just getting to the top of the ramp and turning," Dean said, glancing up from his computer to look in the side-view mirror.

"How far until the first hard turn?"

"About a half mile. You'll be heading hard right into a gradual left. Then you will have another half mile of straight road before the next turn."

"That is where they will engage us. You ready to shoot?"

"Ready as I can be."

"That will have to do," Colt replied coldly. "Reach around and take the AR out of the back seat. There is a switch on the left side that says *safe* and *fire*. Move the switch to *fire*. The black handle below the sight is called the charging handle. Pull it back far enough so you can see the chamber. Is there a silver-colored bullet in there?"

"Yes."

"Okay, release the charging handle and put the rifle into your shoulder. Can you see through the sight?"

"Yeah, but I don't see anything."

"There is a dial on the upper right corner of the sight. Twist it and a red dot should appear."

"Okay, got it."

"Okay, turn back around and hold on, this is going to get rough." Colt expertly removed his foot from the gas and aimed the vehicle at the apex of the first turn. Cutting across the center lane, he took the turn gradually but maintained the majority of his speed. "After we take this next turn I want you to get into the best shooting position you can. That rifle is accurate out to three hundred yards. If they get close enough that you think you can put some rounds into the driver's area, I want you to fire. Do you understand?"

"Yes, I'll do my best."

"We only have thirty-seven rounds, so make each shot count. It will be hard to hit them from a moving vehicle and even harder if they are firing back."

Colt worked the brakes, trying to carry as much speed into the hairpin left as he could without losing control. The front-wheel-drive vehicle's tires hugged the pavement, and although it skipped as the antilock brakes kicked in, Colt never felt the car slide. As soon as the majority of the front of the car was through the turn, he slammed his foot against the accelerator and shot the car forward up the hill.

He watched as the driver of the Charger behind him utilized its rear-wheel drive to spin the car around the hairpin and its larger engine to shoot the car back into the chase.

"This guy is good; this is going to be tougher than I thought."

"You're telling me," Dean responded as he tried to steady the rifle against his shoulder. Colt knew that despite what the movies show, sighting in a target from a moving vehicle traveling at a high rate of speed was not an easy task. He knew that Dean would struggle to keep the gun sight's reticule resting on the tailing vehicle for longer than a split second.

"If you are going to take a shot, you'd better do it

now!" Colt suggested as his next turn came into view. Suddenly the report of the rifle filled his eardrums. The brass casing ejected from the rifle landed in Colt's lap. Looking in his rearview mirror, Colt saw the small hole in the rear windshield, but no deviation from the Charger's driver.

"Son of a bitch! I had the car in my sights for a second and just as I pulled the trigger we hit a bump. I'm pretty sure that completely missed him."

"Turn around and hold on." Colt navigated the Impala through several more turns but realized his gamble with the more powerful Charger was not paying off. The driver appeared to be gaining ground out of every turn. Dean turned around on the next straightaway and was met by several rounds fired at them by a passenger in the Charger.

"They are shooting at us," Dean said, frozen in fear.

"No shit! Shoot back!"

Colt watched Dean snap out of his mental paralysis and begin firing the weapon. The enemy vehicle had moved to within 150 yards of Colt's Impala and Dean should have had slightly less trouble keeping the reticule on target. On Dean's third shot Colt saw the Charger swerve but immediately regain control.

"Nice work. Hold on." Colt steered through several more turns and found them nearing the mountain pass. Recalling his mental map, he knew there were two long, straight sections of road ahead.

"We have two more straightaways ahead, and after that they will be right on top of us. Take your time on the next straight section, but aim for the driver. They are going to be real close once we come out of this turn."

"Okay," Dean replied, with a cool that surprised

Colt. *We have a chance*, Colt thought. Dean's body must have reached the perfect condition for combat. With the right levels of endorphins, adrenaline, and mental clarity any guy off the street could keep calm in the most intense situation.

When they hit the first straight stretch of road the Charger completed the turn right behind them. Dean leveled the rifle and fired until the magazine was empty. The target vehicle was close enough for Colt to see the damage to the Charger's windshield. The spiderwebbing around the impact areas told him that Dean's shots had been too far to the left to hit the driver and too far right to hit the passenger.

"Get down!" Colt yelled. They ducked just before the headrests on both seats exploded in clouds of pale yellow stuffing. The passenger in the Charger was also taking advantage of the straight stretches, and based on the sounds coming from the weapon he appeared to be handling a submachine gun, most likely a MPK5 or a UMP .45.

The submachine guns were not as accurate as the AR-15 at a distance, but they could cut a lot of things down to size if they got close enough. "Hold on!" Colt screamed as they drove over the top of the pass and hit the first hard turn coming down the backside of the mountain. Colt's heart skipped a beat as the Impala momentarily lost traction and started a slide toward the guardrail. The thin metal railing held up by wooden posts would stop a car that was traveling parallel to it, but Colt doubted it would stop a sedan heading straight for it at forty miles per hour.

Dean grabbed onto the dashboard as Colt's knuckles turned white from squeezing the steering wheel, willing the car to turn. Suddenly the tires grabbed the pavement and the Impala brushed against the guard rail before bouncing off it. They were safe but had lost precious speed.

"Drop the magazine using the switch by your left thumb and put this one in. That is our last twenty rounds, but I figure we're dead if you don't take them out before the bottom of this straightaway."

Dean inserted the full magazine, slammed the bolt forward, and took up a firing position. The Charger was close enough now that Colt knew all Dean had to do was bring the sight back onto the windshield every time he pulled the trigger. Colt watched as the Charger suddenly swerved into the guardrail but continued to accelerate and close on their bumper. "Keep shooting!" Colt yelled.

Dean fired the remaining ten rounds with no change to the trailing vehicle. Turning around, he sat down, looking defeated.

"Don't worry about it. Sit down and hold on." Colt risked taking the turn a little slower and in more control. The end of the straightaway turned into a runaway-truck sand bed with two barriers before roughly one thousand vertical feet of cliff face. Both Colt and Dean watched as the Charger missed the sand bed and the barriers before it plummeted off the edge and out of sight.

"That last volley of fire must have taken out the driver. Nice shooting," Colt said as he slowed the Impala down.

"Nice driving. I guess we're alive for a little longer."

"Yeah, but we need to get to your place. We need a new car and more ammunition. I'm down to my sidearm and both of the dead sniper's weapons. That won't cut it against fully automatic weapons."

"My place doesn't have any weapons or ammunition, but we need to make contact with Sam."

"Do you have a phone I can use?"

"Yes, and it is trace-proof."

"Good," Colt kept his attention on the road and the air. He half expected to see another attack helicopter or a black Charger appear at any moment. But he followed Dean's directions, and they soon arrived at the farm without incident.

They could see the owners out on their front porch, sitting in their rocking chairs. Colt could tell something wasn't right, but he followed Dean's advice to drive the squad car into the barn. Closing the door to hide the car, they walked across the lawn to speak with Mr. and Mrs. Anderson.

The closer they got stronger Colt's feeling of unease grew. Dean and Colt both noticed the pair hadn't moved since they arrived. It wasn't until they were close enough to see the blood that they realized the pair were dead.

Colt and Dean found themselves standing in the middle of the yard with no cover for fifty feet in any direction.

28

Farmstead
12:50

Brian Cill drove by the Anderson property in a stolen car. His peripheral vision caught only one dusty old car in the driveway, and better yet the elderly couple appeared to be enjoying their afternoon on the porch. Cill looked in the back seat, comforted by the sight of the long case containing his M21 sniper rifle.

He wasn't worried about this leg of the hunt, but he appreciated how easy they had made it for him. This was a business killing, and the quicker and less complicated the murders the better.

Not wanting to invite any attention, Cill drove on until he found a small service road. Noting the distance on his odometer, he turned onto tire-treaded trail. He followed it until the road was out of sight, then stopped and readied his equipment. After checking his holstered .45

Glock, he donned a tactical vest containing body armor and extra magazines of ammunition. Before leaving the car he slung the sniper rifle over his shoulder.

Cill set out toward the farmhouse at a light jog. The coniferous forest had little undergrowth, allowing him to move smoothly through the trees. When he was a quarter mile from the targets, he stopped to find his sniping position.

Scanning the area, he observed an outcropping of rocks to his left and stealthily moved toward the site. He scaled the boulders and found a spot to lie down, pulling out a set of Leica Viper 8x binoculars to scan his sector of fire. From his vantage point he could see the highway, the barn, and the farmhouse, but most importantly he could see the elderly couple still sitting in their rocking chairs.

His line of fire would not be straight on either of the targets, but even from the side, Cill was content he could still put the rounds were he wanted. Picking up the rifle from its resting place on a rock next to him, he brought it up to his eye and adjusted his support elbow. Drawing the rifle into his shoulder with firm and steady pressure, he picked up his reticule and slowly adjusted his sight picture until he was on target.

Cill drew in a deep breath and then fully released the air in his lungs. Using the pad of his index finger he applied slow, steady pressure to the trigger. He felt the firing pin fall as the weapon fired. The only sound emitted by his rifle was a solid but quiet thud as the releasing gas was controlled by his suppressor.

The old man hardly moved as a .308 caliber round entered his chest through his left arm. The aim point gave the bullet the highest chance of hitting the heart or aorta, instantly shutting down blood flow to the brain. That gave Cill the greatest probability that the old woman would not move or react before his second shot.

As it happened she did move, maybe because of bad timing or an inherent sense that something just happened to the man she loved. Cill's bullet struck her in the shoulder, throwing her back into her rocking chair. Swearing, Cill fired a second bullet. This second projectile grazed her left bicep and entered her side at her armpit. She slumped forward in her seat and fell out onto the porch.

"Shit!" Cill snapped. He had intended to kill the couple as they sat in their chairs so that nothing would appear out of place to anyone driving by or pulling up to the house. He picked up his equipment and ran to the side of the house, where he stashed the sniper rifle. Drawing his sidearm, he listened until he could not detect the hum of tires or the growl of a car engine on the highway.

He moved quickly to the porch and picked up the old woman. She was wearing a blue shirt now stained purple with blood. Righting her in the chair and positioning her arms and legs was easy enough, and after Cill made minor adjustments to the husband he stepped back to admire his work. Pacing off fifty feet, he found that anyone beyond that distance would have a hard time seeing the wounds.

Sweeping the house, he discovered that his intelligence had been spot-on. There was no sign of anyone living in any of the extra rooms. Cill exited the rear of the house and jogged over to the barn. Disturbances in the dirt showed a vehicle had routinely been driven in and out of the barn. He entered the barn through a side door and saw that it was empty.

"Son of a bitch." Cill had hoped to catch Dean Knight

napping, figuratively or, better yet, literally. His plan had been to extract as much information from Knight as he could before forcing him into a vehicle and driving to a remote location to kill him.

Dean's refuge at the farm, it turned out, had a fatal flaw. In a small community, nothing stays secret long, and word spread quickly that a young man had taken up residence in the Andersons' barn. Cill's contacts, gained during his failed mission, advised him of the newcomer. Initially worried that a second agent had been sent to finish his work, Cill began investigating the barn dweller. It was not long before he realized it was Dean Knight and that the programmer's presence was both a danger and a blessing.

Cill had decided his best chance at full freedom was to kill Connelly. However, he lacked the means to track his adversary. Knight would know how to find Connelly; he was famous for his knowledge of Harrison's computer systems and equipment. Cill would never be able to keep Knight captive and alive for an extended time, so he needed to trap the target and work with the time he had.

Cill moved through the barn and located the entrance to Knight's apartment. The rustic room looked like a studio belonging to a man more comfortable living off the land than eating at a diner. The bed was nothing more than a single mattress on an old rusty frame with interlocking springs for support. An old quilt made of mismatched fabric and showing the scars of more than one hastily fixed hole covered the bed. A small square rug next to the bed was littered with dirt and mud. A small olive drab footlocker sat at the end of the bed. Looking inside, Cill found a few changes of clothes but nothing out of the ordinary.

The kitchen consisted of an old wooden cabinet, a wood-burning stove, and a metal utility sink. A card table with a broken leg and an old wooden chair were the only other pieces of furniture. As he looked around the room, Cill thought he might have made a mistake. The man may have only looked like Knight and shown up around the time of Knight's disappearance.

Cill smiled at the thought that he might have killed the old couple for nothing. The murder last night had rekindled old feelings of having ultimate power, deciding who lives and dies. Then, just as he was about to turn and leave, he noticed something odd about the dirty rug near the bed. The sides of the rug matched up perfectly with the edges of the wooden floorboards it sat upon.

Running his hands over the rug, he felt a bump underneath. Upon closer inspection he found that a cut in the fabric of the rug contained a latch. Cill pulled up on it and felt the floor shift. The trapdoor swung open and away from the bed. Anyone on the bed could simply reach down, open the door, and escape to the room below.

A metal ladder led down into the darkness. Cill removed a compact flashlight from a pocket on his vest and switched it on. From his position above the room, he could not see anyone in the void beneath him, and he began his descent.

At the bottom of the ladder Cill found a pull string for a light bulb. At a pull on the cord, the light of a single incandescent bulb flooded the room. He found himself in some sort of cheaply built command center. Maps on corkboards decorated the walls above rickety tables that held computers, strange electronic devices, and miscellaneous parts. This was without a doubt the lair of Dean Knight.

Cill retreated from the hidden room and the barn entirely. As he skirted the rear of the farmhouse he heard the sound of a vehicle approaching on the highway. The tone of the engine and the quieting hum of the tires meant the vehicle was slowing down. Maintaining his position, Cill watched as an unmarked police squad with two occupants pulled into the driveway.

A small pang of fear arose in Cill's chest. He was not sure whether someone had seen him manipulating the bodies or discovered the stolen vehicle. Either way, police presence was not part of his plan.

The sniper rifle was on the far side of the farmhouse; he could get to it, retreat into the woods, and take up the same firing position he had used to murder the old couple. In doing so he risked being seen by one of the officers. It would not take them long to ascertain the situation and call for backup. The roads and hills would be swarming with officers, K9s, and helicopters with infrared and heat-seeking cameras.

He also could not let them get too close to the farmhouse or they would notice the Andersons were no longer among the living. He watched as the vehicle bypassed the small driveway leading toward the house and drove into the barn. Cill noticed bullet holes in the trunk and the damaged back window.

Suddenly it dawned on him that Knight could be in the vehicle. He had to act fast. He couldn't risk getting caught in the open between the barn and the house. Rolling the dice, he entered the farmhouse and took up a position near the window. His decision paid off as the two men came out of the barn and walked toward the farmhouse. Cill recognized Knight instantly, but the sight of Connelly sent a true chill down his spine.

"What the hell is going on?" Cill whispered to himself. He unholstered his Glock and placed the front sight posts on Connelly's head.

Both Knight and Connelly stopped, staring at the Andersons. The window was open, so there would be no interference as Cill pulled the trigger. The gun jumped ever so slightly in his hand as it sent the deadly projectile toward Connelly's head.

29

Frontier PD
1:00

The sound of a heavy key sliding into the cell lock jolted Sam out of his daydream. He listened as the locking mechanism twisted, releasing the large deadbolts. The door swung outward, revealing Officer Richland.

"We are having trouble reaching Detective Sullivan on his cell phone. As I said before, he is working a pretty important case. Are you sure you don't want to talk to someone else? It would probably go a lot faster."

"Officer, I admitted to stealing a car, and you stopped me in that stolen car. I am going to give a full confession to Detective Sullivan when he arrives, and after that I am most likely going to be transferred to the jail and held for at least twenty-four hours. Speed is not a concern of mine; my long-term safety is. As I said before, I don't want to talk to anyone but Detective Sullivan, and I don't want any visitors. But thank you for the offer."

"Okay, I understand. I just wanted to let you know we are running into a delay. Holler if you need anything. Someone will be back to check on you every fifteen minutes or so."

"Thank you, Officer." As the cell door closed, Sam returned to his thoughts. He had always been a pragmatic person, and the uncertainty of the situation was bothering him.

To keep his mind out of the largely uncontrollable future, he recalled William Connelly's arrival at the Vault. Just prior to the arrival of the mortally wounded soldier, Sam had suffered a major setback in the program. His most promising experiment had failed at a catastrophic level.

The botched surgery had involved removing the brain from an agent who was shot and then captured alive by American Coalition Forces in Iraq. The agent had been assigned to assassinate a colonel with the Iraqi National Police. Military Intelligence believed the colonel was selling information to terrorists. The months leading up to the mission had been marked by some of the highest death tolls for U.S. soldiers.

Evidence of the colonel's ties to terrorists was circumstantial at best. Any investigation that failed to result in a conviction would harm international relations. To alleviate the issue, an agent had been sent to end the threat. The agent was ordered to make the death look like a terrorist attack. It would allow Iraqi leaders to save face, while the Americans could plug a deadly leak.

The mission had gone off without a hitch. The agent, dressed in a stolen Iraqi police uniform, had stormed the colonel's office and shot him twice, all the while screaming praises to Allah. His exfiltration from the building had been perfectly planned, but a convoy of American troops happened to be in the wrong place at the wrong time.

The convoy the agent ran into was the remains of an army patrol hit by an IED. The two badly damaged Humvees were limping to the closest friendly base to seek medical attention and security. After arriving at the police station they were informed of the attack on the colonel and spotted the agent attempting to leave the area. The ensuing gunfight resulted in the loss of two more American soldiers' lives and the mortal wounding of the agent. He was brought to a medical center in an attempt to save his life and gain intelligence via interrogation if he survived.

Harrison's men caught wind of the incident and covertly gained access to the agent. His wounds were too severe to ensure a full recovery, but his brain was intact and undamaged. Sam had been tasked with transplanting the agent's brain.

Sam knew that organ transplant rejections occur mainly as a result of the immune system. The job of the immune system is to protect the body from foreign invaders of all sizes. A simple virus is essentially treated the same way as an entire donated organ. If the organ is too different from the host, the immune system attacks and kills the cells of the organ.

Setting aside the fact that the brain is the most complex of the organs and the most difficult to actually attach to the body, it still needs to pass the body's attempt to reject it as a foreign invader. After achieving the best match possible for the new organ, the host body is still given a large dose of immunosuppressive drugs to quiet the immune system.

In the case of the unlucky agent, Harrison provided a living body with little remaining brain function as a host for the agent's brain. The match testing had come back better than expected, and the decision to go ahead with the surgery was confirmed. The grueling surgery and gene therapy resulted in a clean transplant; however, unbeknown to everyone, the host body harbored a deadly disease. The ever-unlucky agent was now dying from the late-stage Hepatitis C carried by the death-row inmate whose body was used for the transplant. Sam had run into this before. Almost half of the prison population is infected with Hepatitis C, compared to less than two percent of people in society.

The screeners always checked the bloodwork of all donor bodies, but this one must have slipped through the cracks due to the expedited harvest of the body. To keep the brain from being rejected, the doctors had to continue with the transplant procedure by administering further immunosuppressant drug regimens, but by doing so they knew they would be allowing the disease to ravage the body.

Their other choice was to stop the drugs and allow the immune system to recover and see if the body could fight the disease, but the healthy immune system would also attack the brain.

As both choices resulted in almost certain death, they chose to ensure the transplant was complete and then allowed the disease to kill the body. A small, silent, undetectable bug had rendered millions of dollars of research, work, and follow-up almost worthless. Worse yet, they lost the agent's brain, which was equally hard to replace.

When William Connelly came in, they knew their odds were even worse. Connelly's wounds were greater, and his massive blood loss meant that some parts of his brain could have been damaged. Exhaustive CAT scans and MRIs suggested that everything was working, but until the process was complete they could not be certain.

Sam reluctantly agreed to perform the operation, and while it was a success, he came close to losing his patient at several junctions. During post-operative care Connelly often slipped into unexplainable comas or awakened out of medically induced comas. As these slips often occurred during Dean's memory rewrites, Sam personally believed Connelly was a time bomb, ready to go off at any moment.

Snapping back to reality, Sam quivered with fear. Any minute now the air inside his cell could smell of bitter almonds as they pumped cyanide gas through the air ducts. He almost jumped the next time the air kicked in. As he settled his nerves, the familiar sound of the lock mechanism turning filled his ears.

"You talk to Detective Sullivan?" Sam asked Officer Richland. Instead he was met by the familiar faces of two of Harrison's agents.

"Detective Connelly is unavailable at the moment," Agent 33 stated flatly. "But if you leave a message I am sure he will never get back to you."

The other agent's pockmarked face broke into a wicked smile. "You'll be coming with us now."

Sam refused to move, frozen in fear. His life was now forfeit. The agents stepped into the cell, grabbed him by the backs of his arms, and utilized their near-inhuman strength to carry him out of the cell.

Sam left behind any hope of surviving the next fifteen minutes. He hung his head and allowed the brutes to carry him off to his death.

30

Anderson Farmstead
1:00

Colt realized they were the potential targets of an ambush. He instinctively crouched to make himself a smaller target, and the bullet aimed at his head missed by inches.

"Shit! Move!" Colt yelled as he directed Dean toward the closest covered position. Several more gunshots rang out as he drew his sidearm from its holster. Without aiming he fired several shots on the move. He had little chance of hitting the attacker, but Colt hoped to force the ambusher to take cover and stop shooting at them while they were in the open.

As his gun ran empty, Colt pulled Dean toward the house. Placing Dean and himself on the front corner of the house, he scanned the exterior. A check of all the windows made Colt confident that the shooter couldn't shoot at them from inside.

"What's the plan?" Dean asked, his voice weak and shaky.

"You stay here. I'll take care of this."

"Shouldn't we stay together?"

"I have our only gun, and we don't know how many of them are inside the house. You stay here. If you hear gunfire, you'd better hope there is only one of them and use the distraction as an opportunity to get out of here."

"I guess it's a plan," Dean replied with disappointment in his voice.

Colt moved from the corner of the house, staying low to the ground and covering potential danger areas as he made his way around the front of the house. As he reached the far front corner he felt himself get lightheaded. He slumped against the wall of the house, and his world went dark.

★ ★ ★ ★

William Connelly woke to find himself pressed against the house with a sidearm in his hand. The world around him was foreign. He tried to remember what he had been doing, but his memory was like a puzzle with the pieces scattered. Assembling a few of the most obvious pieces, Connelly recognized he was under fire and his partner was unarmed. He quickly assessed his situation and decided to try to gain a position of advantage on his enemy.

The house was an older, two-story farmhouse with a large covered porch that ran around the front half of the home. Connelly needed access to the roof of the porch so he could enter the home from the second level. From there he could do a sweep of the upper level before trying to ambush any attackers on the first floor.

The three-foot-high railing around the porch left only a five-foot gap to the lower edge of the roof. Holstering his pistol, Connelly climbed onto the railing. He pulled himself on the roof, then rolled and drew his sidearm to cover the two windows in front of him. Seeing no targets, he quietly moved toward the windows and tried each of them. They were locked, and Connelly did not want to give away his position by breaking the glass. He advanced along the front side of the second story, checking every window.

The last window was unlocked. It was a smaller window that sat higher off the porch roof and led to a bathroom. Placing the Glock back its holster, Connelly started to slide the window open, praying it would not make a sound. He grimaced as it made a small squeak, but he heard no response from inside the home.

With the small window fully opened, Connelly hoisted himself up and through the window. He found himself hanging precariously over the bathtub and painstakingly shifted his weight and his legs while maintaining control of his perch on the windowsill.

Once he had a leg through, Connelly slowly lowered his body until his foot touched the bottom of the bathtub. Sliding his other foot down, he extracted his firearm and moved through the bathroom. He swiftly searched the upstairs rooms and found no enemy combatants. A set of wigs in the main bedroom almost lost the plastic heads they sat on when Connelly cleared the room. The scare was enough to dump additional adrenaline into his system, a gift and a curse at the same time. He then shifted his focus to the stairway to the first level.

Connelly spent a minute calculating the best way to navigate the stairs without walking into an ambush. The steps led to an open portion of the house, and anyone downstairs could see the stairway from several points. Connelly could only see a small portion of the room below, and he would have to blindly expose at least a portion of his body as he made the descent.

Although he feared an ambush, Connelly needed to establish a foothold on the main level in order to hunt down the enemy below. Confident the upper floor was clear, he decided upon an unorthodox method of clearing the danger area.

Connelly lay prone to the floor and crawled toward the first stair. Through the railing he could see the entire foyer and half of the living room. What he could not observe was the area below and to the left of the stairs. If anyone was hiding in that area and had a gun trained in his direction, Connelly would not see the assailant until it was too late.

He desperately wanted a flash-bang, recognizing there was no safe way to traverse the stairs. He was in a classic stalemate with his opponent and had run out of options. A crash from below snapped him to action. The sound of breaking glass filled the quiet house, and Connelly reacted instantly.

Ascertaining that at least one of his adversaries was out of position to view the top of the stairs, he dashed down and moved into the living room. He took a position of defense in the interiormost corner with his back against the two walls. He had established his foothold and now had to wait for his targets to appear or else hunt them down.

Connelly's best course of action was to move to the enemy's last known location. He would rely on his reflexes and the element of surprise. He moved along the living-room wall, staying a few inches away to prevent accidently scraping against it.

At the end of the wall, Connelly "sliced the pie" by moving in a semicircular path around the corner in a slow and methodical manner. This limited the amount of his body exposed to anyone waiting in ambush and kept his weapon in the ready position in case he spotted the target. During his search of the next room he discovered the source of the crashing sound. A broken vase lay among flowers and a puddle of water on the floor.

Connelly could clearly see boot prints exiting the puddle and moving into the next room. Following the tracks, he positioned himself just off the doorway to the next room. The boot prints went through what looked like a kitchen before disappearing around a corner.

He had now cleared a majority of the house and found evidence of only one person. Attempting to stay on the offense, Connelly swung his body around the corner and entered the kitchen. Before his foot struck the ground he picked up movement from the far side of the galley kitchen.

Connelly spun back and moved his gun in the direction of the target, but it was too late. Cill had been waiting for him, and Connelly failed to fire a shot before Cill's rounds impacted his chest. He felt himself falling, and the pain in his chest was unbearable. A cold feeling settled into his bones as he completed his spin back around the deadly corner. His head fell forward, and Connelly slumped against the wall.

31

Frontier PD
1:05

"Hey, gents, hold on a second," a familiar voice called out from behind Sam and the agents. They all turned to see Officer Richland standing at the entrance to the sally port. "We checked out your warrant, and everything looks good, but our policy states we need to book him on our charges."

"With all due respect, Officer," one the agents stated, "our warrant trumps your charges."

"I understand that, Agent Johnson, and with all due respect our policy still states that if someone is held in our facility on any felony charges they need to be properly booked before they can be released."

"Officer, understand this," Agent Johnson replied, sounding irritated. "Your charges don't mean jack shit at this point. This man is a wanted fugitive serving a life sentence without the possibility of parole. He won't see the light of day again, so there is no use in charging him with anything."

"That being said," Officer Richland retorted, "I can't close my case until my arrestee is booked and formally released to your custody. I would much rather close the book on this now and have this done in ten minutes than try to explain to my lieutenant why I violated policy."

The agents looked at each other and rolled their eyes. "Okay, officer. Have it your way, but he doesn't leave our sight."

"No problem. Hell, you can do the fingerprinting, as far as I care. It just has to get done."

"I'll pass," the agent replied. His partner, who had remained silent through the exchange, smirked at Sam.

"I guess you get to live an extra ten minutes," he whispered to Sam.

"What did you tell him?" Officer Richland questioned after noticing the exchange.

"I simply advised him not to try anything funny. Sam and I go way back." The agent let out a smirk that made Richland look uneasy.

"Whatever you say, Agent Smith," Richland replied, motioning with his arm. "Follow me to the booking room, and let's get this over with."

Sam let out a small, unnoticeable sigh of relief. He had just been given an extra ten minutes for Colt and Dean to rescue him. As they walked to the booking room, Sam hoped his friend was in a better position. He had no way of knowing that Dean's best chance at survival had just been shot twice in the chest.

32

Anderson Farmhouse
1:10

Cill let out a sigh of relief. He had spent the previous ten minutes scouring the house, looking for Knight and Connelly. After missing his chance to kill Connelly in cold blood, he had cursed himself as his target's cover fire penetrated his position.

A second string of expletives flowed from his mouth in a near whisper as he attempted, but failed, to reacquire his prey. Cill knew the duo had three options. They could run, hide, or fight back. If they ran, Cill would have to try to take out their vehicle before it got to the end of the driveway. If they hid, he would have to seek them out. But Cill believed it was in Connelly's heart to fight back.

Cill chose to use the natural defenses of the house to his advantage. He locked all the doors and windows. His adversaries would have to damage a door or window to gain entry, and that would make a sound. After five minutes of waiting, he had begun to get impatient. Wondering if he had misjudged his opponents, he looked up and realized his greatest threat was an attack from above.

He found a good defensive position in the living room, beneath the stairs. He couldn't cover the kitchen or rear entry, but he knew both those rooms were secure. Hoping for a clean shot at Connelly coming down the stairs, he had adjusted his position and inadvertently bumped the end table, knocking over the vase.

"Shit!" Cill cursed again under his breath as he retreated to his secondary defensive position. He had chosen the back entryway as a fallback, as it allowed him control over the front and rear entrances as well as the kitchen. The main drawback was his exposure to anyone shooting from the outside.

As Cill moved through the dining room and kitchen, he heard the unmistakable sound of someone running down the wooden stairs. He reached the far corner of the kitchen just as Connelly flew past the base of the stairs in a blur. Too late to take a shot, Cill ducked back around the corner of the kitchen.

Knowing he had lost all of his advantages, Cill looked around for anything he could use in his favor. The sun through the kitchen windows glinted off the wet tracks he had left after stepping in the pool of water from the vase and then while running to his position. *Connelly will see the tracks and follow them, he has to,* Cill figured. *It's a roll of the dice, but an educated roll.*

Cill moved back into the rear entryway and aimed his gun at the entrance to the kitchen. At the first sign of movement he pulled the trigger. Connelly never had time to react. From the distance Cill had shot, there was no doubt he had struck the bastard twice in the chest.

Watching Connelly spin around the corner, Cill waited a few seconds. Keeping the gun trained on the corner he yelled "You dead, Connelly?"

The lack of response did not confirm the kill, but it did bring a smile to his wicked face.

★ ★ ★ ★

Colt felt an intense burning sensation running through his chest. It was like someone had hit him twice with a metal baseball bat and then lit his chest on fire. Looking down he saw two small holes in his body armor. Pulling the armor from his chest he saw there was no blood on the inside. Although it certainly felt like he had been shot, he was happy to see the rounds had not penetrated the vest.

"How the hell did I get here?" Colt whispered to himself. "Better question is, how the hell did I get shot?" He tried to get to his knees, but the pain in his chest doubled him over.

"You dead, Connelly?" A voice called out from beyond the kitchen. Colt thought about remaining quiet, but he needed to buy some time to figure out what was going on. "You're not that lucky, asshole! Who the hell are you?"

"I am disappointed, buddy. We were best friends in the Vault."

Colt searched his memory. Dean's story of Cill befriending Connelly registered. Suddenly flashes of sterile white walls and rooms with computers came and went.

"Brian Cill . . ."

"We have a winner! It's funny how that memory thing starts coming back to you. It took me a while, but I didn't have anyone to help me."

"Why are you trying to kill me?"

"You were programmed to hunt me down and kill me. Just consider this part of my desire to not let that happen."

More memories flooded Colt's brain. They jumped from the Vault to his first day at Frontier PD and ended with Abigail's dead body.

"You still with us over there?" Cill inquired. "Come on, buddy. Talk to me."

Colt decided to try and negotiate. "Just put down your gun and let me take you into custody. You don't need to die here today."

"You're right. I don't need to die here. You can die, and then Knight can die. Then I can get back to what I love best: killing people."

"You could have killed all the people you wanted for Harrison. Why didn't you stay with the program?"

"Killing a person for a purpose isn't as fun. Plus, Harrison makes you play by a set of rules. I was never good with rules. The first person I killed was my sixth-grade teacher. She gave me a C on a paper that clearly deserved an A. I made her a cookie with rat poison in it. The old fatass had heart problems, so they never suspected homicide. I had so much fun I decided to keep doing it."

"Harrison and the president should have never used you. How many innocents have you killed since they recruited you and you broke free?"

"Six . . . well, eight if you count the two on the front

porch. But my favorite was Abby. The love she had for William was too precious. I actually thought of telling her that Connelly was alive before I killed her. But for some reason I just couldn't bring myself to do it. I guess even I have some morals."

Colt was suddenly hit with memories of the dreams he had experienced the night before. "I saw you kill her . . . how the hell is that possible?"

"You were the golden boy. I'd tell you to ask Dean about it, but considering I plan on killing you both, I'll humor you and explain it quickly.

"From my understanding, Mr. Knight's brain works like a computer and he sees *everything* as a computer. In order to make you a more efficient hunter of the assassins, he programmed a wireless transmitter into all of our brains. It reads our brain-waves and transmits the same signals our eyes use. The result is a video-like display of what we see projected into your brain. Harrison is supposed to be the only one that can trigger the process but I figured out how to do it on my own. I wanted to gift you the pleasure of watching me kill your lovely bride."

"I'm done talking to you," Colt said, barely able to contain his anger. "Put down your gun and let me arrest you, or you will die."

"Sorry. No can do, William. After I kill Knight and you, it's much smoother waters for me."

"Your choice," Colt said as he weighed his options. He could circle around and try to engage Cill from the front entryway. Or he could hold tight and hope to ambush the killer if he became impatient and moved. He chose to get on the offensive while he knew Cill's location. He made his way to the front room and moved along the interior wall.

Colt never expected that Cill would predict this movement. He came to the corner containing the broken vase and prepared himself to shoot as he launched himself into the hallway. Pivoting around the corner, he was surprised to see Cill in such close proximity. Before Colt could bring the gun on target and fire, Cill slammed his left arm down on Colt's radial nerve.

Colt's gun dropped to the floor. The surprise in his face quickly turned to despair as he saw Cill bringing his right hand forward and up. In less than a second his life would be over. With nowhere else to go, he fell backwards into the front room as the sound of a single gunshot filled the small hallway.

33

Frontier PD
1:15

"How much longer is this going to take?" one of the agents asked Officer Richland.

"Don't blame me. Blame the machine. I used to be able to roll ink-and-paper prints in less than five minutes. This damn electric piece of junk only works when it wants to work. Here, Sam. Try putting a little more of this on your hands." Sam dutifully rubbed the lotion towelettes on his hands. The lotion moisturized the friction ridges on the skin, allowing them to show up better on the screen.

Sam had figured this out early in the process, and each time he was given the sheet he made sure to leave areas dry so the machine would reject the print.

"Son of a bitch. Let's try that one again."

"Are you kidding me, Officer? We should have been

out of here fifteen minutes ago with this guy."

"Settle down, guys. We're halfway done, and there is no going back now."

"You have ten minutes to finish this up."

"What do I look like? A student taking a test? I'll get this done when the machine lets me get it done. If you have a problem with that, take it up with my supervisor. I am sure she would love to hear it."

"Just hurry up." Sam elected to keep his mouth shut. He wanted to tell the officer that the agents were not really with the U.S. Marshals, but there was no way he was going to get Richland to believe him. Sam also knew that with the agents in close proximity, anything he told the officer would put both of their lives in danger. Richland had done nothing to deserve that fate.

"Jesus, Sam, you must have the driest fingers I have ever printed."

"Sorry to be a bother," Sam replied.

"No worries. We'll get through this. Just keep working with me." Several more minutes passed, and Sam knew he was running out of time. They were printing his last finger when there was a knock on the door.

"Come on in," Officer Richland offered. "Oh, hey Nick, what's up?" Nick walked into the room and looked straight at the agents. "There is an issue with the warrant. You guys better come with me."

"Fuck that! What kind of fucked-up department is this? There is nothing wrong with the warrant . . . just finish up the prints and let us take custody of this guy."

"No can do," Nick stated with plenty of conviction in his voice. "We just got a call from the federal attorney's office out of Denver. This warrant is under review by a federal judge at the request of our attorneys."

"What the hell are you talking about? You can't do that!"

"You know as well as I do. When it comes to courts they would rather err on the side of caution. All we had to do was ask them to look it over, and they are a little busy so they will get to it when they get to it. They don't seem to be in the same rush you two are to get this guy out of here."

The agents looked at each other. "Fuck this. We'll get him some other time."

"Yeah, his days are numbered," the other agent said. "I hope you guys don't like your jobs, because you don't mess with the feds and get away with it. I'll have your badges for this."

Nick just smiled. "You're the hundredth guy to threaten me with my badge during my career. Enjoy the wait in line."

At that the agents slammed the door and left.

"What the hell was that all about?" Officer Richland asked Nick.

"Let's just say that Sam and I have a mutual friend."

"Okay, none of this makes sense to me. Nick, you want to take custody of this guy, or you want him back in a cell?"

"I'll take him from here. Thanks, Richland. Nice work on the arrest."

"Thanks, Nick. Have a good day."

"You too. Enjoy your paperwork."

"Always," Richland replied, leaving the room.

Nick turned to Sam, "How about you tell me what the hell is going on?"

"I wish I could, but it is better off you don't know."

"Story of my life. Let's head upstairs. You can sit in the interview room until I figure out why I just jeopardized my career."

34

Anderson Farm
1:25

Colt awoke, expecting to be dead. He predicted finding a hole in his head but felt nothing other than dry hair and his intact skull. Sitting up, he saw the crumpled body of Brian Cill on the floor. The top half of his head was missing, and what was left was a mess of blood and skull fragments.

Looking past the body, Colt saw Dean standing in the rear entryway with a rifle raised in a firing position. Colt could tell by the look on Dean's face that he was suffering from shock often associated with a first experience with close-quarters combat and violent death.

"Dean, put the gun down," Colt requested softly. He knew that Dean was in a fragile condition. "Dean, you need to put the gun down," his voice now a little firmer. The second appeal had the desired effect. Dean snapped out of his frozen mental state and lowered the rifle.

"His head is missing," the words stumbled out of Dean's mouth.

"You did what you had to do. Thank you for saving my life."

"I didn't know if I could get off the shot. I thought I was going to hit you too."

"I was dead if you didn't shoot," Colt responded. He needed to get Dean's mind off of the killing. "We need to get to Sam. Are you with me?"

"Yeah . . . sorry. Let's go. Take this." Dean handed the rifle to Colt.

"Where did you get this, anyway?"

"I found it on the side of the house. I was getting worried that Cill would figure out the blind spot I was in, so I moved around the house. Then I heard the gunfire and the conversation. I couldn't quite make out what you were saying, so I moved to the rear entryway and found this. As soon as I found the safety I looked in and saw Cill ready to pull the trigger. The door was locked, so I shot through the window."

"It was a hell of a shot. I owe you one."

"You killed the sniper earlier, we're even."

"I think it is fair to say neither of us would be here without the other. What is the best way we can get ahold of Sam?"

"My place in the barn has all we need to hack into some secure networks and figure out what they are doing with Sam."

"Okay, I need to check in with work. I'm supposed to be investigating a homicide, and it doesn't look good when the lead investigator goes off the map for a few hours."

"I have a clean phone in the barn. You can use it to make the call." They ran to the barn and made their way into Dean's hidden room.

"I think you need a hobby . . . and a woman," Colt stated as he looked at the mess of computer screens, towers, and electronic junk.

"This is my hobby, sort of, and it's hard to meet a woman when you are living off the radar."

"I can imagine. Let's find Sam and get moving."

Colt watched as Dean's fingers flew across the keyboards. The screens flashed from program to program in quick succession.

"Oh shit! That's not good," Dean commented.

"What did you find?"

"Sam was arrested by Frontier PD. He was driving a stolen car. They have him at the station, but Harrison has two agents there acting as Feds. They claim to have a warrant so they can take him into their custody."

"Do you have that phone? I'll see what I can do." Colt took the phone and dialed Nick's number. He had wanted to keep Nick out of this, but now he had no choice.

"Detective Nick Lawson, Frontier PD," a voice Colt could identify answered the phone.

"Nick, it's Colt."

"Colt? What the fuck? Where are you? Everyone has been trying to get ahold of you!"

"I know. I went to meet a guy about a lead on the case and my car died. I couldn't get shit for a signal before my battery died. Some yokel without a cell phone picked me up and gave me a ride."

"Jesus. Of all days to get hit with bad luck."

"I know, Nick, but I have good news too. The lead panned out. He gave me the name of a guy who supposedly knows the killer."

"And your lead is credible?"

"Well. He is kind of a nutjob, but it's all we have right now. I need to get ahold of a guy named Sam Mitchell."

"What the hell? Richland just brought in a guy he arrested for driving a stolen car. I think that was his name."

"Nice. See? Our luck is changing."

"Not so fast, Colt. The feds want Mitchell, so they sent two suits down here to pick him up on a federal warrant. What the hell is this all about?"

"Some domestic terrorism bullshit. The feds are all pissed off about a stockpile of weapons, and our victim was a whistleblower. Mitchell is another leak, but if the feds get him they will give half a shit about our homicide, as long as they take down their redneck militia."

"Okay, so what do I do? Tell the feds they can't have the guy on their warrant?"

"Hold on. Let me check something." Colt covered the microphone and whispered to Dean. "Can we make the warrant disappear?"

"Already taken care of," Dean replied with a smile.

Colt took his hand off the receiver. "Nick, just have dispatch run the warrant again. I am pretty sure this guy is clean, and until they can confirm the warrant, he stays in our custody."

"Colt, I saw the warrant. It's good."

"Nick, listen to me. Just have them check it again. Let's just say I have a federal attorney who owes me a favor from a case way back and can at least run some interference for us."

"You realize you could lose your job—maybe go to prison—for this?"

"I'm playing this one close to the vest, Nick. If anyone has to take the fall for it, I'll accept full responsibility. But as your partner, just trust me that this is our only choice and it's the right thing to do."

"Okay, will do. How long is the phone call to quash the warrant going to take?

"Give me two minutes."

"Okay. If it is still in there, I won't be able to do anything."

"I know. I'll make sure it is gone. Just make sure Mitchell stays safe until we can get there and get a few minutes with him."

"Will do. What if I need to get ahold of you?"

"This nice gentleman is letting me borrow his car and cell phone. I'll be at the PD in twenty minutes to talk to Mitchell."

"Okay. See you soon, buddy."

"Yup. And Nick?"

"Yeah Colt?"

"Thanks. I owe you one."

"No, you owe me at least twenty-four . . . beers that is, and a night of babysitting so my wife and I can get away and I can get some."

"Jesus, you ever think about anything else?"

"No."

"Okay. You have a deal. Later, bud." Colt hung up the phone.

"We can't just drive down to police headquarters and grab Sam. They will have it under surveillance," Dean said.

"We can take the Andersons' car. They won't recognize it."

"Yeah, but they will be on the lookout for the two of us. They'll have guys throughout the city looking for us driving anything."

"I have an idea. Grab what you need and meet me back at the house."

Colt ran to the house and found the old woman's bedroom. He removed a wig from one of the plastic heads he had nearly shot during his home search and slipped it onto his head. It wasn't a perfect fit, but he only needed to fool the surveillance from a distance.

Scouring the rest of the closet, Colt found an old floral nightgown. He slipped the nightgown on over his tactical vest. On the nightstand by the bed he found a pair of reading glasses. Looking in the mirror, he found he presented himself as an ugly but passable eighty-year-old woman.

He heard the door open downstairs and called down, "Is that you, Dean?"

"Yeah, I got what I need . . . you ready to go?"

Dean looked up and saw Colt walk down the stairs. "You've got to be kidding me," he said, flashing a smile. "You know . . . that looks just good enough to work."

"All we need to do is get past the surveillance. I can ditch this stuff once we are in the sally port."

"Sounds like a plan. Let's get going." Colt found the keys to the Andersons' Buick. They hit the open road in the dusty old car and headed for Frontier.

"So, after we rescue Sam, what happens?" Colt asked.

"We run and hopefully survive long enough to enact our revenge."

“I have a life here. I have a job and friends.”

“You have to understand. Colt Sullivan isn’t real. William Connelly is real.”

“According to the government, Connelly . . . . I mean . . . me . . . I’m dead.”

“Join the club. Sam and I ceased to exist the day we left the Vault. That’s why it is so easy to kill us. Local police can find bodies, but they need something to identify us by. Forensic pathologists use four methods of identification: visual, dental, fingerprints, and DNA. There is no record of us anywhere, so all comparisons would fail and we would go into the ground as John Doe 1 and John Doe 2.”

“Yeah. We have found several homeless people who died from exposure. With no visual identification, we tried fingerprints and DNA in the database. Out of four bodies, we only received one ID, and that was because he was an Afghanistan veteran and had DNA and fingerprints on file. The other three remain unknown bodies. I can see where that makes killing us very easy.”

“Harrison covered his bases. Okay. Enough talk about death. What is your plan once we get to the station?”

“We have a state-of-the-art interview room. I’ll take a formal statement from both you and Sam. I’ll ask questions about Harrison’s project and your involvement. Then I’ll make copies of the interview and store them both electronically and in hard copy. From there we use it as leverage to keep Harrison off our backs long enough to come up with a way to take him down.”

“That could work, but what if he attacks the station?”

“He wouldn’t be that stupid. We have dozens of trained cops, and they are all armed. He would need a lot of agents, and it would be hard to cover up an attack on a police station."

"True, but I wouldn't put it past him," Dean stated dryly.

Neither man knew that the same conversation was going on inside the Vault as Harrison readied his men for an assault unlike any in the nation's history.

35

The Vault
1:30

Harrison picked up the phone and speed-dialed the tactical operator. "Hello, sir. I was just about to call you."

"What's the update?"

"We intercepted phone traffic on Nick Lawson's phone. Connelly and Knight are driving to Frontier PD as we speak."

"Did our agents secure Mitchell?"

"Negative. Connelly ran interference and had Knight erase the warrant. Lawson advised the agents they would take custody of Mitchell and hold him."

"Where are those agents now?"

"They fell back to their surveillance position."

"How many agents do we have in Frontier?"

"Six."

"How many agents do we have on standby in the base?"

"Six more. The next closest one is in Chicago working on the union boss assassination."

"Twelve should be fine. Did Connelly advise Lawson of the situation?"

"No. He said Mitchell was a domestic terrorist and that the feds wanted him on weapons charges."

"Okay. Prep the six agents and put them on standby. Do not have them move out until I give the order. Tell them to grab heavy gear packages."

"Yes, sir. I'll wait for your call."

Harrison hung up the phone and sat back in his chair. He now had a chance to take out all three targets in one attack. The assault would occur on domestic soil and involve the deaths of innocent law-enforcement officers. It would be a cover-up of extreme magnitude, but if any of the three targets slipped out of his grasp he could lose everything.

He fired up his computer and dug into his files on domestic terrorist groups. He grimaced as he read about the FFR and remembered Cill's failed assignment.

It would not be a stretch to forge a raid on the Frontier Police Headquarters under the guise of an attack by the FFR. The Frontier PD themselves believed they were holding a domestic terrorist, and a squad of agents could easily simulate a squad of ex-military combat veterans hell-bent on rescuing one of their own.

The public outcry after such an event would swing in the favor of Washington, and Harrison would most likely get the nod to pursue further action against the FFR. The losses of Knight, Mitchell, and Connelly could be chalked up to collateral damage, and Harrison would have a clean slate in the eyes of Washington.

According to early reports by Cill, before he defected from his mission, the FFR wore standard army combat uniforms. They sewed their own flags, wore their own rank, and often displayed their freedom names. They carried no government identification during their trainings, and a vast majority of them worked cash jobs to stay off the radar.

Harrison called his control center. "The operation is as follows. At 1430, twelve agents, dressed as members of the FFR, will assault the Frontier police headquarters. They will use all necessary force, to include deadly force, to ensure the capture of Connelly and the killing of Mitchell and Knight. They are to act as members of the FFR and make their intentions known to all witnesses. If all the primary targets are killed, I want photographic and DNA proof. Once all targets are secure, agents are to withdraw, leaving any fallen agents. Surviving agents should follow all security procedures and return to base without compromise."

"Roger, sir. Anything else?"

"Yes. Have intelligence gain control of all FFR media outlets, to include their website, and post vague warning messages concerning an attack on a government installation. After the attack, post an ownership claim for the attack and a warning of future attacks on government facilities."

"Will do, sir."

"I will be coming down there in twenty minutes to personally oversee the operation. None of us can afford for this to fail."

"Understood, sir, I'll advise you of any intel changes."

Harrison lowered the receiver and let out a deep sigh.

In an hour he would either be a hero or a criminal. He took solace in the thought that his agents had killed dozens of war criminals around the world, saving thousands of lives. He would be able to live with the blood of a few police officers on his hands if it meant saving years of hard work by his team.

Turning his head, Harrison looked at a framed picture on the wall. The picture, from Vietnam, showed him and another young infantry officer. The other man was Second Lieutenant Jon Winters. When Harrison conducted a rescue mission the day after the firefight, his platoon had found his good friend tied to a stake in the middle of a Vietcong-controlled village. Winters had been stabbed in the chest with a bayonet and left to die.

Harrison had rushed to his friend's side. A quick look at the wound told him his friend was beyond medical intervention. Holding his hand over the wound, Harrison calmed his friend, who said two words before his eyes rolled back in his head. Those two words were etched on a silver plate in the frame of the photo: "No regrets."

"I've tried to live my life by that motto, buddy, but we'll see how this one plays out." Harrison took one more deep breath before composing himself for the walk to the command center.

36

1:40
Hwy 15

"From our run-ins so far, these guys are well-equipped. You have told me they are well-trained, but what exactly are we dealing with?" Colt planned on using the entire drive to Frontier to gain as much information as possible.

"Equipment-wise, you haven't seen anything yet. These guys have unlimited access to weapons, explosives, and electronic devices. Everything that is made available to Delta Force is equally available to these guys."

"I get the weapons and explosives, but electronic devices?"

"If you can imagine it, these guys carry or have access to it. Everything from concealable communications to full-color night vision displays."

"What about optics?"

"They have high-end cameras, scopes, satellite

imagery, predator drone flyovers, et cetera."

"Great. Anything else?"

"Yeah. We are just breaking the surface. All agents are equipped with on-board cameras, recorders, and vital-sign monitors. Harrison will be able to see and hear everything on the battlefield from his command center. And then there are the upgrades."

"Upgrades?"

"In order to maximize lethality, each agent is screened upon arrival at the Vault. His hearing, vision, and overall physical health are put under a microscope, and any shortfalls are remedied with state-of-the-art surgeries. Agents with poor vision underwent Lasik, and all agents had hearing aids implanted that can pick up sounds much better than the average human ear."

"So these guys are well-trained, well-equipped, surgically enhanced killing machines?"

"That sums it up about perfectly."

"Whatever you do . . . keep your head down," he ordered as the Buick entered the town.

"You don't have to tell me twice," Dean replied, lying down and tucking into a ball in the backseat.

"I'll get us into the non-public parking lot and ditch the costume. I sure as hell won't be able to explain to my coworkers why I am dressed up like an old lady."

"Sounds good. The closer we can get to the station, and Sam, the better."

"That's the idea." Colt's heart thumped in his chest as he checked his rearview mirror and thought he was being tailed. Making several illogical turns, he watched as the suspicious vehicle continued on.

"You can do that all day, Colt, but these guys are

experts at tailing. They probably have three nondescript cars out there right now. If they are on to us, they could follow us for quite some time before we saw the same car twice. If they find us they won't tail; they'll just kill us."

"Good point." Colt drove the remaining few minutes without issue. As the police station came into sight, he scanned the area for any suspicious vehicles. Having worked on the same city block for several years, he knew most of the cars that belonged to any given parking spot at any given time. Seeing nothing out of the ordinary, he pulled into the non-public lot and lost the wig, nightgown, and makeup.

Before getting out of the car he scanned the rooftops of adjacent buildings as well as any open areas that offered a sniper a shot at Colt and Dean. Seeing nothing obvious, he moved quickly and with purpose to Dean's door, unlocking it and letting him out.

"Let's go."

They walked swiftly across the lot and reached the secure door without event. The door clicked when he placed his ID in front of the electronic reader, and once inside the structure, Colt took out Dean's cell phone and called Nick.

"Hey, Colt, we are up in the interview room. I have Mitchell with me, just waiting on you."

"Be there in a second, I gotta grab something from my office first."

"Okay, see you soon."

"Shouldn't we go to Sam ASAP?" Dean questioned.

"The Boy Scout motto is 'be prepared,' and it's not a bad motto to follow. Especially after surviving three assassination attempts in an hour. I wouldn't put it past Harrison to come in here and try to take us with force."

"Just a few seconds ago you said you didn't believe he

would attack the police station."

Sam shrugged. "A cornered animal is the most dangerous kind, especially if it is wounded. Harrison has nothing to lose at this point. If he doesn't try to kill us, he loses, if he does try to kill us and fails, he loses. The only win for him now is to take us out at all costs."

"Damn, you're right. We should warn your coworkers."

"What would I say? Hey guys, any minute now we might be attacked by an army general who planted me here five years ago after transplanting my brain?"

"You have a point. Did it sound that crazy when I said it to you?"

"Yes, but that sniper was awfully convincing." They reached Colt's office, and he opened a cabinet in the back. "Shut the door and close the blinds."

From the cabinet Colt produced an additional bullet-resistant vest and a tactical sidearm holster. Opening a drawer in his desk, he removed two loaded magazines for his handgun. He also grabbed a new shirt and removed all his clothing from his waist up.

"Wow," Dean commented, looking at Colt's chest. Large reddish welts on his skin marked the impact points from Cill's shots.

"That's going to feel good in the morning. Here, put this on under your shirt," Colt said as he handed his concealed vest to Dean.

"At least I know these things work."

Colt changed the rest of his outfit, opting for a more comfortable pair of pants as well as the fresh polo shirt. Re-donning his tactical vest, he strapped on his thigh holster and locked in his sidearm. "Let's go talk to Sam."

37

Frontier PD
1400

Colt and Dean left the office and ran into Angela stepping out of her office.

"Going on a warrant already?" Angela asked.

"Not quite yet," Colt lied. "This guy gave me a lead and I need to go interview him. If all goes well, I'll be doing a search warrant soon. Just want to be prepared if it moves fast."

"Nice work. Need some backup?"

"I'll let you know, thanks for the offer."

"Anytime." Both men found themselves staring at Angela's body as she walked away from them.

"Must be real hard to work with her every day," Dean said, just loud enough for Colt to hear.

"I get by." Colt led them to the interview rooms. "Okay. Follow my lead. Nick is a good cop, so he'll smell bullshit from a mile away. Let me do the talking, and don't open your mouth unless he or I ask you something directly, and do your best to keep up."

"Understood."

"Good," Colt opened the door and saw Nick and Sam sitting on opposite sides of a round table. Nick had set out four chairs, and Colt motioned for Dean to sit down in a chair. Sam's face lit upon seeing Dean, but Dean quickly shot him a glance that sent a strong message that this was not the time and place for a big reunion.

"Nick, this is Dean Knight. He's my lead that ties Sam to the homicide."

"Nice to meet you," Nick replied.

"Same to you."

"Okay, Colt. Why don't you fill me in on what the hell is going on here?"

"Will do. Just a second. Wait, first, are we all clear?"

"Yes, we are," Nick replied, indicating that the video and audio devices were recording.

"Great. Okay, I'll put this as simply as I can. Our man Sam here is involved with the FFR."

"The Freedom Fighters of the Rockies?"

"That's the one. He jumped in with both feet after getting back from Iraq on a civilian security contract a few years ago. Nine-eleven gave him a mid-life crisis and he tried to join the Marines but he was rejected due to his age. He joined up with one of the blackwater type outfits and did two years in Baghdad. The shootout in that courthouse in Montana has him questioning his desire to stay with the FFR. Sam was Dean's boss overseas. Dean saw how distant Sam became after coming back from Iraq and has been trying to talk him out of the FFR.

They were talking earlier today, and Sam told him the FFR killed a woman in Frontier because she was going to give up some of the FFR members to the ATF."

"Shit . . . that complicates things," Nick said.

"Exactly. Dean told me Sam was too afraid to go to the police, so Dean decided to do it for him. Dean met with me, and we decided to go talk to Sam but got delayed due to my car and phone problems. When I finally got ahold of you and found out Sam was in our custody, it was a godsend."

"Until you found out about the feds."

"Yeah. If the FFR finds out that Sam talked to the feds, he'll be tucked away or killed. I want justice in our case, and as long as we have Sam we stand a much better chance of bringing down the killers."

"Okay. So where do we go from here?"

"Sam," Colt turned to the prisoner. "I am going to need some names of individuals who were directly or indirectly involved in the murder. I can't use their assumed names, I need their legal names."

Sam jumped, so involved in the story that he had almost forgotten his role in it. "I can't give the cops their names. If I do I'm a dead man."

"So you do know the names . . . thanks for clarifying that fact, Sam," Nick stated.

"I never said that."

"Sure you did. Instead of telling us you don't know them, you told us you can't give them to us. So you do know the names—"

"Come on Sam! Tell them what they need to hear so they can protect you," Dean interrupted.

"Like hell they can!"

"Sam, they are cops. I know you don't like them, but you have to put that aside for now."

"Sam, I realize you don't trust us, but they killed Abby because they thought she was a whistleblower. What do you think will happen when word spreads that you were down here talking to us? If you tell us who did this, we will arrest them and we can protect you," Nick replied.

"No offense, Nick. I want to talk to Dean and Colt alone right now. Dean told me I could trust Colt, and he never let me down in Iraq," Sam replied.

Colt turned to Sam, "Just give Nick one name, in good faith. Nick can go look him up while we chat. That way we know if you are telling us the truth and not just looking for five minutes of fame."

Sam appeared to think about the dilemma. Finally he sheepishly replied, "David Leadstrom. He's not the killer, but he's involved."

"Thanks, Sam. I'll be right back." Nick left the room, and Sam hopped up and hugged Dean.

"It's good to see you again! For a while there I thought we were both dead," Sam exclaimed.

"I'm amazed I'm still alive. Nice work getting out. Did everything work according to plan?"

"Everything except the vent covers being padlocked. I had to use the escape tunnel. That was a real bitch."

"I can imagine. Okay, enough talk, what is the next move?"

"Colt is going to get us to give a statement about Harrison, the Vault, the agents, everything. Then we will use that statement as a bargaining chip for our freedom."

"That's a start. Let's get going," Sam said, rubbing

his hands together.

"Okay, gentlemen, have a seat. I have to go start a new recording. How long do we have before Nick figures out David Leadstrom isn't involved?" Colt asked.

"No idea. I pulled that name out of my head. I figured it was popular enough to have a few records but not so common it sounded like bullshit."

"Nice work. If I know Nick he'll look for a good half hour to avoid coming back empty-handed." Colt left the room to set up a new recording, then returned and sat down at the table.

"Okay, gentlemen. Everything you're going to tell me will be recorded. While I can't make you swear on a Bible, I want anyone who watches this tape to know that you guys are telling the truth."

"I wish it were one big lie, but everything that comes out of our mouths will be the truth," Dean offered.

"Okay, why don't we start with Sam and have him explain his history. Then explain your involvement in the Vault and everything that has led up to today." Colt sat back as Sam spilled his story. Several minutes went by before Dean took over and did the same.

"So, to summarize. You both were recruited to work for Harrison. And your job was to create these assassins, also known as the agents?"

"That is correct," Sam replied. "We did the research, the surgeries, the programming, all of it."

"But you also did it under duress, as you were not free to leave the program at any point."

"That is correct," Dean replied. "We were misled to believe we were working on a project that would save human lives, not ruin ours as well as hundreds of others."

"Okay, anything else you want to add?" Both Dean and Sam declined to add any other comments. Colt looked at the wall and realized twenty minutes had gone by. A knock on the door announced Nick's return to the interview room.

"Come on in," Colt shouted. Nick entered the room and glared at Sam.

"These guys tell you anything valuable?" Nick asked.

"Not really. Just more beat-around-the-bush crap from Sam here," Colt stated, acting frustrated.

"I found nothing on any David Leadstroms. Where does he live?" Nick questioned. "If he even—"

"I don't know the address, but I can show you on a map," Sam interrupted.

"That's a start," Colt remarked. "Is it far from here?"

"No. He lives about a half hour—"

Sam fell silent as the sounds of nearby gunfire permeated the room.

38

The Vault
1425

"The men are in position," the controller advised General Harrison, who was leaning over his shoulder.

"Have the lead agent report the scene dynamics. I want to know traffic levels for vehicles and pedestrians, civilian foot traffic in and out of the police station, and their ability to secure the scene."

"Agent 33 reports very light levels of civilian traffic in the area. They have witnessed four civilians entering the building and three exiting. The only one unaccounted for could have been an employee. There are no children in sight, but the local high school will let out in less than thirty minutes."

"Our men will be done by then. What about scene security?"

"The building has two main doors, the public and

non-public entries. The sally port doors are secure at the moment, and several squad cars are missing from the parking lot. Agent 33 has assigned four agents to hold at the doors and take down any units responding to back up their comrades inside."

"Okay, advise the agents to move into pre-assault position and await my word. They are also ordered to not assault any civilians or unarmed personnel inside the building. They may subdue as needed, but they are to not apply harm to non-sworn personnel. Connelly is a take-alive target; I want him back here in a chair in front of me in an hour. Knight and Mitchell are shoot-on-sight."

"Copy, sir." Harrison stared at the wall of monitors in front of him. He did his best to imagine he was ordering this attack on a Taliban stronghold or even a Cold War–era Soviet KGB headquarters. The idea of attacking Americans on domestic soil was still not sitting well with him, but he had been through every other scenario.

Waiting for Connelly, Knight, and Mitchell was not on the cards. They had to be dealt with immediately in order to ensure the safe continuation of the program. After several tense minutes of watching the agents get into position he ordered the attack.

"All agents, you are green light for Operation FFR. Commence your assault on the objectives and report in on progress," the controller stated as he selected the camera view and life monitor for the lead agent. Each agent donned a black mask and gloves to prevent identification.

The cameras became a hornet's nest of movement as men exited vehicles and rushed toward the police department. Working in teams of two, they moved toward the two entrances. A breach team from each element led the way to both doors. Normally the team would have used firearms, explosives, or a ram to gain access to a locked door. This time the agents had key cards, thanks to yet another Dean Knight program created to hack security systems and create universal access cards. Harrison allowed himself to smile for a second as he counted the number of Knight's and Mitchell's own projects that were being used against them during the assault.

The camera on the first agent to enter the public door showed a large foyer. Scanning the room from left to right, the agent saw interview rooms to the left, a receptionist behind thick glass, a door to the front, and a set of stairs leading to the second level on the far right.

"Show me your hands!" one of the agents yelled at the receptionist, ready to fire through the bullet-resistant glass if needed. Other agents searched and secured the remainder of the foyer. During the search a uniformed officer suddenly appeared at the top of the stairs. Seeing the armed men, he drew his firearm and was able to get several shots off before he was taken down in a hail of gunfire.

"They know we are here," Harrison commented as he watched the video feed. "This is when it gets ugly." He watched as six more agents entered the non-public door, meeting no resistance.

"The agents have a foothold in the building. I am noting one officer down and no agents injured at this time."

"Advise them to emplace rear security personnel and conduct a sweep of the building. Their primary objectives are still the three main targets. I want regular progress reports."

"Copy, sir." The controller relayed the information

and watched on the screens as the two agents at each found cover and prepared to take out any responders.

"There's no going back now," Harrison said to himself as he watched the screens. "Tell the assault teams to move into the building and capture Connelly, and put a couple extra rounds in Knight and Mitchell for me."

39

Frontier PD
1430

Screams rang out down the hall as the detectives sprang into action. Nick ran out of the room toward the sound of gunfire. Grabbing Knight and Mitchell, Colt rushed them out of the interview room and into a maintenance room. "Lock the door and stay in here."

Knight and Mitchell complied. Colt ran down the hallway and met up with a handful of detectives and officers. When the small defense force reached the landing above the foyer, Colt found Nick and asked, "What the hell is going on?"

"No idea. I made it as far as the landing above the stairs. I saw Ramirez shot up and retreated up here to gather the troops. It sounds like there are quite a few of them down there."

"Who the hell are they?"

"They have been shouting stuff about the FFR, but your guess is as good as mine." Just then they heard the sound of gunfire from a distant location in the building. "Fuck, they made it in the back too . . . We need to protect Knight and Mitchell."

"What the hell are you talking about?"

"I can't explain it all, but these guys are after Knight and Mitchell, just trust me on that."

"I don't care who they are after. They killed Ramirez!"

"And they won't stop until they kill Knight and Mitchell. These guys are well-trained and heavily armed. We need to get to the SWAT room and even the odds a little."

"I'm with you on that, but the SWAT room is on the main level. There are only two ways down, and if they're smart they will occupy both of the stairwells.

"Hold on! Let me take a look," Colt moved around the officers who had taken up defensive positions at the top of the stairs. "Benson. Let me have a look," Colt said as he tapped the patrol officer on the shoulder. He took a very quick look down the stairs and into the foyer. Two agents with AKS-74s trained on the stairs opened fire at the sight of the movement. Several 5.45mm rounds punched through the space Colt's head had recently occupied.

"Thanks, Benson. I wouldn't recommend doing that," he said as he maneuvered back to Nick.

"You've got to be crazy. You nearly lost your head," Nick greeted Colt.

"I know. But it was worth it. There are two guys with guns trained on the stairs. They won't leave their backs exposed, so that means there are one or two more with guns pointed outside."

"That still doesn't help us with how we stop this."

"Well, I'm guessing they didn't come here to set up camp in our lobby. They plan on carrying the assault further into the building to kill their targets."

"How can you be so sure of that? What if they are terrorists who want some form of ransom?"

"If money is what they want, they could rob a dozen banks or armored cars with their firepower and coordination. These guys are on a mission. You don't walk into a police department shooting unless you plan on doing some damage."

"Unless you are crazy or suicidal."

"If it was one person. I'd agree with you: suicide by cop. We have at least four and probably closer to ten. We need some information. You stay here and help out Benson and the others. I'll check the back stairwell and see what I can find."

"Shouldn't we stick together?"

"You are one of the best shots in the department. I want you to protect my back in case these guys charge up those stairs. I'll be back in less than a minute, just hold tight." With that Colt took off down the hallway and found the maintenance room.

"Knight, Mitchell, it's Colt coming in." Inside, Colt saw Mitchell standing with a broom handle held like a baseball bat and Knight holding a mop in a similar fashion. "I'm glad I warned you guys."

"It's not much. But it's all we have in here," Knight responded, lowering his mop.

"I know. I'd give you guys something better, but I

just have my sidearm. We are going to try to get to the SWAT room, but it's on the first floor and we can't get there without going past an assault team. I need to know their weaknesses."

"Easy answer," Sam stated. "They have none. But they are humans, not robots. If you shoot them, they will bleed."

"Great."

"Good luck. We are all counting on you," Dean rested his hand on Colt's shoulder. "You can do this. You were trained for it."

"You mean Connelly was trained for it?"

"He's with you, and he may respond to this," Sam suddenly spoke.

"What do you mean?"

"The barriers that we built are weak. I don't have time to explain it, but there is a good chance this is the last time we will see you as Colt Sullivan."

The sound of more gunfire quickly brought them all back to the urgency of their situation.

"Go, your partners need you!" Dean exclaimed.

Colt was already out the door and moving down the hallway. Turning the corner he heard the door from the stairwell open and watched as a small cylindrical canister rolled out into the hallway. Recognizing it as a flash-bang, he tried to avert his eyes, but the sudden explosion of light and sound doubled him over.

An agent tactically moved into the hallway. Seeing a disoriented target, the first agent raised his rifle and put Colt in his sights.

40

The Vault
1435

"We have had no emergency communications from inside the station. Agents are preparing to move farther into the building," the controller advised Harrison.

"Copy," Harrison stated, scanning the monitors. "Where was Connelly's office?"

"Second floor, above the rear stairwell."

"Agent 43's sector covers that office. Put his live view on the main screen."

"Yes, sir." The controller moved the live view for the requested agent onto the wall-sized screen at the front of the command center. They observed the agent moving up the stairwell with his partner.

"How many communication attempts have been made?"

"Hundreds. We have successfully blocked all radio,

phone, and Internet communication from the building. The only shots fired were inside the building, and traffic outside the building has remained normal."

"Did we shut down communication at the county dispatch center as well?"

"Yes. We have ensured that no communication will reach any mutual-assist agencies."

"Good work. We should have target confirmation in less than five minutes, exfiltration in less than ten, and with any luck we'll be in the clear in twenty." Harrison knew he was tempting fate, but he felt confident that his agents could take down a police station with roughly ten officers inside.

"Agents 43 and 26 are approaching the second floor, rear stairwell," the controller noted.

"Stay with Agent 43." They watched as the man's partner removed a flash-bang from his tactical vest, primed it, cooked it off, and threw it into the hallway. The resulting explosion shook the cameras on both agents, and it took a second to settle as the door opened and the agent rushed through.

The camera showed a lone detective, dressed in tactical gear, standing in the hallway. "That's Connelly!" Harrison exclaimed. "Tell them to take him alive."

"Roger, sir. Agent 43. Do not engage that target! Secure the target and deliver to security personnel on the first floor."

They watched in disbelief as the agent raised his rifle and took aim at Sullivan. "Agent 43, do not engage, that is an order!" barked the controller.

"What the hell is he doing?" Harrison screamed. "I want him alive." The whole encounter dragged into slow motion in Harrison's eyes. It was only a matter of a second before the agent pulled the trigger and killed Connelly, rendering the whole mission a disaster.

An instant later, the camera view whipped backwards and the agent's life-monitor alarms sounded. His heart rate, breathing, and blood pressure fell to zero.

The controller instinctively switched to the live-view monitor for agent 26. The screen showed rapid movement and the agent taking up a position at the far end of the hallway.

"Agent 26, report," the controller ordered as he moved the agent's live-view monitor to the large screen.

"43 took fire from an unknown location. I believe a target appeared in an area blocked from view by agent 43's body. I was hit twice in the back, but the armor held."

"Is the target still in sight and incapacitated?" Harrison asked, keying up his microphone.

"Hold on, sir. Let me check." The agent did a quick peek down the hallway. The camera answered the question before the agent did. The hallway was empty.

"Goddammit!" Harrison yelled. "Get 26 another agent from the rear-door search element, and tell them to get Connelly!"

"Yes, sir," the controller replied. Relaying the commands, he watched as agent 13 moved up the stairs. The agents coordinated their movements and covered for each other as they regained a foothold in the hallway.

Moving together down the hallway they found that it was a T intersection with a hallway lined with doors on either side.

Time was running out for everyone—especially Colt.

41

Frontier PD
1435

Connelly awoke in a small office with the face of a gorgeous woman inches from his eyes. "Colt, wake the fuck up!"

"Colt?" Connelly felt a distant connection in his memory to the name. "I don't know who you are. And I have no idea who Colt is."

"What the hell are you talking about, Colt? I am looking right at you."

"I'm not Colt, my name is William Connelly."

"Connelly? Is this some kind of a sick joke? Colt, wake the fuck up! The PD is under attack."

Connelly grabbed Angela by the shoulders and stared into her eyes. "This is no joke! I'm William Connelly. I don't know why you think I am Colt, but I don't care right now. Just tell me what the hell is going on!"

Angela looked like she was going to challenge him again, then backed off. "Fuck. I still don't know what the hell is going on, but we'll figure it out later. I was in my office when the attack began. I tried calling on the radio and the phone and nothing worked. I even tried e-mailing Dispatch, but our Internet is down. I ran down the hallway to help the officers at the top of the front stairs and learned that several armed men were in the lobby and they had killed one of our officers.

"Nick told me you went this way to try and gain access to the SWAT room. I figured you could use some help, so I doubled back but couldn't find you. I was heading back to Nick when the flash-bang went off. I came around the corner and saw a man dressed in camouflage with his gun raised in your direction. I shot him in the head. He had another suspect with him, but his back was turned. I shot twice and hit him in the back, but he fled down the hallway. Must be armored pretty good. I grabbed you and dragged you back to my office. You were out of it for about fifteen seconds."

Connelly had dozens more questions, but time was critical. "Who are these guys and what are they equipped with?"

"Nick told me they are claiming to be FFR, the Freedom Fighters of the Rockies. They are a domestic terrorist group based here in Colorado. They are armed with assault rifles, although I am not sure of the model."

"Why are they attacking?"

"Your guess is as good as mine. We know they are a well-armed group of ex-soldiers who believe in states' rights, but they have never been this radical."

"Something changed, there has to be a reason they

attacked. Something your department said, did, didn't do . . . maybe an arrest that was made."

"Everyone here has been focused on the homicide. Well, that and a guy we found driving a stolen car. He was brought in earlier. He wanted to talk to you. I think it had something to do with the murder."

Connelly thought hard for a second, trying to draw forth some memories of the past hour. His mind was a jigsaw puzzle that was missing too many pieces. "Fuck it. How many of them are there?"

"It sounds like four to six in the front, unknown in the back."

"Minus one, thanks to you," Connelly stated. "You said his partner ran down the hall."

"Yes, but that was a minute ago. I have no idea where he would be now."

"He's most likely looking to gain some revenge. Do you have a map of the building in here?"

Angela grabbed the emergency-exit plan from the back of the door. "We are here," she said, handing it to Connelly. "They came up this stairway, and I shot the guy here."

Taking the map, he looked it over and quickly developed a tactical plan. "They will bring more guys and push down this hallway. They'll want to clear these offices. We don't have much time. Chances are they are out there right now."

"What are we going to do?"

"Does your window have a ledge?"

"Yeah, but the window doesn't open."

"All windows open. Be ready to follow me." He faced the window and grabbed a three-hole punch from

Angela's desk. He drove the end of the heavy punch into the corner of the window, which collapsed with a minimum of noise. "Watch the shards."

Angela followed Connelly onto the small ledge. "It won't take long for them to figure out which office we were in and where we went," Angela remarked.

"I know. The map showed a roof access from that rear stairwell. If we can get to that access point we can double back behind them and take them out." Connelly grabbed the ledge of the roof and pulled himself up.

"Take them out? How about get out of here and call for help?"

"No offense, but who are you going to call for help? You're the police."

"I know, but we have ten officers out at the homicide. We could use their help."

"With your radios down, the only way you are going to get ahold of them is in person."

"I can drive there. It shouldn't take more ten minutes round-trip. We could double our numbers."

"Okay. Find a way down, get a car, and get out of here. They will have the exits covered, and when you come back expect a shootout at both doors."

"I will. Good luck."

"Thanks. You too." Connelly covered Angela as she made her way along the ledge beneath him. She was able to lower herself from the ledge onto a large utility box next to the parking lot and then jump to the pavement. Using parked cars to block the view from the rear exit, Connelly watched Angela move through the lot and climb into a squad car.

"Nice work," he said aloud as he resumed his climb

to the rooftop. Connelly used a large metal downspout to aid him in reaching the edge of the roof. After pulling himself up onto the roof he heard the sound of a revving engine and squealing tires. Angela was on the way to procure reinforcements.

Suddenly the cough of a suppressed and fully automatic weapon sounded on the rooftop. Sprinting across the roof, Connelly observed a man dressed in camouflage and tactical gear reloading his assault rifle.

The enemy was thirty yards away. Connelly knew his first shot needed to count. Putting his front sight post on the enemy's head, Connelly focused on squeezing the trigger. His only hope, as the bullet left the gun, was that it had found its mark fast enough to save Angela.

42

The Vault
1440

“What the hell is taking so long? We should have cleared by now!” Harrison was fuming. The operation was not a failure—not yet—but his men were not gaining ground as he had hoped.

The police department had seventy full-time officers, but a weekend day meant there should only have been five patrol officers working. The department had called in additional help for the homicide investigation, but most of those officers and detectives were confirmed on assignment at the crime scene.

The Vault had sent twelve highly trained, heavily armed agents into a small police department and expected to walk through the place. Killing a few officers and eliminating or securing the target personnel should have been an in-and-out job.

Instead he had lost one agent during the only chance so far at securing the main target. His front-lobby agents were making slow gains on the first floor, and his rear agents had found nothing so far in their search of the second floor.

"He can't disappear into thin air. I want the cop who shot agent 43 killed, and I want Connelly taken alive."

"Agent 26 reports they found an office with a broken window. It appears the targets fled onto the roof."

Harrison cursed himself for not leaving snipers outside to block anyone from fleeing via the windows. It was a rare oversight on his part, but a large one. "Advise a search-element member to go outside and check the roof."

Within thirty seconds they had a live view of the roof. Large air-conditioning units and the uneven rooftop made it difficult for the agent or the command center to see much of anything. The agent reported his findings and began a full search of the roof.

The agent moved from the access hatch through the maze of HVAC equipment. Seeing no targets on the roof, he was looking for an ambush location when he heard the sound of a car door slamming and an engine starting. He reported his findings, and the general gave him a green light to take out the vehicle. He fired several shots at the engine block and tires of the escaping vehicle.

A small smile crept across the agent's face as he watched small craters erupt in the car's metal body. As the last round cleared his magazine he watched the vehicle go over a curb, and crash into a tree.

The smile evaporated as the slap of a bullet passing by his head was quickly joined by the sound of a handgun firing nearby. The agent dove for cover behind a brick half-wall and rapidly reloaded his weapon. Two more shots followed. Dust and debris rained down as slugs hit the bricks above his head. Rolling to his right, he popped up to a knee and fired a quick burst.

His volleys hit empty air. The roof of the building was devoid of targets. Heating and cooling equipment offered the most likely path of egress for the unseen shooter. As the agent moved toward the noisy machines, he lost the ability to track by sound. He was now tracking an adversary he couldn't see or hear.

Walking through the large metal boxes, he expected at any moment to see his quarry fleeing the rooftop. He saw nothing. His prey must have gone down the hatch or over the edge of the roof. Turning around, he paused for a second to calculate his next move.

He felt the air beside his neck and right ear move ever so slightly. His right knee buckled, and a single arm pinned both sides of his neck.

The agent dropped his rifle as he grabbed at the vise-like arm. His strength left him as his world went black.

43

Frontier PD
1440

Connelly knew he'd pulled his first shot before it left the barrel of the handgun. He tried to compensate, but the trained enemy dove for cover before Connelly could bring his sights back on target.

Cursing himself for jerking the trigger, Connelly fired two shots at the half-wall hiding the agent. Both rounds struck the top of the wall and sent two tiny debris clouds up into the air. It would only be a matter of seconds before his better-armed adversary could recover and return fire. He ran for the cover of the air-conditioning units.

As he dove into the space between the large metal cooling units, he heard the punch of the suppressed rounds. They dissected the empty air he had just vacated. Connelly knew he was facing a fully automatic AKS-74 submachine gun with a thirty-round magazine. His semiautomatic handgun had only eleven rounds left.

There was no question that his adversary held the advantage in the showdown. If he didn't die going toe-to-toe with his opponent, there was still a high likelihood of taking some of the enemy's rounds. Injury would put him at an insurmountable disadvantage against the roughly ten additional opponents he needed to hunt down.

Pushing himself up from the ground, he looked around and saw a maintenance entrance on one of the larger cooling apparatuses. The man-sized hatch allowed technicians access to the inner workings of the units. Squeezing through the small opening, Connelly realized it would be impossible for him to hear his opponent over the deafening fans. Luckily for him, the sun was still high, and light spilled through the air vents on the side of the unit.

Within moments, the space darkened as the agent passed by the vent. Connelly made a quiet exit from the hatch and moved rapidly behind his stalker. Up close, the man presented quite a threat in hand-to-hand combat. He stood a few inches taller than Connelly and had him by thirty pounds of solid muscle. Connelly opted for the silent and effective takedown known as the lateral vascular neck restraint.

Holstering his handgun, Connelly struck the bigger man in the back of the right knee. As his opponent dropped his weight down and to the right, Connelly shot his right arm past his foe's right ear and hooked his arm around both sides of the stronger man's neck.

Connelly felt the man go limp in his arms and lowered him to the ground. Pulling a pair of zip cuffs off the agent's tactical vest, Connelly secured the man's hands behind his back and removed his weapons. When he was ready, he slammed an open palm between his adversary's shoulders, bringing him out of his cataleptic state.

As his enemy's eyes gained focus, Connelly applied a swift kick to his ribs. The pain would sharpen the large man's senses and ensure he understood Connelly was in charge. "Who are you and why are you doing this?" Connelly questioned, making sure the other man knew he was unafraid.

"Fuck you. I ain't telling you shit, you pig," the man replied.

"You aren't in a position to make that choice," Connelly replied, giving the man a kick to common peri-neal nerve bundle in the side of the man's leg.

"You're a cop! You can't do shit to me."

Connelly knelt down on one knee, took out his side-arm, and put it to the side of the man's head. "You've got it all wrong. I'm not a cop. So none of those rules apply to me." He then turned the gun around and struck the captive man in the side of the head. The force was enough to dust out some cobwebs, but not enough to fracture or cause any internal bleeding.

"Fuck, man, all right. I'll tell you what you want to know, but only because you are as good as dead."

"Brave words coming from a man with a gun to his head. I don't think you understand how easy it would be for me to kill you."

"I'm no fool, Connelly. I know how many agents you have killed."

Connelly was taken aback that the man knew who he was. "What do you mean by agents, and how do you know my name?"

"Shit. They really did wipe your mind. You're Harrison's goon. You hunt us down and kill us when we fail."

"Who is Harrison?"

"Harrison is the guy in charge. He runs the program, makes the calls. You went off the reservation, and he sent us in here to kill you. You and—" The man's head jerked to the side, and his shattered brain and pieces of his skull struck the cooling unit.

Connelly brought the dead man's AKS-74 up and began firing behind him. A brief glimpse along the bullets' path revealed two men with weapons aimed at him. Connelly dropped his shoulder and rolled. One of the assassins took three rounds to his upper torso.

Dropping his gun, the man fell over in a pile of pain, grabbing at his chest. The armor-piercing bullets had bored through his body armor and struck his heart. Connelly risked another look to evaluate. Death would not be instantaneous, but it would be unavoidable in ten to fifteen seconds as the man's heart stopped and blood flow to the brain slowly shut down.

The other agent was holding a strange-looking sidearm. Connelly heard a pop and felt his body lock up in pain. Cramps took hold of his entire body, and he fell to the ground. After what felt like an eternity the pain released him.

Connelly looked up to see the man fumbling with the device. The Taser shot had caused Connelly to drop his rifle. He drew his handgun and fired five rounds in less than two seconds. The fumbling man took all five rounds and fell backwards to the ground.

Looking at his chest, Colt found two small electronic

barbs buried in his body armor. The barbs had thin filament wires running out of them, back toward his deceased opponent. The wires only ran for a few feet before they broke from the remainder of the wire. Connelly's fall had severed the Taser's wires and cut the circuit.

Pulling the barbs from his chest, he gathered his weapons and moved to the two newly slain men on the rooftop. Two small round holes on the face of the man holding the Taser told the story. Although the three handgun rounds had lacked the capability to pierce the man's body armor, nothing had stopped the .45-caliber hollowpoints from crushing the man's skull.

Connelly searched the lifeless men, gathering up extra ammunition, a few flash-bangs, and a spare AKS-74. He needed to get off of the roof as soon as possible but feared running into an ambush at the roof hatch. Doubling back to the broken window, he returned to Angela's office.

He had been lucky so far, but the problem with luck in combat is that it has to run out.

44

Frontier PD
1444

Connelly moved out of Angela's office, alert for additional agents. Considering what he had learned from his captive on the roof, he sacrificed precious time to search his jumbled memories for more information.

Although most of the recollections remained spotty, the clear vision of a maintenance room in the hallway formed in his mind. He found the room and opened the door. Something told him to duck just as a broom handle struck a glancing blow off the top of his head.

His weapon at the ready, Connelly was about to pull the trigger when he heard two questioning voices. "Colt, is that you?"

"No, it's Connelly."

"Oh shit . . . sorry, man," came a reply from the dark. As Connelly's eyes adjusted he started to make out the outlines of two men huddled in the back corners of the small room. "I guess it makes sense that you didn't announce yourself."

"Who the hell are you guys?"

"Sam Mitchell and Dean Knight," Dean announced. "We don't have time to explain a lot right now, but we are on your side."

"What are you doing hiding in a closet when this place is under attack?"

"We are scientists. We don't have weapons and aren't really trained for this," Sam replied sheepishly.

"I can fix the weapons part, but first you need to tell me what is going on."

"Short version. You are a secret government weapon created to police a secret government assassination program housed at a secret military installation from which we both escaped," Dean answered.

"That's a lot of secrets. Why is this station under attack?"

"The general who runs the program wants the three of us dead in order to keep everything nice and secret," Dean continued.

"Harrison?" Connelly questioned, recalling the name brought up in his short interrogation on the roof.

"That's right. He sent a team of agents to kill us," Sam responded.

"Why can't I remember anything?"

"You brain was reprogrammed and you were given an alternate personality," Dean replied.

"Colt?"

"Yes, you were Colt Sullivan, a police detective assigned to this station," Dean explained. "For the past five years Harrison has hid you here in plain sight to determine if, and to what level, his assassins could be reprogrammed. He also used you when he needed to track down other agents who failed their missions."

"Missions?"

"Assassination missions. The agents are sent into some of the hottest conflicts, both political and military, to carry out homicidal and sometimes suicidal missions to remove someone from power. If they fail, you are sent in to clean up," Sam replied.

"But something went wrong with me?"

"Your mind broke down. The façade that was your life fell apart. Dean intercepted you and gave you enough knowledge to destroy Colt's control of your brain," Sam stated.

"That explains enough for now. Can you guys fight?"

"If you give us weapons, we can join you. Keep in mind, though, we are mostly untrained," Dean advised.

"Take these," Colt said, handing over the spare AKS-74 and sidearm gleaned from the rooftop attackers. "As long as you keep your finger out of the trigger well until you are ready to fire, there is no reason to have the weapon on safe. If we run into the enemy, do your best to point the weapon at the bad guy and pull the trigger."

"Sounds like a plan," Sam said, taking the sidearm. "Dean has experience with a rifle today; he'll take the larger gun."

"Okay, you each have full magazines, and explaining a reload will take too long; just make your shots count. Let's go, and no matter which way we move, watch my back." Connelly led them out of the room just as the sound of an explosion shook the hallway.

A heavy volley of gunfire, most of it suppressed but still audible, echoed down the hallway. Connelly broke into a jog toward the sounds of the firefight. With Dean and Sam in tow he moved slower, but he appreciated the security behind him.

Reaching a security door at the end of the hallway, he estimated the source of the gunfire to be on the other side. The sustained sounds of gunshots had died out; it was now limited to the occasional pop of a handgun followed by the barking of several suppressed assault rifles.

The enemy soldiers had most likely gained the advantage, and Connelly opted to turn the tides. Slinging the AK over his shoulder, Connelly removed one of his two borrowed flash-bangs from his tactical vest. He readied it by pulling the pin and releasing the spoon.

With his free hand, Connelly swiped his keycard and cracked the door. He slid the flash-bang through the opening and flicked his wrist. There was a moment of silence before the blast slammed the door back against his bracing shoulder. Connelly leveled his weapon and kicked his way through to a bloody scene.

Several police officers lay unmoving on the floor with blood pooling beneath their bodies. The only movement came from the three enemy combatants standing stunned at the top of the stairs. Connelly leveled his weapon and held down the trigger. Dean and Sam moved to either side and contributed to the deadly wall of lead.

The agents wilted to the ground. The closest enemy lay unmoving while the other two writhed in pain. Connelly finished off the remaining rounds in his magazine by double-tapping the surviving enemies.

"Colt," called a raspy voice from a corner of the landing. Connelly turned to see a man with a badge on his belt and a gun in his hand. "Watch out!"

The warning came too late as a fourth agent appeared at the top of the stairs. The agent pointed his weapon at Connelly and pulled the trigger. At fifteen feet away, there was no chance the agent could miss, and although the injured detective raised his gun to take down the threat, he was too late.

45

Frontier PD
1453

Sam saw the movement out of the corner of his eye a half second before Nick shouted the warning. His first instinct was to raise his weapon and fire, but he knew without thinking that there was only one option. Shoving Connelly away, Sam fell into the path of the bullets and took both shots to the chest. Nick's bullets found their marks in the agent's neck and forehead, and the attacker's body fell and rolled back down the stairs.

"No!" Dean screamed as he ran to his fallen friend. Sam lay on the ground with two crimson circles steadily growing on his chest. Placing his hands over the wounds Dean looked his friend in the eye. "Don't you die!"

"Dean. I'm not going to make it." Sam coughed up a little blood.

"Don't talk like that. We'll get you some help," Dean replied.

"I can feel the cold. I'm not going to make it," Sam stated, his voice becoming weaker with each word.

"Just hold on Sam! You'll be okay," Dean pleaded.

"No, I won't." Sam coughed up more blood and tried taking a breath, but his failing chest wouldn't move. "At least I didn't die in that damn Vault."

"Sam—" Dean felt his friend go limp in his arms. "Sam!" Dean shook the now-lifeless body, hoping for one last response.

"He's gone. We need to move on," Connelly said. He knew it sounded cold, but there was no way around it. A battlefield was no place for emotion. As long as they were under attack they needed to keep pressing forward.

"Before you flashed the room, I heard them calling out to at least one more suspect down the stairs," Nick interrupted. Connelly moved over to the injured man to assess his wounds.

Nick's left shoulder was a mess of blood and torn skin, and he had taken two bullets to his left shin. None of the injuries looked life-threatening, but the man would not be able to assist in the fight.

"Colt, these guys are animals. They executed Benson, Williams, and Moyer after they threw the flash-bang. I fired at them as they shot Williams, but I hit the guy center-mass and he just laughed it off. I took cover behind this railing, but I couldn't get my left side to cover," Nick stated, waving his good hand at his injured shoulder.

"You'll be okay," Connelly replied.

"Whatever you say, Colt, you don't have three holes in your body right now," Nick replied with a grimace.

"Only thanks to Sam," Connelly went over to Sam.

"I owe him my life." Connelly picked up Sam's sidearm and tucked it behind his belt. "That makes eight dead agents."

"With one or two still in the lobby and likely another one or two at the back door," Dean commented. "Harrison risked everything for this attack. He won't call off his guys."

"Who is Harrison?" Nick asked.

"It's a long story," Connelly replied. "Dean, stay with him and keep him safe. I am going to end this."

"Colt, that's suicide!" Nick advised. "At least take him with you. I'll be fine."

"No, I need someone to watch my rear in case they try to come up the back stairwell."

"I don't like it," Nick replied.

"I don't care if you don't like it. I have to do this for Sam."

Connelly made his move down the stairs toward the lobby. He paused at the bodies of Ramirez and the agent who killed Sam. Readying his last flash-bang, he tossed it and waited for the explosion before charging headlong down the flight of stairs.

Seeing movement, Connelly aimed his rifle and fired. The rounds landed true. The head of an agent poised to ambush Connelly disintegrated. As the agent's body descended, Connelly scanned the remainder of the room. Turning the corner at the bottom of the stairs he came face-to-face with his target.

The agent had tracked down a civilian employee and was holding a gun to the side of her head. Connelly knew the agent could twist his gun in the matter of a second and fire a round at Connelly before he had time to react.

With his gun sight trained on the agent's head, and without hesitation or negotiation, Connelly fired one shot.

The middle-aged woman began screaming as she felt the man's weight fall forward against her back. Connelly rushed forward and took her by the shoulders and sat her down. Her body was shaking, and he feared she would go into shock.

"You are going to be okay," Connelly reassured her. He ran to the base of the stairs. "Dean, get down here. I need you."

Dean ran down the stairs and met up with Connelly. "Stay with her, Dean. Make sure she keeps talking to you and keep her safe."

"Okay." Connelly sprinted back up the stairs to Nick, who was still propped up against the wall.

"The lobby is clear. That just leaves the rear entrance."

"Nice work. I thought you were a goner."

"Not yet. Do you think you can move if I help you?"

"I can try. How far do you need me to go?"

"Just down the hallway to the top of the rear stairs. I am going to need a distraction."

"Help me up." Nick reached for Connelly, who pulled him up by his right side. Giving Nick his left side to support the weight on his good leg, Connelly slung his rifle and took out his sidearm. They would be most vulnerable as they moved to the top of the rear stairwell.

Upon arriving at their destination, Nick whispered, "Ask me again if I can move and I am going to tell you to go fuck yourself. I can't believe I didn't pass out."

"You did great. All I need you to do is count to sixty. Once you get to sixty, open the door and fire some shots into the top of the stairs. Can you do that?"

"Let me see." Nick sat against the wall on the right side of the door. He set down his handgun, reached up and opened the door quietly. He picked up the handgun and stuck it through the small opening. "Yeah, I can do that."

"Okay, start counting," Connelly sprinted down the hallway. Keeping count in his head, he barreled down the stairs. He passed Dean, who was still trying to calm the traumatized receptionist.

Connelly followed the main hallway as it wrapped around and arrived at the back hallway with seconds to spare. He was just around the corner from the rear stair entry. At exactly sixty seconds Connelly heard several shots from the top of the stairwell.

Using the sound of the gunfire to mask his movements, Connelly snuck around the corner. As he entered the rear foyer he saw one agent slowly making his way up the stairs while another covered the door. Connelly used one five-to-six round burst to bring down the agent on the stairwell.

The agent at the door whipped around and fired in his direction. The hurried shots went wide as Connelly leveled his own weapon and pulled the trigger. The agent took two shots to chest and one to the head before falling forward.

Connelly scanned the last two agents for movement. After the agent on the stairs stopped twitching, Connelly moved in to check pulses. Confident neither agent had a pulse, he stayed on alert for any other targets and searched the rest of the building.

Finding no more agents, he searched the exterior of the building and found Angela in her car. She was alive and breathing, but unconscious. He picked her up and carried her into the building and set her next to Dean and the receptionist.

Assisting Nick down the stairs proved to be a painful and difficult task, but with Dean's help they were able to load all three of the surviving police personnel into a vehicle.

Dean agreed to drive them to the hospital and drop them off. Connelly told him to drive to the homicide scene and tell a bystander what had happened. The bystander could then tell thc police, and Dean could make an exit without getting pulled in for questioning.

Afterward, Connelly and Dean would meet up at a tertiary spot. There were going to be more questions than answers after this, and neither of them would ever stop being a target. Connelly had to leave the life of Colt Sullivan behind.

Before leaving the department, Connelly gathered up all the weapons and ammo he could find. He carried Sam's body to an unmarked SUV. After loading the body and the equipment, he left the gruesome scene.

★ ★ ★ ★

They buried Sam in a makeshift grave high in the mountains. Dean could think of no other way to part with the body of a man who didn't exist. Connelly read a few verses from a Bible and Dean shed a few tears before they left their fallen friend behind.

They both knew they had a long, hard road ahead. Their hellish day was over, but their journey was just beginning.

46

The Vault
1800

The phone rang twice in quick succession; Washington was calling for answers. Harrison had spent the last twenty minutes contemplating suicide. The bottle of Wild Turkey sat open on his desk with a full shot glass at its side. He emptied the contents of the glass into his mouth before picking up the phone.

"Harrison here." His speech was slightly slurred from forty minutes of hard drinking.

"What the fuck is going on over there, General?" the unmistakable voice of the secretary of defense yelled into the phone.

"The situation is not as bad as it seems," Harrison lied.

"How the hell can't it be as bad as it seems? You have two rogue operatives, a classified document leak, and a police station full of dead cops and your dead agents!"

"I know, sir. But hear me out . . ." Harrison paused.

"I won't hear you out. My plane will be landing in half an hour. You will be on it, and you will report to Washington for a full debrief of the situation. If you aren't on that plane you will be arrested and thrown into the worst prison I can find."

"Understood, sir." Harrison realized he was talking to dead air. He hung up the phone and poured himself another shot of bourbon. Picking up the 1911 from the desk, he felt its weight and admired its simple but effective design. Holding the gun in one hand and the shot in the other, he downed the shot and then put the sidearm to his temple. His finger moved into the trigger well as the alcohol burned down his throat and moved into his stomach.

Just as he was about the pull the trigger, the phone rang again.

Letting out his breath, Harrison picked up the phone. "Harrison here."

"General Harrison, my name is Alan Graves and I work for the president."

"Save your voice, Graves. I know I fucked up. You'll be rid of me soon enough."

"Just get on the secretary of defense's plane. We'll talk when you get to Washington."

"And if I don't?"

"Let's just say this is a once-in-a-lifetime get-out-of-jail-free card . . . you don't want to pass this up." Graves hung up the phone without another word.

Harrison stared at the receiver and realized he still had the gun in his other hand. Setting both on the desk, he poured himself one more shot before shaking his head. "No regrets . . ."

EPILOGUE

Frontier, CO
Three days later

A cold rain fell on the small gathering of mourners at the gravesite. Abby Connelly was not well known, but a few coworkers showed up to pay their last respects. Some cried and others felt almost a sense of relief, thinking that she was finally going to join her husband in heaven.

William Connelly stood in the distance, the rain running unnoticed off his head. Hot tears ran from his eyes and mixed with the cold precipitation on his cheeks. He watched as the casket was lowered into the ground. The priest said a few words, and people retreated with haste to their cars.

When the crowd had fully dispersed, William walked over to the grave containing his wife. The cemetery workers were busy removing the apparatus, and they paused as they watched William walk to the site. He nodded his head, indicating that they should just continue their work, and stood at the gravesite.

Abby's name and date of death already occupied half the tombstone. William could hardly believe it had only been three days since she died. He grimaced as he thought how long the five years she lived without him must have felt to her.

The other half of the tombstone contained his name. Abby had already purchased and prepared the headstone with William's information. Her will clearly dictated that if anything happened to her, she was supposed to be buried in Frontier with the ashes of her dead husband at her side.

Connelly knelt down in the sodden grass and touched the headstone. From the pocket under his coat he produced a single rose and set it on the stone.

"I know you never gave up hope that I would come home. I know for five years you lived in pain, missing me and wishing I could be by your side." Connelly wiped a tear from his eye.

"The man who did this to you is already dead. But there is still a man out there who is responsible for keeping me from you. I will avenge the injustice that kept us apart, and then when it is my time I will join you. I know it is a lot to ask of you to wait for me up there, but I will come eventually. I still have work to do. But know that I love you and I will always be thinking of you."

With that, Connelly stood up and walked away from the grave.

★ ★ ★ ★

For the past two days Dean had been hacking into secure networks to determine the fate of Harrison and the Vault.

From what he could decipher, Harrison had boarded

a plane for Washington. Under orders from and review by the secretary of defense, the Vault had been shut down and all personnel had been reassigned. Their reassignments were hidden so deep that even Knight couldn't find any more answers. It was as if Harrison, the agents, the Vault, and all the base personnel just disappeared overnight.

★ ★ ★ ★

Knight and Connelly knew they weren't out of the woods yet, not even close. With the cemetery in his rearview mirror, Connelly left Frontier. He drove to the farmhouse and helped Knight load his gear. Leaving the mountains behind, they aimed the vehicle at the East Coast.

They were hunted relentlessly. Colt Sullivan faded from Connelly's memory and he focused on revenge. He knew the day would come when he could settle the score but first they needed to survive. They managed to avoid detection for three months until they made a fatal mistake and once again found themselves in Harrison's crosshairs.

ACKNOWLEDGEMENTS

This book would not have been possible without the help of many great people. To my beautiful wife, Brea, thank you for all your patience and understanding. I couldn't have done this without you. You are my true love and make my life better every day. To my wonderful sons, Keegan and Declan, thank you for being an inspiration for the future. To my parents, I have always appreciated your love and support and wouldn't be the man I am without you.

Huge thanks to all my friends who suffered through my early drafts and provided me with helpful feedback that strengthened this novel. Blake, OJ, Brian, and all my rough draft and beta readers—your contributions are greatly appreciated.

To the staff at Beaver's Pond Press, thank you for giving me a chance to succeed and for your guidance. A special thanks to Dara and Kim for believing in me. Thank you to Kellie Hultgren, a very talented editor—without your help this book would still be one giant "info-dump." Thanks to Jay Monroe for his outstanding design work.

With a heavy heart I thank Steph and Mac for allowing me to dedicate this book to the memory of their infant son, Dane. His big blue eyes will always watch over us, and his heart will always remember your love.

For all my military brothers and sisters with whom I served, and those stationed around the world, keep up the good fight and stay safe. For all my brothers and sisters in blue, including my co-workers and anyone else who fights for justice, remember: Blessed are the peacemakers, as they will be called the children of God.

ABOUT THE AUTHOR

Dan McCarty is a veteran of the U.S. Army. He served as an infantry team leader during peacekeeping operations in Kosovo. Dan is currently a full-time licensed police officer in a suburb of Minneapolis. He lives in Minnesota with his wife and two sons.

Check out **DanMccartyBooks.com** for information on additional books and events, and to contact the author.